Big Lake Burning

By Nick Russell

Nick Russell
1400 Colorado Street C-16
Boulder City, NV 89005
E-mail Editor@gypsyjournal.net

Also By Nick Russell

Fiction
Big Lake
Big Lake Lynching
Crazy Days In Big Lake
Big Lake Blizzard
Big Lake Scandal
Dog's Run

Nonfiction
Highway History and Back Road Mystery
Highway History and Back Road Mystery II
Meandering Down The Highway;
A Year On The Road With Fulltime RVers
The Frugal RVer
Work Your Way Across The USA;
You Can Travel And Earn A Living Too!
The Gun Shop Manual
Overlooked Florida
Overlooked Arizona

Keep up with Nick Russell's latest books at
www.NickRussellBooks.com

Author's Note

While there is a body of water named Big Lake in the White Mountains of Arizona, the community of Big Lake and all persons in this book live only in the author's imagination. Any resemblance in this story to actual persons, living or dead, is purely coincidental.

My thanks to Mac McCoy, Oregon State Fire Marshal's Office (retired) and, Stu McNicol, Division Chief, Anne Arundel County (MD) Fire Department (retired) for all of their technical assistance in researching this book. They patiently answered countless questions and explained points of fire science, firefighting techniques, and arson investigation. Any errors in these areas are totally my responsibility.

To my son Travis, who has traveled many roads to become the man he is. I love you.

Prologue

The first fire started in an old wooden shed at the back of Tom Cotter's property two miles outside of town. Nobody was home at the time. Cotter was in his eighteen-wheeler hauling a load of tires back west from the Cooper Tire factory in Findlay, Ohio. He had been on the road almost three weeks this trip, first dropping off a shipment of produce in Minneapolis that had originated in California's Coachella Valley, then picking up a load of dog food bound for New Jersey before he deadheaded back to Ohio. Tom missed his wife and was looking forward to getting home in a few days.

Seven years younger than her husband, Jill Cotter had been lonely during his long absences from home. In the early days of their marriage she had accompanied Tom on a few runs, but she didn't enjoy long days staring out at the world through a windshield. She found sleeping to be impossible in the tiny compartment behind the truck's cab with the noise of idling diesel engines parked next to them in truck stops and highway rest areas, and let's face it, Tom wasn't much for conversation either. She had tried reading books to pass the time, but was prone to motion sickness when she did. After a particularly miserable trip to Liberal, Kansas, Jill had crawled out of the Kenworth on shaky legs and vowed never to get back in again.

It didn't take long for boredom to set in and she had tried different types of craft projects to keep herself occupied. When she realized she had no talent for creating things, Jill began searching for something else to fill up the long, empty days and nights.

She found just what she was looking for in Brian Spangler, a dark haired man two years her junior who fancied himself a country singer, even though he couldn't carry a tune and had a terrible time remembering the lyrics to every song he attempted to sing. That didn't matter to Jill, who was busy moaning in passion in Brian's bed on the other side of town at the time a neighbor smelled smoke and discovered the shed was on fire. In a small town, a girl gets her diversions where and when she can.

By the time Big Lake's volunteer fire department arrived on the scene the shed was fully engulfed and all they could do was water down the grass and trees to keep the flames from spreading. A couple of old bicycles, a broken lawnmower, and an assortment of junk were lost in the fire. After the fire was out, the firemen couldn't determine what had started it, and since it was a minor incident, there wasn't an investigation.

Love is blind, so when he got home Tom Cotter accepted Jill's claim that she had been shopping at the WalMart in Show Low at the time of the fire without question, and set about cleaning up the rubble of what had been his shed.

***

One unexplained fire may not get much notice, but two in less than a week in a town the size of Big Lake does. Four days after Tom Cotter's shed burned, flames were discovered shooting out of the roof of an abandoned barn on Santa Fe Lane. Since it was a mile outside of town, and because they had to cut a lock off a gate to get to the barn, by the time firefighters got to the scene it was too late to do anything to save the decrepit old building. As with the first blaze, all they could do was watch it burn and be on the alert to keep the fire from spreading to the grass around the barn.

"Any idea who owns this place?" Sheriff Jim Weber asked Fire Chief Steve Harper as part of the barn's roof fell in, sending a shower of sparks skyward.

Harper shook his head. "It was part of the old Mayer place, but I think the bank took it over a while back after Henry died and it went into foreclosure. You might ask Wally McKnight over at the real estate office."

"I remember Henry Mayer," Weber said. "Always wore bib overalls and no shirt, summer or winter. Didn't he have a kid? A boy?"

"Mark," Harper told him, nodding. "He got cancer or something and died a couple of years before Henry did. Broke that old man's heart. I think that's what really killed him."

Kevin Upchurch, who worked as a maintenance man for the school system when he wasn't responding to fire calls, joined them, wiping sweat off his forehead. Upchurch and Harper had been best friends since childhood, had joined the Army and served as part of the peacekeeping mission in Korea together, and then came home to Big Lake, where they married local girls and raised their families on the same street. While Harper was the smaller of the two by several inches and easily 75 pounds, he was the unquestioned leader in everything they did. Upchurch had always seemed happy to let his friend blaze the trail, while he followed happily along, covering his back.

Upchurch nodded at Weber and took a long pull from the plastic water bottle Harper handed him. "We haven't had a fire all summer long, and now we've got two this week. What's that tell ya?"

"Makes a man think," Harper said. "Could be a coincidence, I guess."

"Could be," the bigger man said. "Or maybe we've got us a firebug."

"Let's hope not," Weber said. "You guys mind poking around and seeing what you can come up with once this cools down?"

"We'll stay until it's good and out, but it'll be dark by then," Harper told him. "I'll come back tomorrow and see what I can find, if anything."

Weber thanked them and left the two firemen to oversee the mop-up operation. As he pulled away and started back to town, he hoped Upchurch was wrong and that this second fire coming so close on the heels of the first one was just a coincidence. But he'd worn a badge long enough that he didn't believe in coincidence any longer.

Chapter 1

Three days after the barn burned an old International dump truck parked next to Max Woodbury's plumbing shop went up in flames. Woodbury lived in a small apartment attached to the back of the shop and was frantically trying to keep the flames from spreading to the building when the fire department arrived.

Woodbury seldom used the worn out old rust bucket except to haul trash to the dump, and while it wasn't much of a monetary loss, the fire was confirmation of what Weber and Chief Harper had already suspected.

"So much for coincidence," Harper said, staring at the blackened hulk as his firefighters rolled their hoses up and stored their equipment away.

"I'm sure glad you guys got here when you did," Woodbury told him. "I was doing everything I could with that there garden hose but I was losing the battle."

"You did the right thing hosing down the side of the shop instead of trying to put the truck out," the fire chief said. "You've got some scorched wood there but that's about it. You could have lost the whole damn place."

"That old truck was on its last legs anyway. I figured I could buy another truck for a lot cheaper than rebuilding."

"Any idea what caused it yet?" Weber asked.

Harper shook his head and spit, "Diesel fuel's not as volatile as gasoline, but the way that thing went up, I think somebody used an accelerant."

"An accelerant?" Woodbury asked. "You mean like gasoline or something, Steve?"

"I think so," Harper said. "We've had a couple of other suspicious fires this week."

"Why would somebody set fire to my place? Who'd I piss off that bad?"

"I don't know. You tell me," Weber said. "Do you have any disgruntled customers who could be holding a grudge?"

"What the hell's that supposed to mean?" Woodbury asked defensibly. "You know me, Jimmy. I do good work and I charge a fair rate. I don't stick it to folks or try to pad the bill."

"I know you don't," Weber said, holding up his hands dismissively. "No offense meant, Max. I just wondered if some customer expected something for nothing and got mad when they didn't get it?"

"Not that I know of. But you know how some of these flatlanders are. I guess it could happen. But still… set a fire instead of at least complaining first?"

"I'm just grasping at straws," Weber told him. "Forget I even said anything."

Max seemed to relax and Weber asked, "When did you spot the fire?"

"I didn't. I was asleep until Grace Rood came driving by and saw the flames and started pounding on the door," Woodbury said. "I owe that lady a bouquet of flowers or something."

"Anybody see anything suspicious?" Weber asked.

"Not that I know of. Sunday morning, folks are either in church or sleeping off Saturday night," Harper said.

"I need to talk to Grace. Where did she go?"

"She was all gussied up, I expect she was on her way to church," Max replied.

"I don't think Grace's ever missed Sunday morning services in her life," Harper told the sheriff. "I remember a couple of winters ago we had a big storm and the whole town was snowed in. I was out shoveling snow away from the front of the fire station and there came Grace in that little orange Bug of hers, plowing her way along. I think she was the only one at church that morning except for the preacher. And she had to wade through the snow to the parsonage next door to get him. Said if she could make it to church, so could he!"

They walked back to the fire truck, and as Harper pulled off his turnout gear, Weber stared back at the fire scene, watching as Woodbury stood looking at the rubble with his hands on his hips, shaking his head.

"As soon as I get the truck's water tank refilled and get back to the garage I'm going to sit down and write a report on this fire, and tomorrow morning I'm calling the State Fire Marshal's office down in Phoenix. This scares me, Jimmy. I think we might have a serial arsonist on our hands, and whoever's doing this is stepping up the pace. The fires are happening faster and this one is right here in town and so close to a house."

"I was just thinking the same thing," Weber replied. "I don't know much about how a firebug's mind works, but I know it's going to keep getting worse until we stop him."

"I'll do what I can to help you, but that's your job and the Fire Marshal's. Mine's to put out the fires. And I don't have much to work with as it is."

"Still no luck with the Town Council on funding?"

"Meeting's this week but I'm not very optimistic. Chet Wingate sees the Fire Department as a money pit with no return on investment."

"Chet's an idiot," Weber said, referring to Big Lake's mayor, a short, heavyset man who appeared to have been born with a sour attitude.

"You'll get no argument from me on that, but he holds the purse strings to the budget."

"I'll be there to give you whatever support I can," Weber promised.

"I appreciate that, Jimmy. And I'd appreciate you catching this son-of-a-bitch before he starts another fire and hurts somebody."

"You think it could come to that?"

"Could have today if somebody didn't wake Max up," Harper said.

"Did you find anything out at that old barn that went up the other day?"

Harper shrugged his shoulders and tucked a pinch of Skoal into his mouth, then offered the can to Weber, who shook his head. "I poked around but there wasn't much left. Leastways, nothing I could find. But keep in mind, Jimmy, I'm a small town guy and the only firefighting training I had was in the Army. And that didn't include investigations. So unless I see an empty gas can and a box of matches, I'm way out of my league. The only training our volunteers get is our monthly drill, if they can get away from work to show up. I'd like to do more, but with no budget…"

Weber knew where the man was coming from and sympathized. While he had been involved in more than one battle with the Town Council over funding constraints, the Sheriff's Department budget was still many times higher than the pittance they allowed the Fire Department.

"The last time I went begging to the Town Council with hat in hand, Chet said all we do is sit around playing cards and washing the fire truck. Then Gretchen asked what we did with all of the money we got from our fundraisers. She must think we sell a bunch of food at our three fish fries every year."

Councilwoman Gretchen Smith-Abbot was a thin, severe woman who favored drab gray business suits, her hair always pulled into a tight bun on the back of her head. She was the mayor's right hand and strongest supporter, and the two seemed joined at the hip.

"They only need you when they need you," Weber said, "the rest of the time you're the redheaded stepchild."

"Are you saying that because I'm a redhead or a stepchild?"

"Maybe because you're so childlike in your innocence?" Weber suggested.

Harper laughed and said, "Yeah, childlike, let's go with that." Then he dispelled the childlike image with his next comment. "Oh shit! Max, hold on, damn it!"

The plumber had backed a blue Chevrolet pickup next to the burned truck and was shoveling debris from the fire into the bed.

"I need you to let that all sit there for a while. I'm going to try to get the State Fire Marshal to send an investigator up here to see if they can figure out how the fire started."

"I can't let it just sit here. Once it dries out all that ash is going to get all over the place."

"How about we get some plastic tarps and cover it up and stake it down for now?"

"You going to help me with that, Steve? I'm just one man. And who's going to pay for the tarps?"

"Stop being such a cheap bastard," Harper told him. "You've got more money buried in Mason jars in the back yard than I'll ever make."

"Maybe yes, maybe no. Ain't none of your business. But I'll still need help, you little runt."

"Then you're buying me lunch when we're done."

"Hell, the time you waste standing here flapping your lips, lunch will be long gone and it'll be time for dinner before we're done."

"Sounds like a lot of work. I'll leave you two to hammer out those details," Weber told them, walking back to his Ford Explorer. "Steve, call me after you talk to the Fire Marshal."

The fire chief was too busy warning the plumber that if he threw out his back helping cover the burned truck there would be hell to pay, so Weber left them to their banter and drove to the New Hope Baptist

Church in search of a devout lady in an orange Volkswagen Beetle.

Chapter 2

Reverend Goldhatch was standing outside the church door shaking hands with the congregation as they left, and nodded at the sheriff as Weber got out of his vehicle. Weber returned the nod and walked across the parking lot to where Grace Rood was talking with two other women. They interrupted their conversation, which sounded more like gossip to the sheriff, and Grace smiled at him. The other two women scowled, though the sheriff knew that it wasn't his presence that made them scowl. Both wore the expression most of the time

"Why, Jim Weber. I can't remember the last time we saw you at church. It's about time," said Lois Burgee.

"Technically, he's not *at* church," Rita Zimmerman said, "Services ended ten minutes ago." Weber remembered Mrs. Zimmerman's high school English class and how much of a stickler she was for accuracy in every detail. To the longtime teacher, a misplaced comma or semicolon was on a par with truancy or robbing a convenience store. The fact that she was as tall and broad shouldered as a football fullback only added to her intimidation factor in the minds of students and other faculty members alike.

"Ladies," Weber said, tipping his hat, "how are you this fine morning?"

"Some of us are washed in the blood of the lamb," Lois told him. She was a slender sharp faced woman who took her religion seriously and who changed churches on a regular basis, whenever her current pastor or fellow worshipers offended her by not being as pious as she herself was. Lois made the circuit at least once a year between Big Lake's Baptist, Pentecostal, Methodist, and Lutheran churches. She avoided the Mormon's, whom she considered a cult, and the Catholics, who she felt stood too much on ceremony and because they used wine in the Blessed Eucharist. Weber suspected that in an earlier century Lois would have been quite happy as a member of the Inquisition or attacking saloons with Carrie Nation.

Grace said, "I imagine you want to ask me about the fire this morning at Max Woodbury's place."

"Max Woodbury," Rita said the name as if it left a bad taste in her mouth. "A terrible student, he never applied himself. I'm not at all surprised that he turned out to be such a failure."

Weber was tempted to tell her that some people would consider anyone who started a business from scratch and made a name for himself based upon hard work and honesty was far from a failure, but he knew that in the former teacher's eyes, anyone without a college degree or who worked with his hands would never measure up to her standards. In truth, even those who did further their education would not make the grade with Rita Zimmerman.

Instead, he said to Grace, "I hear you were quite the hero this morning, waking Max up and saving his place and all."

"The proper term is heroine," Rita said. "Hero is masculine, heroine is feminine. You would know that if you would have spent your classroom time paying attention instead of daydreaming."

"If Max would have been awake and on his way to church where he belonged, nobody would have had to wake him up in the first place," added Lois.

"Be that as it may, Mrs. Rood here still saved the day for Max. I need to ask her a couple of questions. Would you ladies mind excusing us for a minute?"

"A minute is sixty seconds," Rita told him. "You should say moment, which is a short indefinite period of time, unless all you require is sixty seconds."

Weber remembered why he had skipped English class so many times as he led Grace away. They stopped next to his Explorer and Weber asked her to tell him what had transpired that morning.

"Well, I was on my way to church about 7:45, and when I passed by Max's place I saw the truck was on fire so I pulled in and pounded on the shop door. Nobody answered so I went around back and saw the door to the apartment and started pounding on it and calling for help. Max came to the door and I told him about the fire and he ran outside and grabbed a hose and started squirting water at the truck. He told me to call 911 so I went inside the apartment and called. Then I went to church."

"You went to church? You didn't stay to help him put out the fire?"

"Of course not, Sheriff. Services start at 8:30 and I had to be here in time to get the bulletins ready to hand out as people came in."

"Did you see anything out of the ordinary at Max's place this morning?"

"Yes, his truck was on fire."

Weber knew he had that one coming and let it pass. "Besides that. Anything suspicious? Maybe somebody else there or nearby?"

"If somebody else was there I would have told them to get help and kept on going. I told you, I had to be here in time to get the bulletins ready to hand out."

"Yes you did," Weber told her, feeling like he was wasting time. But he pressed on, hoping to get lucky. "So you didn't see anybody else? Maybe walking nearby or running away? Or a car taking off?"

"No, nothing like that."

"Was the truck burning all the way when you first saw it?"

"No, just the inside was on fire."

"The inside? Inside the cab or inside the bed?"

"The part where the driver sits."

"The cab?"

"I guess so, if that's what you call it," she said. "Flames were coming out the window."

"But the rest of the truck wasn't on fire?"

"Not then, but by the time Max got out there, it was burning all over."

"Did you hear anything, Grace? Like a big whooshing sound maybe?"

"No, not that I recall. I was pretty worried and may not have noticed if there was. I'm sorry."

"Nothing to be sorry about. Like I said, you're a hero. Or heroine, I guess. I'd have been worried too, if I were in your shoes and dealing with a fire."

"Oh, I wasn't worried about the fire. I was worried about getting to church on time. I had to be here to get the bulletins ready to hand out."

"Grace? Are you about done? If we wait much longer we won't be able to get a seat."

"Oh, sorry Rita," Grace called and turned back to Weber. "We usually have Sunday brunch at the Wagon Wheel. It gets crowded if we wait too long. Do you want to come with us? You can ask me any other questions you have."

Of the few dining options the small town offered late on a Sunday morning, and the tablemates he might choose, brunch with the three women was about as far from Weber's first choice as could be.

"No, thank you Grace. I appreciate it, but I need to get back to work. Thanks for your time."

The crowd had thinned out and the minister made his way to Weber. "Nice to see you, Sheriff. I'm just sorry it wasn't inside for my sermon."

"Yeah, I need to do that," Weber told him. "It's been a while."

Goldhatch raised his eyebrows. "A while? I read somewhere that God has a rule about fibbing, my friend."

Weber laughed, "You got me. It's been a long time. This job tends to keep me busy."

"I also read somewhere that God created the heavens and the earth in less than a week. *That's* busy. Maybe you need to work on your time management skills."

Weber laughed again. "I'll get right on it."

"Please tell me that if the reason for your visit here today isn't to save your soul, at least it wasn't to take one of my congregation away to the hoosegow. I need to keep all of them that I can."

"No, nothing like that. We had a fire at Max Woodbury's place this morning and Grace Rood saw it and alerted him. I was just following up with her."

"Grace is a wonderful woman and works very hard for the church. If she's not teaching a Sunday school class or making cookies for our bake sale, she's busy passing out bulletins. She even comes in on Saturdays to make sure the church is clean and ready for Sunday services."

"I wish I had deputies that dedicated," Weber said.

"Well, we don't pay anything but we've got a great retirement plan," Goldhatch said.

"Let's hope all of us have a good long time before we have to collect on it," the sheriff said as he got into his vehicle. "But if you happen to get there first, put in a good word for me, will you?"

"No need to wait for that," the minister told him, "I'll do it today. We never know, after all."

"I appreciate that," Weber said. "I need all the help I can get."

As he waved and drove away, the sheriff had no idea just how much help he was going to need in the days ahead of him.

Chapter 3

Paul Lewis, the portly owner of the weekly *Big Lake Herald* newspaper, was not in a good mood when Weber plopped himself down in a chair in his small office, where it seemed like every available space was piled high with newspapers, file folders, books, and photographs.

"Will you look at this piece of crap," Paul said, throwing a newspaper across his cluttered desk.

"What did you do now? Print another picture with a dog taking a dump in the background?"

A few weeks earlier Paul had run a front page story on the grand opening of the new Hi-Country Market that included a four column wide photograph of the store's manager and the Town Council preparing to cut the symbolic red ribbon. But he had failed to notice Arley Beeson's large red Irish Setter doing its business in the background. Nor had Margie Shores, the newspaper's combination receptionist, proofreader, and bookkeeper. Gary Jackson and Joe Kraemer, who worked part time helping print the newspaper had missed it, too. But when the telephone started ringing on Margie's desk as soon as the new issue hit the street, it seemed like everybody between Big Lake and Springerville had seen the defecating doggie.

"No, not that, *this*," Paul said, stabbing a round stubby finger at the newspaper. "Did you know anything about this, Jimmy?"

Weber unfolded the paper and stared at it for a moment, then whistled. "Where did this come from?"

"I saw it sitting on the counter at the ButterCup Café when I went in for breakfast this morning. A big stack of them. They're also at the Fast Stop, the Town Pump, the Wagon Wheel, and all over town."

The words *Big Lake Truth* spread across the top quarter of the front page in bold black type, with the subtitle *The Real News You Need To Know*. Three of the front page's five columns were surrounded by a black border under a headline that said *It's Time For The Truth*. Weber read the first three paragraphs, shaking his head as he did:

It's time for the people of this good community to know the truth and we are here to deliver it. The truth that the established newspaper and certain people in power here in Big Lake don't want you to know. The truth that has been hidden from you.

Truth such as the fact that certain business owners in Big Lake have long curried favor from the press and some members of the Town Council. Truth such as the fact that the Good Old Boy system is alive and well in this town, shutting out anyone who dares to stand up to the establishment and creating an atmosphere that strangles commerce.

The truth that corruption and incompetence reign superior and that certain well known business owners and Town employees have been allowed to make their own rules and take advantage of their position to attack anyone who challenges them. That all stops today! We're here with the *Truth*!"

"Where did this come from, Paul?"

"Keep reading, it get's better," the newspaper publisher said.

We are not afraid to name names and expose those who have hidden behind a cloak of fear and intimidation until now. We are not afraid to pull them from the shadow world they inhabit and show you the seamy underbelly of this town. Because the *Truth* shall prevail!

The citizens of Big Lake need to clean house and this publication is the broom that will do the job. Starting with the Town Council and working our way through the School Board, Maintenance Department, Fire Department, and especially the Sheriff's Department, we promise to make a clean sweep. Out with the corrupt, incompetent old and in with the bright and shining new!

"Wow, muckraking at its best," Weber said. "Who's putting this rag out?"

"The masthead on Page 2 says the editor and publisher is Darron Tovar."

"Never heard of him."

"I have," Paul said. "The name rang a bell with me. Young guy who just graduated from NAU with a journalism degree. He sent me an unsolicited resume a while back, but I didn't need anybody so I didn't respond. About a month ago he showed up here with the ink still wet on his diploma, trying to convince me that I needed him. I told him this little old paper of mine barely pays the bills and that I can't afford any more help and he went off on me. Telling me that he didn't need to work here, that the old stodgy guys like me were history and that the new wave was going to wash us away."

"Okay, so he's pissed at you and wants to put you in your place, but why go on the attack against the whole town?"

"Who knows? Maybe he thinks it will get him some readers. And he's not attacking the whole town. A couple of people seem to be doing a great job. Read the editorial there on the same page."

The editorial blasted several Town Council members, the entire School Board, and Weber himself as incompetent, and promised to expose their sins in future issues. However, it also gave high praise to Mayor Chet Wingate, Councilwoman Gretchen Smith-Abbot, and Councilman Adam Hirsch, all of whom it referred to as enlightened, progressive, and committed to the best interests of the community.

Weber thumbed through the rest of the eight page newspaper, most of which was compromised of boilerplate filler; crossword puzzles, an astrology column, canned movie reviews, and three pages of classified advertising. There were only two display ads, a full page for Wingate's Hardware & Lumber and a half page for Mountain Auto supply.

"It looks like they've got a lot of yard sale ads, but the only big ones are from Chet Wingate and Todd Norton."

"Those classifieds all came from my last issue," Paul said. "He copied them all, almost word for word."

"He stole your ads? Why would he do that? Is it even legal?"

"Classified advertising isn't copyrighted, so technically he didn't *steal* them. And the reason he has them there is because a lot of people read a paper just for the ads."

"Yeah, because calling out so many people in the local government isn't enough," Weber said sarcastically. "So how did he get Chet and Todd to take out ads?"

"Obviously Chet has an agenda, so he supported it," Paul told him.

"Chet *always* has an agenda," Weber said. "But you've been around forever. Why would he support this new guy? And with such a big ad?"

"Our good mayor has been mad at me because I wouldn't give him a weekly column on the front page, where he wanted to share Town Council news. What it actually was going to be was a puff piece telling the world how wonderful he is. So he pulled his weekly ad a month ago, out of protest. As for Todd Norton, he never advertised much at all anyway. Don't know why he took such a big ad in this thing."

"He's pissed at me because I told his wife to talk to an attorney during their divorce, since he was cutting her out of everything," Weber said. "Maybe he wants to help this guy stick it to me."

"Do you ever feel like a pin cushion in a room full of porcupines?"

"All the time," Weber replied with a chuckle. "So what are you going to do about this thing?"

"Hell, maybe I'll let him run me out of business like he wants to," his old friend said. "I'll spend my golden years watching late night infomercials on TV and sleeping all day, and let him deal with everything it takes to run a small town paper like this. That would serve him right."

Chapter 4

Weber was swearing in the Sheriff's Department's new Citizen Volunteers; five men and two women who had undergone a month long training program learning the basics of traffic control, radio procedures, routine patrol, and first aid, to be able to assist regular officers at special events or when a crime or disaster occurred that taxed the department's available manpower. Weber was impressed at how much they had learned in their twice-weekly evening classes and made a mental note to compliment Deputies Dolan Reed and Chad Summers for making the program become a reality.

Paul Lewis was taking photographs of the proud new volunteers posing in their uniforms with the sheriff when Mary Caitlin turned from the dispatch desk

"Jimmy, we've got another fire. And Chief Harper says it's bad!"

***

As soon as the Explorer came out of the trees, Weber could see the thick black smoke billowing into the sky up ahead. He sped through the open meadow and took the SUV into the long curve that followed Beaver Creek at twice the posted speed, his tires howling against the blacktop in protest as he expertly fought the steering wheel for control to prevent a sideways skid that could end in a rollover.

Up ahead the road was blocked by Big Lake's two fire trucks, and men in yellow turnout gear were working hard to subdue the flames that shot into the air from a small cabin. The blackened hulk of an automobile was parked next to the cabin.

Weber stopped behind the fire trucks, the acrid smell of burning rubber and plastic filling the air. Even from that distance the heat of the fire assaulted his face and his eyes stung as soon as he stepped outside of his vehicle. It was obvious that despite their best efforts, Chief Harper and his volunteers had already lost the battle.

"Anybody inside?" Weber asked the fire chief.

"No idea, Jimmy. Won't know until we can get inside. And that's not going to be anytime soon," Harper said, and then interrupted himself to shout orders at one of his men, "Ronnie? Put some more water on that propane tank! We don't need that thing going up, too!"

He watched as the fireman sprayed a stream of water on a horizontal propane tank at the back end of the driveway, then turned back to Weber and said, "The car's gas tank went off just as we pulled up. Damn thing must have been full, because it made a hell of a fireball."

Dolan Reed and Chad Summers joined them and Dolan said, "Hell of a way to break in our new volunteers. What can we do for you, Steve?"

"Not much anybody can do," Harper said. "It's a dead end street and there's only a couple more cabins up there and nobody in them, so we don't really need any traffic control, except maybe at this end to keep the gawkers at a distance."

Before Dolan could assign any of the volunteers to the end of the road, the first of those gawkers arrived in the form of Big Lake's mayor.

"What's the status at this point?" Chet Wingate demanded. "Is anybody inside that cabin?"

"You can see the status," Harper told him. "It was burning bad when we got here and we haven't been able to enter yet. There's a vehicle there, but I don't know if the place was occupied when the fire began."

"And you didn't go in to look?" the mayor asked incredulously.

"No. It's not safe."

"What if there's somebody trapped in there?"

"If there was anybody in there, they're dead," Harper told him.

"You can't know that until you get inside. Send somebody in to check!"

"No way! Are you crazy?"

"Do it! That's an order."

"Now you listen here, Chet. I know you're the mayor, but I'm the fire chief and I'm not going to order any of my men in there until it's safe. As bad as this place was burning when we got here, it was too late to do anything for anyone who might have been inside."

"What are you doing here, Chet?" Weber asked. Usually the mayor was busy criticizing the sheriff for the way he ran his department, but Weber found it just as irritating when he poked his nose into any place where it didn't belong.

"I'm doing my job. I have voters who are concerned about the safety of this town, Sheriff."

"Well how about you go on about your business and let us do *our* jobs," Weber told him. "All you're going to do here is get underfoot."

The mayor started to raise a finger and object, but before he could say anything there was a frustrated shout from the fire scene and one of the firemen ran back to a truck and flipped a switch. The sound of the generator powering the truck's pump was silenced and two firemen worked quickly to unhook water hoses from the truck.

"What's happening? Why are they taking the hoses off?"

"The truck's out of water," Harper told him. "They need to refill it."

"Out of water? How can it be out of water?"

"It holds 2,000 gallons, and once it's empty we have to refill it. The closest water source is Shoat's Pond. It's gonna take them at least half an hour to get there and fill up and get back here."

"And what happens in the meantime?"

"We'll pump water onto the propane tank from the brush truck, but it's only got a 250 gallon tank so that won't last long. Meanwhile, we'll try to keep the fire from spreading using shovels and hoes. That's all we can do without fire hydrants."

"That's not enough. Do something," the mayor demanded.

"What would you have the man do?" Weber asked him.

"I don't know. Something besides just stand there while the place burns!"

"Well I'll tell you what," Harper said, "how about I give you a helmet and coat and you can go up there and piss on it? Maybe that'll do the trick."

"You can't talk to me that way. I'm the mayor," Chet shouted.

"And I'm the goddamn fire chief," Harper said, leaning forward until the two men were almost nose to nose. "So how about you trot your fat ass back to your office and do whatever it is you do and I'll stay here and do my job?"

Though Weber enjoyed seeing somebody else in Chet Wingate's crosshairs for a change, he knew that both men were hotheads afflicted with little man's syndrome and decided he should intervene before they came to blows, actually before Harper made it physical. He had dealt with Chet Wingate long enough to know that while the man was a blowhard, he was all bark and no bite. Harper, on the other hand, was a redheaded Irishman who never let his size keep him from wading into battle when he was pushed. And as much as Weber would have enjoyed seeing the mayor knocked onto his rear end, he didn't think it was worth all of the paperwork that such an incident would generate. As much as the sheriff disliked the mayor, he loathed paperwork even more.

But before he could do anything, he heard Dolan yell, "What the hell are you doing? Get off of there!"

Weber turned to see a young man with long brown hair tied in a ponytail standing on top of the fire department's pumper, busily snapping photographs of the fire. On the ground, Dolan and two firemen were shouting at him to climb down but he ignored them and continued taking pictures.

"Get down, dammit," Dolan shouted. "They need to take this truck to get more water."

When the man didn't do as ordered, Kevin Upchurch shook his head in frustration and climbed behind the wheel of the truck. Putting it in gear and pulling forward slowly, he dumped the stranger into the cabin's gravel driveway. As soon as he was on the ground, the other fireman jumped into the truck and they sped off toward Shoat's Pond.

By the time Weber reached them, Dolan had the man on his feet and a firm grip on his arm as he tried to pull away. "Stop resisting or I'll put you in handcuffs."

"Let go of me, I've got a right to be here," the photographer said, "I'm with the newspaper. You're interfering with my freedom of the press!"

"What's your name?" Weber demanded.

"Darron Tovar. Now make this storm trooper of yours let go of me. I've got a job to do."

"So do these firemen," Weber told him. "What were you thinking, climbing up there on that truck like that? And why didn't you get down when Deputy Reed told you to?"

"Because I was busy."

Before Weber could reply, Chet Wingate stormed up and ordered, "Deputy, release that man right now!"

"Shut up, Chet," Weber said.

"Don't tell me to shut up!"

"Back off, Chet. I mean it."

Chet pointed a finger in Weber's face and said, "Sheriff, you're stepping way over the line. Do I have to remind you that I'm the mayor of this town? I want this man released right this minute or I'll have both of your badges."

Weber was rethinking his position on Chief Harper punching the mayor out when Darron Tovar raised his camera with one hand and took their picture. The sheriff wasn't sure which irritated him the most. Before he could decide, everybody had to step out of the way while Claude Finley backed the brush truck up as close to the cabin as was safe and started deploying the truck's water hose from it's reel.

"What do you want me to do with this idiot?" Dolan asked.

"Deputy, that's no way to talk to a citizen," Chet said.

Weber ignored him and stepped in front of the young man. "If we let you go, will you stay out of the way so the firemen can do their job?"

"I have a right to be here."

"Don't bust my balls," Weber told him. "I didn't say you can't be here. I asked if you'd stay out of the way while you get your pictures. Now, can you?"

"Yeah, fine. Whatever you say."

"All right, then. Dolan, let him go."

"We seem to have gotten off on the wrong foot," Weber said, extending his hand to the newcomer. "I'm Jim Weber, the sheriff. Why don't you stop by my office once we're all done here and we'll get acquainted."

"I know who you are and we're as acquainted as we need to be," Tovar said as he walked away and resumed taking photos.

"Well thank you very much," Weber said to his back and shook his head at the man's arrogance. He had a feeling that, despite what Darron Tovar had said, the two of them were indeed going to get better acquainted.

Chapter 5

By the time the fire was extinguished, all that was left of the cabin was a burned out shell. Weber breathed a sigh of relief when they were able to get inside and ascertain that no one was killed in the inferno.

"Damn, Jimmy. This is bad," Harper said as they stood in what had been a bedroom but was now nothing but a blackened trash heap of sodden bedcovers and the remnants of furniture. They wore paper masks over their mouths and their eyes burned. Weber wondered what kind of carcinogenic gases they were inhaling from the cabin's burned insulation, upholstery fabric, and other materials.

"Did you get a chance to call the Fire Marshal's office yet?"

"First thing this morning. All I got was a runaround from some clerk telling me I needed to make a formal request and what forms I needed to fill out to do it. She faxed them to me, but I got the idea that she didn't think an old truck or a barn that was already falling down was much of an issue."

"Well, this damn sure makes it an issue," Weber said. "We've gone from empty sheds and barns to a truck parked next to an occupied structure to a cabin fire, in what? A week? Eight days?"

"I'm going to call again as soon as we get the trucks refilled with water and fuel. And this time I'm not taking no for an answer until I talk to somebody who can actually do something."

"You go do that now," Weber told him. "I'll have my guys tape the place off to keep people out."

"Thanks, Jimmy. This is way past my ability. I'm in over my head."

"I've got a bad feeling that we both are with this one," Weber said.

***

Weber barely had time to get back to the Sheriff's Office and wash some of the soot off his face when the mayor and Councilwoman Smith-Abbot came through the door to his private office.

"Sheriff Weber, I want to talk to you."

"Didn't your mother ever teach you how to knock?" Weber asked.

"What happened out there this afternoon was an outrage. An outrage, I tell you! What are you going to do about it?"

"Which outrage are you referring to, Chet? The outrage of your interfering with Chief Harper's job at the fire or the outrage of you interfering with Dolan doing his job? Because anybody in his right mind would find both pretty outrageous."

"I'm talking about Deputy Reed and Kevin Upchurch's actions. I want both of them suspended for the way they treated Mr. Tovar."

"It's very fortunate Mr. Tovar wasn't seriously injured," Councilwoman Smith-Abbot said.

"Mr. Tovar is just lucky he's not sitting in a jail cell right now," Weber replied. "Where did you come up with this idiot, Chet?"

"I don't appreciate the way you are referring to one of this town's newest business owners," Smith-Abbot said. As Chet Wingate's ardent supporter and almost constant shadow, some in Big Lake wondered if their relationship extended past their official duties, though the idea of either one of them ever having any emotion that wasn't harshly critical or coldly clinical tended to dispel the thought.

"I didn't see you at the fire today, Gretchen. Were you afraid that if you got any water splashed on you that you'd melt like that witch in the Wizard of Oz?"

"How dare you!"

"You weren't there and didn't see anything that happened, so all you have is hearsay. And as for you Chet, Dolan was doing his job and I'm damn sure not going to suspend him for it. And Kevin Upchurch is a volunteer fireman. I don't see how anybody can suspend a volunteer."

"Then I want him charged with assault. He could have killed Mr. Tovar with that fire truck."

"Come on, Chet. He was trying to get water to fight the fire. The same fire you were screaming at Steve Harper to put out just a minute before."

"So you're not going to arrest him?"

"No, Chet, I'm not."

"And you're not going to suspend Deputy Reed?"

"Nope."

"Why do I even bother trying to talk to you, Sheriff Weber? It's a total waste of my time."

"I don't know, Chet. Why *do* you do it? I'd think you'd learn by now."

"Do I have to go over your head, Sheriff?"

At 5'10', with a medium build, Weber wasn't a big man, but when he stood up from his chair he was still taller than the mayor, and when he took a step forward the shorter man took an involuntary step backward.

"If you plan to go over my head, you'd better bring a stepladder, Chet. So how about you and your charming pal here get the hell out of my office and go find one?"

"You can't talk to me like that!"

"I just did, Chet. Now go away."

"This is so like you, Sheriff Weber," Councilwoman Smith-Abbot said. "You are a bully and a ..."

"You too, sister. Don't let the door hit you where the Lord split you," Weber said.

The woman gasped in shock at his words as the mayor said, "I'm taking this to the Town Council. We'll just see what they have to say about your latest act of disrespect and insolence."

"Out!" Weber roared, pointing a finger at the door. The look on his face and the tone of his voice left no doubt that he was prepared to eject them both bodily if they didn't comply with his order, and the mayor and councilwoman nearly tripped over themselves on the way out the door.

Two minutes later an attractive 60ish woman with mischievous blue eyes and a thick mane of graying hair knocked and poked her head inside the door. "Is it safe to come in?"

"I don't know. Are you bringing coffee or paperwork?"

"You're too tense for coffee and I'm holding off on the paperwork until you're in a better mood, so I can spoil it, too," Mary Caitlin said. Weber's administrative assistant was more than an employee, or even a friend. She was almost like a mother to Weber, or at least a favorite aunt. The wife of Weber's mentor, former sheriff Pete Caitlin, Mary had an almost encyclopedic knowledge of the people of their small town. She seemed to know everybody in town not just by name, but also their family background and tidbits of useful personal information. Mary wasn't a gossip by any means, but Weber, who had been born and raised in Big Lake, was amazed that she could always tell him who was married to who, what man was raising a child whose paternity was suspect, what bride had walked down the aisle a short six or seven months before giving birth, who had been in trouble with the law in the past, and who was struggling to get by in the town's often shaky economy. And if she didn't know, she always found out. Mary didn't let him down this time either.

"You asked me about Darron Tovar. He's from Payson but he's got a local connection."

"Okay, what is it?"

"First, let me tell you a little bit about him," Mary said, referring to the yellow legal pad she carried. "It seems he's an overachiever, to say the least. Straight A's all through high school, president of his senior class, went to Northern Arizona University on a full scholarship, where he finished in three years and graduated with honors, then he earned a master's degree. Did I tell you he has a local connection?"

"Yes you did, what is it?"

"I don't think I told you that he ran the school newspaper in both high school and at NAU, did I?"

Weber knew the routine well and leaned back in his chair, knowing that Mary was not going to give up her information easily. "No, Mary, you didn't tell me that."

"Or that he had job offers from half a dozen newspapers and TV stations?"

"No, you didn't tell me that either."

"But I did tell you that he…"

"Yes, Mary, you did tell me that he has a local connection. And from that smirk on your face, I know you're dying to tell me all about it, but you want me to work for it, don't you?"

"Am I that obvious, Jimmy?"

"Yes, you are, Mary."

"But you love me, right?"

"With all my heart."

"And who's your buddy?"

"You are, Mary."

"And who's the smartest, sexiest woman you know?"

"You are, Mary. And if you don't tell me right now, I'm going to boot your smart, sexy ass right out that door I just sent Chet and Gretchen through."

"You'll catch more flies with honey than with vinegar, Jimmy."

"Mary…"

"Gosh you're a grouch sometimes," she said, sticking her tongue out at him, her eyes twinkling at the game.

"Don't make me kill you, Mary."

"Okay, okay. But you're going to love this one."

"Uh huh?"

"Darron Tovar has an aunt here in Big Lake that thinks he has the face of an angel and walks on water."

"I see. And do I know this woman, Mary?"

"Why, yes, you do, Jimmy. In fact, you just threw her out of your office a few minutes ago."

Weber's jaw dropped and he leaned forward in his chair.

"No way!"

"Yes, way."

"Really?

"Really. Darron Tovar is the son of William and Doris Tovar. His father is the sales manager at the Ford dealership in Payson and his mother is the former Doris Smith, the younger sister of your dear friend Councilwoman Gretchen Smith-Abbot."

Chapter 6

News that a serial arsonist might be on the loose spread through Big Lake as fast as the flames that had devoured the cabin on Beaver Creek Road. People talked about it in the shops along Main Street, at the counter of the ButterCup Café, and as they stood in line at the Timber Savings Bank.

Some people believed it was the work of teenagers with time on their hands during summer vacation, probably out of town kids who were part of the invasion that happened every summer as people fled the desert heat in Tucson and Phoenix to escape to the cooler pine covered mountains of Arizona's high country. "We never had problems like this before those damned developers started building all those cabins and vacation homes," more than one Big Lake native said. And somebody would always nod their head in agreement and say, "The old days were so much better."

The *old days* were back when the small mountain town was still undiscovered, except for the occasional fishermen who came to town hoping to hook a trophy from the lake that gave the town its name; a three mile long body of deep cold water teeming with fighting trout that drew anglers from across the southwest. That was before developers cast their eyes upon the scenic mountainsides that towered over the community and envisioned summer cabins, lodges, and expensive custom log homes.

Within a decade, the little town's year-round population of 4,000 was tripled in summer as the weekend warriors arrived in their expensive automobiles and SUVs, with their designer jeans and seemingly unlimited budgets. While many old timers cursed the newcomers, especially those who had abandoned California with its earthquakes, mud slides, wildfires, and urban violence, at least they could take comfort that it was only for a few short summer months and then things would get back to normal. But that was before they built the ski lodge, and now even winter was a busy time of year. Now when the snow piled up, cars and sport utility vehicles carrying ski racks brought crowds of powder lovers to the mountains.

Of course, while many residents publicly cursed the loss of the small town atmosphere and quality of life they had long enjoyed, they secretly appreciated the extra dollars these newcomers brought to town. Land that had long sat idle and unwanted was suddenly in high demand and more than one Big Lake resident had traded a property tax bill for a hefty deposit into their bank account.

Some were not convinced the fires were started by bored youngsters from the city.

"It ain't kids," George Holman told Candy Phillips as she handed him two blueberry donuts at the Sweet Seductions bakery. "It's these damn developers settin' them fires."

"Now why would they do that?" Dale Burglehaus asked him as he emptied the third packet of sugar into his coffee. "Makes no sense at all."

"Sure it does," George insisted. "The handwritin's on the wall. This here boom ain't gonna last forever and they know it. So they're tryin' to cash in by settin' the fires and then collectin' insurance."

Holman was an average looking man of medium build in his mid-thirties who wore a perpetual look of woe. And who could blame him? George was convinced that he was smarter than the rest of the world, and even though he had spent much of his life sharing that knowledge, the world never seemed to get it and appreciate him.

"That's the stupidest thing I've ever heard," Ray McDermont said. "None of the fires were at anything any developer built. So why would they burn down an old barn or set fire to Max Woodbury's truck?"

George shook his head at the other man's ignorance. "Ya gotta understand how their minds work, Ray. They're sittin' a president."

"A president? What the hell are you talking about, George? What does the president have to do with anything here in Big Lake?"

"Not that kind of president," George said. "A *legal* president. That there's when things is done a certain way so we come to expect it."

"Do you mean a precedent, George?"

"Ain't that what I just said, a president? See, once word gets out about these here fires it sits a president. Then when they burn up a whole bunch of them there specalatin' houses they built, why the insurance companies will just think it's part of the same pattern."

Ken Strodel shook his head as he listened to the two men debate

Big Lake Burning 33

the origins of the fires, but at the word president he couldn't help but interject his own opinion into the conversation. "It's not the developers. It's the damn government doing it. And it starts back in Washington at the White House."

"What do you mean?"

"It's simple, Ray. They want to stop development here and have this whole region revert to primeval forest. You watch and see, before they're done the whole damn town will go up in flames"

Like many western ranchers, Ken hated the Bureau of Land Management and the Forest Service, and was convinced they were trying to put small operations like his out of business.

Before Ken could expound any deeper on his theory, the door opened and Sheriff Weber and Deputy Chad Summers stepped inside the bakery. They nodded to the three men at the table and Weber said, "George, you taking a day off?"

"Why no sir," George said, standing up so quickly he knocked over the chair he had been sitting on. "Nope. Just headin' that way now, Sheriff."

"I was planning on stopping by your house sometime this week to say hello, but since we've already crossed paths, you give your missus my regards when you get home tonight. Tell those kids of yours that I'll swing by one of these days and let them blow the siren on my unit, okay?"

"I'll sure do that," George said as he made his way to the door.

Once they got their coffee and were seated Chad said, "So old George is still going to work every day. What's it been, six, seven months now? And I hear he's helping Susan around the house and with the kids. I'd have never believed it."

"Well, when a man's got enough incentive, he'll stick to something," Weber observed as he bit into a buttermilk long john.

What he didn't add was that a private conversation between himself and the chronic slacker that had taken place in the parking lot of the Antler Inn the previous winter had been just the incentive George had needed.

"Any news on those fires?" Ray McDermont asked.

"Somebody from the State Fire Marshal's office is supposed to be up here tomorrow," Weber said.

"Instead of coming here, they need to be headed to Washington," Ken Strodel insisted. "No offense to you, Sheriff, but I think this is way more than you're equipped to handle. This goes all the way to the top. It starts right there in the Oval Office!"

"Well I'll sure rest easier when you catch whoever's starting these fires," Candy Phillips said.

Weber wasn't convinced that Ken's idea was correct, since the man saw everything from drought to grazing leases as a government plot to make the lives of the working class miserable, but if he had to admit it to himself, he wasn't yet willing to accept Candy's assumption that he would catch the arsonist. At least, not anytime soon. Weber had a bad feeling about the string of suspicious fires, a feeling that the worst was yet to come.

Chapter 7

Normally not well-attended, Tuesday night's Town Council meeting was packed with concerned citizens wanting to know more about what was being done to stop the rash of fires. Those who arrived too late to find seats were standing in the back and along both sides of the room.

Mayor Chet Wingate opened the meeting with a call to order and the Council quickly dispensed with the routine reading of the minutes from the last meeting. Then two smaller items were addressed; approving a stop sign at the intersection of Main Street and Hacienda Road to make it safer for shoppers to get in and out of the parking lot of the new Dollar Store, and voting down a request by Aaron Bagley to build a go cart track on three acres of land he owned next to the medical center that served as Big Lake's only hospital. Bagley was upset and vowed that he would see every councilmember out of office come next election.

Once Bagley stormed out of the room, the mayor said, "We have personnel matters to discuss which do not concern any of you, so does anybody in the audience have anything to say before we adjourn this portion of the meeting?"

"Yeah, what are you doing about the fires?" Timothy McKay demanded to know.

"We'll be addressing that in our closed session," the mayor said.

"Closed session? We have a right to know, before our homes and businesses go up in smoke next," objected Lois Miles, and the crowd murmured loudly in agreement.

"Order!" Chet said, rapping his gavel.

"Why do we need a closed session?" Councilman Kirby Templeton asked the mayor. "These people have serious concerns and I think they have a right to know what's going on. As a resident and a business owner, *I* have serious concerns about these fires."

"I think it's best that we discuss this in private," the mayor said, but was quickly overruled by the majority of the Town Council.

"All right then, if you insist we'll do it your way," the mayor said, though it was obvious he was frustrated. "Our next order of business is the Fire Department. And I have to tell you that I am very unhappy with the performance of Chief Harper. *Very* unhappy. He has shown a complete lack of professionalism and it's my opinion that he should be replaced immediately."

"Hold on there, Chet," Frank Gauger said. "I think Steve Harper's done a fine job given what he has to work with."

"A fine job? A *fine* job? Do you call preventing these fires a fine job, Councilman Gauger?"

"I don't believe it's the Fire Chief's job to prevent crimes," Gauger said, "Assuming that these fires *are* the work of an arsonist. Chief Harper, have you and Sheriff Weber been able to determine the origins of any of the recent fires yet?"

"It's my belief that they are arson," Harper said from where he was seated next to Weber in the front row. "I've spoken to the State Fire Marshal's office down in Phoenix and they are sending up an investigator tomorrow."

"So you don't *know* if they are arson?" Mayor Wingate asked. "You're just *guessing* at this point?"

"I'm not trained in arson investigations," Harper said. "I'm giving you my informed opinion."

"So you're just guessing?"

"Call it whatever you want to," Harper said.

"There you go! He's the Fire Chief and the best he can do is *guess*," the mayor told the council. "I move that we replace this man immediately."

"Replace him with who, Chet?"

"I have a candidate in mind."

"And would you mind sharing who that is with the rest of us?" Templeton asked.

"Yes, Archer Wingate," the mayor said primly.

"Archer? Your *son*? Are you kidding me, Chet?" Templeton's question was drowned out by hoots and laughter from the crowd.

Wingate rapped his gavel sharply and demanded, "Why not? Archer has already proven himself as a more than capable deputy. I think he'd make a splendid Fire Chief."

"Oh Lord," Weber murmured. The mayor had foisted his underachieving overweight son off on the Sheriff's Department two years earlier, and in the time that had elapsed since then, Archer had done little to demonstrate he was capable of doing much more than showing up for work, usually in a rumpled uniform and half asleep.

"Chet, we are not making your son Fire Chief," Templeton said. "First of all, we already have a Fire Chief. And unless you can demonstrate why he should be replaced, we don't need anybody else."

"What about these fires?" the mayor insisted. "Aren't they proof that he isn't doing his job?"

"No, Chet. I think the Chief and his volunteers have done a very good job. Keep in mind that one thing on the agenda tonight is the Fire Department's budget. The same budget you have refused to increase two years in a row."

"Why give him more money to waste when it's not doing any good anyway?"

Weber leaned closer to the fire chief and said, "Every time this idiot opens his mouth he sticks his foot in it."

"Let's hear from Chief Harper," Councilman Gauger suggested. "Chief, give us an overview of your Department and what you need to accomplish your job."

Harper was not comfortable with public speaking and had to refer to his notes as he spoke. "We've got sixteen members on the Fire Department. I'm the only paid employee, the rest are volunteers. The only ones with any formal training are me and Kevin Upchurch, and that was in the Army. We drill twice a month and the guys show up when they can."

"Are you telling us that they're not *required* to attend training sessions?" the mayor asked incredulously.

"No, they're not. They're volunteers. They have jobs and families. Sometimes things get in the way," Harper replied.

"Well there you go," the mayor said sanctimoniously as he folded his hands across his stomach and sat back in his chair. "We have a Fire Chief with little training who doesn't even require his men to attend training sessions. A bunch of incompetents under the direction of an incompetent. And you wonder why we have a problem?"

Harpers' face turned red and Weber could see his anger building. "My men are not incompetent! They are dedicated volunteers. They buy their own turnout gear, which costs each one of them $250, if they can scrape the money together. Some can't. They use surplus radios and worn out equipment. They drop whatever they're doing and show up when there's a fire. Now, if you want to put me down and make me look bad in front of the Town Council and all these people, I guess that's your right, Chet. But I'm not going to stand here and let you talk bad about my men!"

By the time he was done speaking, Harper was shouting and the mayor rapped his gavel.

"That's the next thing," he told the council. "Besides not being capable of doing his job, this man is dangerous! Here, look at this. He almost attacked me yesterday!"

He held up a photograph of himself and the fire chief screaming at each other at the cabin fire.

"What were you doing at the fire scene, Chet?" Templeton asked.

"I was doing my job. Trying to get this man to do *his*!"

"The only thing you were doing was getting in the way and slowing us down," Harper retorted.

"Enough!" Templeton said loudly. "Chet, I've heard from three different firemen that you were there, getting underfoot. We're not going to debate this all night. Chief Harper, you requested $60,000 dollars and I have your report on what you plan to do with that money, but for the sake of the citizens gathered here, can you tell us what it's going to go for?"

"We have a thirty year old pumper truck that holds 2,000 gallons of water and a small truck we use for brush fires that holds 250 gallons. We pump about 95 gallons of water a minute and then we have to go refill them. There's a military surplus 6x6 pumper truck sitting in Deming, New Mexico that the fire department there isn't using. We can buy it for $15,000 and it will take another $5,000 to have it hauled up here and get a couple of mechanical things done and put new tires on it to put it into service. It would give us another 2,000 gallons of capacity. We don't have any breathing apparatus so we can't even enter a structure that's burning. For $2,500 per man I can buy ten complete turnout sets with breathing equipment."

"That's $25,000 right there," the mayor said, "and for just ten men?"

"Do you remember yesterday when you wanted me to send somebody into that burning cabin? How did you expect my men to do that without any way to breathe?"

"Quit being so damned cheap! Give them the money they need to get the job done," somebody shouted from the back of the room. Other voices agreed, though there were a few who wanted to know if that would mean increased property taxes.

"Quiet," the mayor said, rapping his gavel. "So that's a total of $45,000. What's the rest of the money for?"

"Better radios. We need to upgrade our hoses, and we'll need to put up a structure of some kind for the other truck if we get it. The guys said they'd do the labor, but there's materials…"

"And on and on and on," the mayor interrupted. "And we still don't have any guarantee you can do any better than you've been doing all along."

Before Harper could respond, Ladonna Jordan, the newest member of the Town Council, spoke up. "You said this truck down in Deming needs some mechanical work. Is it going to be a lemon? I mean, has anybody actually looked at it so we know what we're getting?"

"Me and Kevin drove down and checked it out," Harper said. "The tires are weathered and definitely need to be replaced. It also needs all new water hoses and a good cleanup. Randy Laird over at the garage said he'd donate his labor, so all we'd need to pay for is any parts."

"And how big did you say the tank on this truck is?" Councilwoman Jordan asked.

"2,000 gallons. So we're doubling our capacity. That will make a big difference. If we would have had it, we might not have lost that cabin yesterday."

"That's your opinion," the mayor said. "Personally, I believe better management of the Fire Department is the answer to this problem, not just throwing money at it. Before this goes any further, I make a motion that Chief Harper be dismissed," the mayor said."

"Really, Chet? You're going to push this?"

"Yes, I am, Kirby."

"Motion seconded," said Councilwoman Smith-Abbot, as she had done with every motion the mayor had made since she was seated on the Council.

"Fine, let's have a vote," Templeton said. "All those in favor of firing Chief Harper?"

Only the mayor and councilwoman said "Aye."

"Opposed?"

The nays by the other councilmembers brought a deeper scowl to the mayor's face.

"Motion overruled," Templeton said. "And as long as we're voting, I make a motion to approve Chief Harper's request for $60,000 for a truck, breathing equipment, and whatever else it will buy. These folks are putting their lives on the line for us, the least we can do is give them the equipment they need to get the job done."

"Before I second the motion, I have a question," Frank Gauger said. "Chief Harper, can you whittle that $60,000 figure down at all?"

Harper shook his head. "I've already whittled it down. It would take twice that to really get set up. We can't do it holding fish fries and raffles."

Gauger nodded and then said, "I second your motion, Kirby."

The motion was approved by a vote of five to two and Weber was sure the mayor would grind a layer of enamel off his teeth with his frustration.

Hoping to gain *some* yardage out of the meeting, Mayor Wingate attempted to introduce a debate about the treatment of Darron Tovar at the hands of the Sheriff's Department at the previous day's fire scene. But since the young man who was the alleged victim was not present, it quickly died on the vine and the meeting was adjourned.

"I'll be damned. I won one for a change," Harper said as the meeting broke up.

"You won a battle. Trust me, the war's not over yet," Weber cautioned him. "But I have to say, it was nice seeing you in the barrel instead of me for a change."

Chapter 8

Weber was surprised to find Deputy Archer Wingate was at work on time and wearing a clean, pressed uniform when he arrived at the Sheriff's Office on Wednesday morning.

"Jimmy, I need to talk to you."

Usually when Archer wanted to talk to him it meant that he had done something stupid and wanted to explain why it wasn't his fault. Like the time he had left his police car running in front of the Town Pump while he had run in to purchase a candy bar and Coke, only to come back outside and find that unknown pranksters had hidden the car behind the store. Was it *his* fault that car thieves were on the loose in Big Lake? And how could you blame Archer for leaving his gun belt and duty weapon hanging on a coat hook inside the toilet stall at the ButterCup Café? Accidents happen.

"What did you do now, Archer?"

"Nothing."

"Did you lose your car again?"

"No."

"I see you're wearing your gun, so it's not that. Did you have another accident?"

In Archer's time with the Sheriff's Department he had had two fender benders and also torn the exhaust system off his cruiser when he drove over one of the concrete parking lot bumpers at the Arby's. It seemed that many of Archer's mistakes and mishaps happened at places where food and snacks were sold.

"No, Jimmy. I didn't do nothing. I just wanted to talk about the Fire Chief's job."

"Forget it, Archer. Steve Harper is the Fire Chief and that's not going to change. And do you really think you're qualified to be the Fire Chief?"

"No sir," Archer said, shaking his head. "I know I'm not. And I don't want Chief Harper mad at me or thinking I'm trying to steal his job. That's all my dad's doing. He thinks I should be Fire Chief but I don't *want* to be and I told him so. I'd be lousy at that. I'm a lawman, not a fireman."

Weber wanted to tell Archer he wasn't qualified to be a lawman either, but before he could say it the door opened and Deputy Dan Wright ushered in a thoroughly unhappy George Holman.

"I'm tellin' you, I paid that darn ticket over a month ago! You got no right to treat me like I'm some common criminal."

"And I told *you* the computer still shows it as outstanding," Wright told him.

"Sheriff, I'm glad you're here," George said. "Will you tell this here man that I ain't no criminal!"

"What's up?" Weber asked Wright.

"I pulled him over for running a stop sign and when I ran his license it came back with an outstanding warrant for an unpaid ticket."

"I paid that ticket," George said again. "I went right in there to Leslie and paid it as soon as the next Friday come around. This here is harassment is what it is!"

"Just relax and have a seat and we'll get it figured out," Weber said.

"Well I hope you get it done fast. I'm a workin' man and I got responsibilities to tend to."

"Judy, can you run Mr. Holman's license for me," Weber asked the dispatcher, handing her the man's drivers license.

She nodded and typed his information into her computer, and a moment later said, "I show a warrant for failure to appear for a ticket originally issued May 19th of this year."

"I'm tellin' you, I paid that ticket," Holman said. "You can call Susie and ask her. She handles the money these days, what with me bein' so busy with my career and all. She gave me the money, $52, and I went right in there to the Town Clerk's office and paid it."

"Did you get a receipt?"

"Heck, Sheriff, I don't know. Are you all callin' me a liar?"

"Well, George, you're credibility *has* been a bit questionable in the past. I better not find out you took that money and blew it at the Antler Inn."

"No sir! I ain't been in that place in months. The last time I was there was when I had my pifany."

"Your pifany?"

"Yeah, that's when you have one of them there life changin' experiences. A pifany."

"I think you mean an epiphany."

"Well, ain't that what I just said? A pifany!"

Weber remembered Holman's epiphany very well, since he himself had been the catalyst of the event, when he had administered a bit of street justice to the chronic slacker, and after George was able to get back on his feet and draw a couple of deep breaths, the sheriff had explained to the man that it was time to get a job, support his family, and stop mooching off anybody that would give him a handout. And he had to admit that ever since that incident, the feedback he had been getting was that Holman was indeed stepping up to the plate and acting like a responsible citizen. An opinionated and often irritating citizen, but a citizen nevertheless.

"This is easy enough to settle," Weber said. "Come with me. But I'm warning you right now, George, if I find out you're lying to me..."

"I swear, Sheriff, I paid that ticket," Holman said, holding his hand up as if in testament.

As they started out the door, Archer stopped them. "Jimmy, will you talk to Chief Harper for me? Tell him I'm not looking to take his job?"

"Sure, Archer," the sheriff said, though he doubted that Steve Harper was very worried about competition for his job from Archer.

Weber led Holman and Dan Wright outside and across the parking lot to the Town Hall, where Town Clerk Leslie Stokes was standing behind the counter shuffling through a thick stack of papers in a folder as a stylishly dressed woman stood across from her with her arms folded and a scowl on her face.

"I'm sure it's here, Mrs. Hartford. Just give me a minute to look it up."

"Surely you must have a better way of dealing with things than this," the woman said sarcastically. "I mean, after all, it *is* the twenty-first century. Or didn't you get that memo?"

Leslie's face reddened, but she continued searching as she said, "I'm sorry. I'll find it."

"Would it be easier for you if I returned again in the twenty-second century? Do you think you might have it by then?"

"Is there a problem here?" Weber asked.

The woman turned and gave him a look of disdain. "Oh, no problem at all. It's not like I have anything to do with my time but stand here while this... *person* bumbles her way through life."

The woman epitomized everything Big Lake natives disliked in the newcomers who had invaded the community in recent years; privileged, spoiled, and with a superior attitude that looked down on anyone not in their own social strata as an inferior life form.

"No need to be rude," Weber told her.

"Rude? Rude is my having to come in here and waste half my day while this *public servant* attempts to do a job any high school student could have done in minutes."

"Just what is it you need done?" Weber asked her, trying hard to hide his irritation at the woman's attitude.

"I paid our water and sewer bill for the year months ago, and last week I got a past due notice. For some reason it never got recorded and now she can't find any record of it."

"Do you have a receipt or a cancelled check?"

"Is there any reason you need to know all of this..." she read Weber's name from the metal clip on his shirt, "Sheriff Weber?"

"Just trying to help," he told her.

Before the woman could reply, Leslie said, "Here it is," and pulled a sheet of paper from the folder. "Yes, Mrs. Hartford, I show you paid cash, $107, on March 1st."

"Then why did I get this past due notice?" the woman asked, jabbing her finger on an envelope on the counter."

"I'm very sorry. It was a computer error on our part. I'm going to go in right now and reconfirm your payment."

Leslie sat down at an ancient computer terminal and began typing, and a moment later a tired old dot matrix printer on a stand behind her chattered to life and printed out a receipt. She pulled the finished receipt from the printer, handed it to the woman, and apologized again. Instead of thanking her, or even acknowledging Leslie's existence, the woman just shook her head as she stuffed the receipt into a leather Tory Burch handbag that Weber thought might well have cost more than Leslie earned in a week.

"Don't you have a squirrel to shoot or something?" she asked Weber as she walked past him and out the door.

"Well wasn't she a breath of fresh air and sunshine," Weber said, as he watched the woman get behind the wheel of a white BMW Z4 convertible and drive away.

"It's been one of those mornings, Jimmy. What can I do for you today?"

"There seems to be some confusion that we need to get straightened out. Mr. Holman here got a ticket back in May and he said he came in and paid it, but today when Deputy Wright stopped him for something else, the system shows a failure to appear warrant was issued July 1st."

"Do you have a receipt?" she asked.

Holman shrugged. "I don't know, but I came in here and paid you myself."

Leslie shook her head sympathetically. "The computer system just automatically spits out a list of unpaid tickets after about six weeks and I take them over to Judge Ryman and he issues warrants for failure to appear. I can check and see if there was some kind of mistake. Sometimes our computer doesn't save a payment for some reason and I have to go back and look it up. But that's usually something like a business license renewal or tax payment."

"Or Mrs. Hartford's water and sewer bill?"

"Yeah," Leslie said, nodding her head ruefully.

"Can I use the phone to call home and see if Susie has my receipt?" George asked. "She's real good at keepin' track of things like that, us bein' on a limited budget and all."

"Sure, but let me check first," Leslie told him. "It won't take but a minute. When was it you paid?"

"It was the very next Friday when I got my paycheck."

"So that would be May 25th," Leslie said, referring back to a desk calendar. "Hang on just a second."

She went into another room and Weber heard a file cabinet drawer being pulled open and then closed a moment later. She returned to the office with a thick ledger and said, "Yep, here it is. George Holman, cash, $52. I'm *so* sorry Mr. Holman. I'm glad it wasn't next door in the records room or I'd have kept you waiting even longer."

"Well, there you go," Holman said, nodding his head righteously. "I told you guys I paid it."

"I'm sorry," Dan Wright told him. "All I had to go on was what our computer tells us."

"Computers," Holman said derisively. "Darned things are more trouble than they're worth."

"Okay, you can go," Weber told him. "Sorry to waste your time, George."

"It ain't about wastin' my time, though Lord knows I'm a busy man," Holman said. "What about my public humilatin' and all? Bein' treated like a common criminal."

"The word's *humiliation*, George, and everybody has apologized.

What more do you want?"

"Again, I'm really, really sorry sir," Leslie said. "It wasn't their fault, it was here in our office."

"Well, ain't I due some compensatin' for my pain and sufferin' and all?"

"George, how about if Deputy Wright here gives you a pass on whatever he pulled you over for today and you get out of here before you *do* experience some suffering?"

"That's the best deal ya got for me?"

"It's all you're getting, George."

"Well all right then. I'm a reasonable man and I know these things happen. How about if you forget today's ticket and reimburse me $100 for my time and we'll call it square?"

"How about I lock you up and throw away the key?"

"Okay, I'm going. But it ain't right, I'm tellin' you that right now."

"George…"

"Goodbye," Holman said, seeing the look on Weber's face and making a quick exit.

"I'm really sorry about all this," Leslie said once he was gone. "Our old computer system has seen better days and this happens more and more. I keep asking the mayor to authorize an upgrade, but you know how that goes."

"Oh yeah, I surely do," Weber assured her. "That man could pinch a nickel until the buffalo squeals. Don't worry about it, Leslie. No harm done, and George has something new to complain about. It's all good."

What wasn't good was that Gordon Hahn was waiting for him at the Sheriff's Office when Weber returned. Now *that* was something to complain about.

Chapter 9

The Bureau of Indian Affairs investigator assigned to the nearby White Mountain Apache Reservation, Gordon Hahn was a crude loudmouth who tended to bull his way through life, counting on his bulk and demeanor to cover up his lack of professional skill and social grace. Weber, and most other people, found him to be thoroughly dislikable, and for good reason.

"Hey, Jimmy!" the big man said when Weber came through the door. "How they hanging, son? You getting any?"

"What do you want, Hahn?"

"Nothing. Not a thing at all. I just got tired of living among the war whoops and decided to come to the big city for the day and check out the available nookie. Hell, the ugliest woman here is a damn sight better than them squaws on the Rez."

He stepped closer to Weber, and when he spoke, the sheriff winced at his rancid breath. "Hey Jimmy, do ya know the difference between a bowling ball and an Apache squaw? You can only get three fingers in a bowling ball!"

Weber scowled and wondered, not for the first time, why Hahn had not been found beaten to death on some back road on the Reservation years before. Hahn made no pretense of hiding his dislike for the Apache people, and Weber knew the feeling was returned from Whiteriver, the headquarters of Apache government, to the small outlying villages like Cibecue and McNary that were scattered across the 1.6 million acres of the Reservation.

"So I hear you got yourself a firebug," Hahn said.

"We've had some suspicious fires," Weber acknowledged, not wanting to get into a discussion with the man, in the hope that he would get the message and leave. Of course, Hahn was too dense to ever understand how unwelcome he was wherever he went.

"I wish you'd send whoever it is down to Whiteriver," Hahn said. "Burn that whole frigging place down and turn a bunch of those blanket asses into crispy critters."

Hahn guffawed at his own humor, ignoring the harsh stares from

Weber and the rest of the people in the office.

Weber was trying to decide if it would be better to beat the florid faced man to death or just shoot him and get it over with when Steve Harper came through the door with a woman that Weber could only describe as beautiful. She was tall, well built, with thick red hair that hung past her shoulders, and green eyes. Full lips highlighted a sprinkle of light freckles across her nose.

Weber tried not to gawk at the woman when Harper introduced her.

"Sheriff Weber, this is Deputy Fire Marshal Colleen Callahan. Colleen, this is our Sheriff, Jim Weber."

"Call me C.C.," she said, shaking Weber's hand firmly.

"It's nice to meet you, C.C.," Weber told her. "My friends call me Jimmy. This is Deputy Dan Wright, Deputy Archer Wingate, and Gordon Hahn from the Bureau of Indian Affairs."

She shook Dan and Archer's hands and nodded curtly at Hahn.

"What, no hug for an old buddy?" Hahn asked. "Not even a handshake?"

"Hello Hahn," she said. It was obvious there was history between the two of them, and judging by the woman's attitude, it wasn't pleasant history.

"Oh, don't play hard to get, you know you want me," Hahn said. He clapped Weber on the shoulder and said, "Big Red here and me, we go way back. We spent a lot of hours snuggled up in my car one cold winter, trying to stay warm."

Weber stepped sideways enough to dislodge the man's hand, but the BIA man did not notice. He was busy examining every inch of Colleen Callahan, from her toes upward. Weber had herd the term "undressing her with his eyes" before, but had never actually seen it until that morning in his office. He felt dirty just standing beside the man and was about to tell Hahn to shut up and get out, when C.C. proved she was no pushover and said, "It was cold because I had to keep my window open so I could breathe, being so close to you."

"So does that mean you don't want me come wash your back in the shower tonight?" Hahn leered.

"Hahn, you need to know that as long as there's one filthy, stinking, toothless bum living under a bridge somewhere watching the pus run out from under his scabs, there will always be at least one man standing in line ahead of you."

Weber tried to stifle a laugh, but Hahn was unfazed by her reply. "Aww... come on, just one time, C.C. At least let me take a peek and see if the carpet matches the drapes."

"You're a disgusting pig," she told him, "Now, unless you want me to kick your flabby scrotum up somewhere around your lungs, get out of my face."

It was obvious that the woman loathed the repugnant oaf, but Hahn wasn't ready to give up yet and tried one more attempt at his foul humor.

"Hey, Jimmy, ask her how she knows what my scrotum looks like."

"That's enough, Hahn," Weber said. "Get out of here before somebody shoots you. Somebody like me."

Hahn shrugged and said, "Geez, what's your problem, Jimmy? I was just having fun with the lady, no offense intended."

"You offend the whole world just by waking up every morning," Weber told him. "Now do us both a favor and get out of my sight."

"Yeah, well, I know you guys are busy and I've got things to do anyway," Hahn said, hitching his belt up over his large belly. "I'll catch you all later."

He shuffled out of the office and C.C. turned to Weber with fire in her eyes. "I don't need you to fight my battles for me, Sheriff."

"I was just trying to get rid of him," Weber said.

"No, you were being a typical macho man protecting the weak little woman. Well here's a news flash for you. Most women don't *need* protecting! When you pull that kind of bullshit you're just as bad as guys like Hahn."

Weber felt his face flushing and the anger rising within him. He raised his hands as if to ward off an attack and said, "Whoa, easy lady!"

"Don't *whoa* me," C.C. said heatedly, "I'm not some filly you can throw a lasso on, so cut the cowboy crap!"

Weber was tempted to take the woman by the arm and march her out the same door he had just sent Hahn through, but he bit back his first reply and instead said, "I wasn't protecting you, I was just throwing his nasty ass out of the office. I'd have done it whether you were here or not. It wasn't the first time, and knowing Hahn, it probably won't be the last. So get over yourself, okay lady?"

The woman stared hard at him for a moment, and then relented and nodded. "Sorry. That guy just pisses me off."

"He pisses everybody off," Weber told her. "It's what he does best."

"Tell me about it," C.C. said. "Two years ago I was on the Rez investigating a series of fires on new home construction. We spent a couple of nights staking out one of the building sites and it was all I could do not to puke being cooped up in a car with him. Not to mention having to hear him tell me what a bull he is and how he could really ring my bell."

She shuddered at the memory, and then said, "Okay, let's talk about these fires of yours."

***

Before Harper ran down the list of recent fires, C.C. asked if there was a map of the town that they could refer to. Weber had Dan Wright pin a map to a corkboard in his office and Harper stuck yellow stickers at each fire site, marking them 1 through 4 to designate the sequence of the fires.

C.C. studied the map for a moment and said, "I don't see any pattern yet."

"What do you mean by pattern?" Weber asked her.

"If the fires were all concentrated in one part of town, it could indicate that either the perp lives nearby, or else has a problem with a certain class of people. For example, let's say the fires were all in those new summer cabins going up all over the place; one could make an assumption that they were being set by somebody who is mad about the newcomers in town, or resents their wealth."

Weber knew that there were locals who thought every newcomer to Big Lake, whether they just spent weekends and summers or came to town to stay, was ruining the way of life they had always enjoyed. And there were a handful of miscreants who probably weren't above setting the fires, but as C.C. said, there wasn't any pattern that he could see either. Tom Cotter was born and raised in Big Lake, Henry Mayer had been dead for years, and Max Woodbury was another Big Lake native. Only the cabin on Beaver Creek was owned by out-of-towners, a couple from Glendale who bought the property and built the cabin three years earlier, and only spent weekends in the mountains.

"This is all assuming that these fires really are arson in the first place," Weber said.

"Oh, they're arson all right," C.C. replied.

"How can you be sure without even seeing the scenes?" Harper asked her.

"How many fires do you have in a normal month, Chief?"

"Not many," Harper said. "One or two in the winter, usually chimney fires or a hot ember popping out of a fireplace and landing on a rug. In the summer we get a few grass fires from careless smokers or campfires. But nothing like this."

"There you go. It could be a string of coincidences, but do you really believe that?"

"If I did, you wouldn't be here," Harper said.

"Well then, let's go look at your fire scenes, gentlemen."

Chapter 10

Wearing a pair of jeans cut off nearly at the crotch and a tube top that was almost as skimpy, Jill Cotter led them into the back yard and stood off to the side smoking a cigarette and watching impassively.

Except for the woman's display of flesh, there wasn't anything to see. Tom had already cleaned up the debris from the fire and hauled it to the dump, leaving a bare spot in his back yard and a small area of blackened grass where the fire had spread before it was extinguished. C.C. took photos of the bare earth and sketched a small map in a notebook she carried, then squatted down at the edge of the dirt where the shed had been and studied it carefully.

"I don't see any power lines. Were there any to the shed?" she asked as she stood up.

"No, it was just one of those little cheap things you store junk and lawnmowers in," Harper said.

C.C. walked around the yard for a while, then into the pine trees that bordered the back end of the property, eyes on the ground as she went. A few minutes later she rejoined the two men in the yard and said, "Let's go see the barn."

***

"Have you ever had an arson fire here before, that you know of?"

"The only one I know of was last summer, and that was a local heavy equipment operator who set fire to his own bulldozer to collect the insurance money."

"Dutch Schmidt," Harper said with a scowl. "I never did like him."

"Is he still on the street?"

"Yeah," Weber said. "First offense. He did 90 days and got a big fine. Last I heard he was living over in Heber."

C.C. shook her head. "It wasn't him. Guys like that, it's a one time thing, maybe even twice if they get away with it the first time. A serial arsonist is a different type of criminal. They always escalate."

"You sound like you know your perps," Weber said, as they climbed out of the Explorer at the old barn.

"I do," C.C. replied. "That's why I get the big bucks." She surveyed the scene and said, "Here we go, we'll find something here."

"I don't know what," Harper said, waving at the burned ruins, "There isn't much left but a couple of walls and lots of rubble."

"There's always some evidence left, no matter how hot the fire was," C.C. told him. "You just have to know what to look for."

"I'm not trained in fire investigation," Harper said with a slight edge to his voice. "This isn't the big city."

Weber knew that Harper had a short fuse, and his brief encounter with C.C. after he threw Gordon Hahn out of his office earlier that day had shown him she had a temper, too. He wondered if he was about to see another fire erupt at the same scene, but the Deputy Fire Marshal put things at ease.

"Ease up, Chief." C.C. said, "Nobody's faulting you. Be glad this isn't the big city or you'd see way too much of it. I'm not here to bust your balls, just to help you catch whoever's behind these fires."

"Sorry," Harper said, nodding his head. "I guess this whole thing has me all twisted up inside."

"Well then, what do you say we catch this SOB and get life back to normal around here?"

She carefully climbed over the rubble and into what was left of the barn, warning, "Watch your step. Lots of nails sticking out of stuff."

C.C. spent a few minutes poking through the rubble, then walked to the far end of the barn where two blackened walls still stood. She turned around, squatted down to get another perspective like she had at Tom Cotter's, and carefully studied the barn from that angle, then stood up and said, "The fire started over there in that corner," pointing to the far corner of the barn, now nothing more than a pile of ashes and a few odd pieces of charred wood sticking up at a odd angles.

"How can you tell?" Harper asked.

"Come here," C.C. said. "Do you see how the damage is the worst over there, and as the fire moved in this direction it was less? Fire always forms a V pattern as it burns. Follow that V backward and you'll find the point of origin."

It took Weber a moment to see what she was pointing out, but once he did, the burn pattern was obvious.

"Damn," Harper said and whistled, "you're good."

"Did you have any doubt?" C.C. asked with a sardonic smile, then led them to where the fire had started. "Either he got lucky or our perp knows what he's doing. When you start a fire in a corner like this, you have two walls to burn at once. So it burns twice as much for the same effort."

"So now we know where it started," Weber said. "Any idea *how*?"

"Not yet," C.C. said, "But I will before we're done. Right now, let's go see the other two fire sites."

***

"Grace Rood, the lady who spotted the fire, said it was burning inside the cab when she first saw it," Weber said as Max Woodbury pulled the blue tarp off the old truck. "She said flames were coming out the window and by the time she pounded on the door and Max got out here the whole truck was burning."

C.C. stepped up onto the running board and pulled the driver's door open. All that was left inside the truck's cab was ashes and the springs from the seat. The misshapen top half of the steering wheel still hung from the column, the bottom melted away.

"Mr. Woodbury, do you remember if the windows were rolled up before the fire?"

Max shrugged. "Probably not. Darn windows tended to fall out of the tracks all the time and I got tired of fighting with them, so I usually just left them down."

Wearing heavy gloves, C.C. carefully swept aside the debris under the seat and said, "Chief, Sheriff take a look here." She pointed at some white globs mixed amid the ashes. "Do you see that stuff? That's leftover phosphorous from a road flare."

"Max, did you have any flares in here?"

"Not that I can remember, Sheriff. Don't think I've had any flares around in years."

C.C. pulled a plastic evidence bag from a pocket and carefully scooped up the phosphorous residue on a knife blade and deposited it in the bag.

"Grace told me she didn't see anybody around when she first saw the fire," Weber said. "But if the truck's windows were down it wouldn't have taken but a couple seconds to light the flare and toss it in and be gone."

"Was there much inside the cab, Mr. Woodbury?"

"Not really."

"Any fast food wrappers, foam coffee cups, things like that?"

"Yeah, probably. I'm not real good at keeping it clean. It was a trash hauler, that's all."

"A hot fire source, plenty of fuel between the seat material and whatever junk was inside. An easy target," C.C. said as she stepped down from the truck and pulled her gloves off. "Let me take some pictures, and then you can cover it back up."

"I'd really like to get this thing out of here," Max said. "Is it okay to haul it to the scrapyard over in Show Low yet?"

"I'm sorry," C.C. told him. "It's evidence. I may still need to look at it again."

"Damn truck wasn't worth all this effort."

"You know there were other fires, right?" Harper asked.

"Yeah, Steve, I know it. It's not like I've been on a desert island or something. The whole town knows."

"Then I'm sure you can understand why we need to preserve every piece of evidence we possibly can," C.C. said.

"What evidence? It's just a burned up old truck."

"Evidence like the residue from the flare that started the fire," C.C. said. "If we find more at another fire site we can run a chemical DNA profile on it and see if it came from the same kind of flare, even what lot they were all in."

"Okay, I guess that makes sense," Max said. "Here, Steve, help me get this tarp back over it."

"Do I look like your personal assistant?" Harper asked, and ignored Max's retort as he grabbed one end of the tarp.

Weber and C.C. walked a few steps away as they bickered.

"Those two sound like my grandparents," C.C. said.

"They're cousins, been squabbling since they were in diapers," Weber told her, then asked, "Can you really get DNA from a road flare?"

"Damned if I know," C.C. said. "But it sure sounds all techy and professional, doesn't it?"

***

The cabin took the longest time to examine. First C.C. photographed the outside from all angles, then she entered and moved from room to room, stepping carefully over piles of burned debris, pushing aside the remnants of furniture and fallen pieces of the roof as she explored the fire scene. After an hour she stood up and stretched her back, then said, "This one was more sophisticated. We're not dealing with a kid here."

"What do you mean?" Weber asked.

"We don't know anything about the first fire at the shed, and since the owner already cleaned up and hauled everything away, we probably never will. At the barn, it would have been a simple case to pile a bunch of whatever trash was laying around inside into a corner and set it on fire. Maybe even an old hay bale or two if there were any. The place is far enough out of town and behind a locked gate so the chances of being seen were pretty slim. The truck was quick and easy in and out. Light the flare, toss it in, and hightail it out of there. But this one was different. He took his time here."

"How do you know?"

"First of all, the wall's bowed outward on this end of the house. Now look at the stove," C.C. said. "See, the burners are all set to the On position. Now follow me."

She led them out of what had been the kitchen, past a waist high half wall, and into the living room, where she squatted in a corner and pointed to a splotch of soft material on the floor. Scraping some of it up on the blade of a small pocketknife, she held it up for inspection. "See this?"

"What is it?" Harper asked.

"Wax."

"Wax? Like a candle?"

"It *was* a candle," C.C. said. "The perp set a large candle here on the floor and lit it, then went in the kitchen and turned on all of the burners on the stove. If there was a pilot light, he blew it out first, then he left. The gas started filling the place up and when it got to the candle flame, Boom!"

"How long would that have taken?" Weber asked her.

"Hard to say, Sheriff. Propane is one and a half times heavier than air, so it sinks to the floor and pools as it spreads. In a place this size, I'm guessing an hour, maybe more."

"So whoever did this had plenty of time to get away before it went off."

"That's right," C.C. said.

"How did he get in?" Harper asked.

C.C. shrugged her shoulders. "Who knows? Maybe broke a window and crawled inside, maybe kicked a door in. But like I said, this isn't a kid, so it could have been something more subtle. I'll leave that to Sheriff Weber to figure out."

"Half the time people leave a key under a planter or something on the front porch, or above a doorjamb," Weber said.

"So we've confirmed what we already knew but hoped we were wrong about. We have a serial arsonist on our hands," Weber said. "Now what?"

"Well gee, Mr. Sheriff, I've done my job," C.C. said, blinking her eyes innocently at him. "The rest is up to you."

Chapter 11

While Weber had been busy with the fire investigation, things had been busy in town, too. The second edition of the *Big Lake Truth* had hit the street with a front page picture of Mayor Chet Wingate facing off with Fire Chief Steve Harper while the cabin burned behind them, under a page-wide headline that declared *Fire Chief Argues While Home Burns!* The story under the photo wasted no time declaring that Harper and the entire Volunteer Fire Department were incompetent:

Even the intervention of Big Lake Mayor Chet Wingate failed to motivate the Big Lake Fire Department to save a burning cabin on Beaver Creek Road on Monday. Fire Chief Steven Harper, pictured above, seemed to prefer to spend critical moments arguing with the mayor, who tried to get Harper to make an attempt to save anybody who may have been trapped inside the inferno.

As if his lack of concern for anyone endangered by the blaze wasn't troubling enough, Chief Harper actually allowed two of his men to leave the scene in the middle of the fire with the Department's main pumper truck, leaving only a small truck with a slide-in water tank and a single hose to make a feeble attempt to deal with the conflagration. When this reporter tried to take photos of the fire scene he was first assaulted by a member of the Fire Department, and then a deputy from the Big Lake Sheriff's Department. Only the intervention of Mayor Wingate prevented what may possibly have been serious injury at the hands of these two uniformed thugs.

While we prefer to keep editorializing on our Opinion page, one has to wonder how long the good citizens of Big Lake will be forced to depend on such incompetents who seem more interested in victimizing those they are sworn to serve and protect than in doing their jobs.

There were three more paragraphs along the same vein, but Weber tossed the newspaper onto his desk and shook his head in disgust.

"Oh, it get's worse," Mary Caitlin said. "In the editorial they talk about how Chief Harper buffaloed the naïve Town Council into giving him sixty grand to waste on a worn out piece of junk from out of state, and how valiantly Chet Wingate and Gretchen Smith-Abbot tried in vain to save the taxpayers money."

"I bet Harper's mad enough to chew nails," Weber said. "This guy Tovar's a real piece of work."

"So's Paul over at the *Herald*," Mary said. "I went over to pick up some copies of the pictures he took of the new volunteers being sworn in and he looked like he was about to blow his cork. It looks like the new paper picked up half a dozen new advertisers, including a quarter page from the Antler Inn."

That didn't surprise Weber. He had had many run-ins with Margo Prestwick, the overweight bleached blonde with a perpetual bad attitude who owned the bar. The Antler Inn was a run down tavern housed in a cinder block building located on the outskirts of Big Lake. For years the tavern and the rough crowd it attracted had been a thorn in the side of the Big Lake Sheriff's Department.

"So do you suppose old Margo took an ad out just to spite me, or because young Mr. Tovar is such a handsome young man that he set her hormones all atwitter?"

"And that woman from the Fire Marshal's office called Gordon Hahn a pig," Mary said in mock dismay. "Go figure."

"Yeah, life's a mystery," Weber told her, picking up the newspaper again to see what else Darron Tovar had to say.

***

"So what did you guys figure out with that lady fire marshal?" Larry Parks asked.

"She confirmed what we already thought. The fires were all arson. She's sharp. She saw things we never would have known to look for."

"Easy on the eyes too, from what I hear," Parks said, slathering butter onto a roll.

"Enough with the calories and cholesterol," Marsha Perry said, nudging Big Lake's resident FBI agent in the ribs.

"Damn, woman, an active man like me has to eat to maintain my fighting weight. Don't you know that?"

"The only thing you're fighting is love handles," Marsha said. "And don't think I didn't smell chocolate on your breath when you kissed me this afternoon, buster!"

"I just munched on a tiny bit so I'd be as sweet as you," Parks replied.

"Don't bother trying to play all innocent and blameless with me," the short, dark haired woman shot back, snatching the roll out of his hand midway to his mouth. "I also know all about the double order of fries and the big chocolate shake you had at lunch."

"Man, I'm telling you. This woman has more snitches than a prison cellblock," Parks told Weber. "I can't get away with anything in this town!"

"That's right, Mr. Smarty Pants, I've got eyes everywhere. And don't you forget it," Marsha warned.

"Geez, I thought Steve Harper and Max Woodbury argued like an old married couple," Weber said. "Why don't you two just tie the knot and get it over with."

"This isn't arguing," Parks said, inching his hand across the table toward the basket of dinner rolls until Marsha slapped it away. "This is what's called verbal foreplay, Jimmy. You see, these days women want more than rock hard abs and a chiseled jawline. No sir, they're looking for a man who's not only breathtaking, but also challenges them mentally as well."

"Well then, you've got a long way to go," Weber said. "A mental midget with love handles."

"Let's get back to the lady fire marshal," Robyn Fuchette said as she set a platter of pork chops on the table. "Just how easy on the eyes is she, Jimmy?"

Weber looked at her warily, deciding how to answer. Both the Big Lake Sheriff's Department's only female deputy, and his girlfriend, Robyn had a streak of jealousy in her that she tried hard to control, not always with success.

Seeing the look on his face, she grinned impishly and said, "Relax, I don't expect you to be blind. Besides, I've already got the rundown on her. What was it Dolan called her? Oh, that's right, a redheaded firecracker."

"She's got her spies, too," Parks said, grinning at his best friend's discomfort. "So tell us about this here *firecracker* of yours, Sheriff."

Weber was literally saved by the bell, in this case Robyn's doorbell, and a moment later Archer Wingate and his new wife Kallie Jo joined them. For once Weber was glad to see his deputy, and especially Kallie

Jo, who always talked a mile a minute, with a thick southern accent she brought with her when she came west to meet Archer in person after their relationship had begun online.

No one was more surprised than Archer when she actually showed up in Big Lake, unannounced, and everybody expected the pretty young woman to take one look at the bumbling Archer and make a beeline for the next bus back home to her native Georgia. But Kallie Jo had surprised them all by being just as enchanted with Archer as he was with her, and wedding bells had soon followed. Weber knew that with Kallie Jo carrying the dinner conversation, they probably wouldn't get back to the subject of C.C. Callahan.

"Sorry we're late. Archer's daddy called just as we was walkin' out the door and it took me forever to get him off the telephone. He's just convinced that Archer ought to be the fire chief, even though he's told his daddy over and over that it's not what he wants to do with his life. Archer knows the best way he can serve his community is as a deputy, not a fireman."

Weber wanted to suggest that maybe Archer might be better suited for the job of dog catcher, but he was sure there were animal rights groups who would object, and rightly so. But he didn't have to say anything at all, because Kallie Jo was just getting started.

"Well now, Miss Robyn, don't you just look positively gorgeous," Kallie Jo said, hugging Robyn, then turning to embrace Marsha. "And look at you! I swear, girl, you're lookin' as pretty as the first flowers in springtime. Ya'll need to stop being so gosh darned pretty or the rest of us ladies here in Big Lake might as well just go jump into that there ol' lake 'cause we ain't nothin' but straggly ol' weeds compared to you two. And that's a fact!"

"Oh, you're too kind," Marsha said, returning the hug.

"And look at that there feller sittin' next to you," Kallie Jo said, pointing at Parks as she sat down at the table. "How are you doing, Mr. Larry? I hear tell you been takin' flyin' lessons over there at the airport in Show Low."

"Just looking at the world from a different perspective," Parks told her.

"Well now, I'll tell you what," Kallie Jo said, "I know you're competent at everything you do, but you be careful now, you hear? 'Cause I still can't forget my grandpappy always sayin' that if the Good Lord wanted us to fly, he'd a' givin' us wings. Now wouldn't that be funny, if we all had wings? 'Course, angels have wings now, don't they? But angels ain't really people anymore, so maybe that don't count."

"Are you feeling okay?" Robyn asked, interrupting Kallie Jo's monologue as she looked at the woman's face.

"I'm fine," Kallie Jo said, though Weber couldn't help but notice the dark circles under her eyes, and though she was a small woman to start with, it did seem like she had lost weight.

In fact, both Kallie Jo and Archer had lost weight recently, come to think of it. Weber had noticed just the day before that Archer's uniform shirt no longer gaped at the buttonholes across his belly. And if Weber had to admit it, Kallie Jo *had* been a good influence on Archer in other ways. He noticed that the deputy's normally dull shoes and gun belt were now always polished to a gloss, and Archer was clean shaven every day.

Of course, that didn't stop him from falling asleep anytime he sat down, or nodding off during staff meetings. But then again, Weber knew Rome wasn't built in a day, and he didn't expect Archer to become a competent deputy overnight. Hell, he didn't expect *that* to ever happen!

"Jimmy? You in there?" Robyn asked, touching his shoulder.

"Huh?"

"Kallie Jo asked you to pass the potatoes."

"Oh, sorry," Weber said.

"Thank you, Sheriff," Kallie Jo said as he handed her the bowl of mashed potatoes. "Now tell the truth, where was you at just now? My mama Billie Rae always says that there's like your brain went on a little vacation, but your body stayed right here at home. Is that what you was doin', Sheriff? Takin' a vacation with your brain?"

Before Weber could form a response, Kallie Jo was off on another tangent, telling everybody about the time her whole family; her daddy Buster, her mama Billie Rae, her sister Sarah Beth, and assorted cousins and other kinfolk all went to Myrtle Beach, South Carolina one summer. She told them how they all got terrible sunburns, and her cousin Audrey got caught sneaking back into the hotel in the wee hours one morning after a tryst with a blond headed surfer she had met the day before. But everyone knew, as Kallie Jo pointed out, that Audrey, bless her soul, didn't have a lick of sense and was sadly lacking in the morals department, too.

By the time dinner was over and the dishes washed and put away and they had retired to the living room of Robyn's small house, everyone knew even more about Kallie Jo's large extended family, who seemed to make up most of the population of Pierce County, Georgia.

Robyn, Marsha, and Kallie Jo returned to the kitchen to serve up slices of fresh strawberry pie, a procedure that seemed to involve a lengthy hushed discussion.

"Did you forget about us out here?" Parks called. "Don't make me wait too long for dessert, Marsha. I've got a Hershey bar, and I'm not afraid to use it."

"Hush, we're having girl talk," Marsha called back. "You won't starve, you just left the table ten minutes ago."

When the women did return with the pie on dessert plates, Parks rubbed his hands together with glee, but Marsha made it a point of making sure he got the smallest slice, which was still a generous portion. Parks whined for a moment, but when he saw Archer's eyes on his plate he quieted down and made do with what he had.

The conversation drifted from what a nice summer evening it was to the fishing report from the lake, and on to Parks giving a description of his first solo flight. Weber noticed that twice Kallie Jo yawned, and the second time she did it, Archer said it was probably time for them to head home. Kallie Jo insisted she was fine, and tried to join the conversation, but after she yawned a third time, Archer said it was time to go.

Soon after they left, amid hugs and a promise from Kallie Jo that she was going to have everybody over to their mobile home soon for a down home dinner of southern fried chicken with "all the fixins' like Mama always makes." Parks and Marsha lingered a while longer, but left just after 10. Weber and Robyn cuddled on the sofa for a while, watching a sitcom on television and then the news out of Phoenix.

"So what was all that "girl talk" about in there earlier?" Weber asked.

"Oh, just that. Girl talk."

Robyn seemed slightly troubled, and Weber asked, "Is Kallie Jo okay?"

"What do you mean?"

"I don't know," Weber said, shrugging. "She looks different."

"Different how?"

"It looks like she's lost some weight, and her eyes look kind of sunken. And then she sat there yawning."

Robyn turned to face him and said, "I have to tell you something, but you have to keep it to yourself, okay?"

"She's leaving him, isn't she?"

"Leaving him? No," Robyn said shaking her head with bewilderment. "Why in the world would you think that?"

"I don't know. Because he's Archer?"

"No, Jimmy, she's not leaving him. Kallie Jo's in it for the long haul."

"Then what's the problem?"

"Well," Robyn said, "How do I say this delicately? Archer and Kallie Jo… they've been, ah…."

"What Robyn? They've been…?"

"They've been going at it like a couple of bunnies on crack," Robyn said. "Apparently since they were both virgins before they got married, they have a lot of… passion stored up. Well, I think maybe Kallie Jo's exhausted some of that passion, but not Archer, apparently. Jimmy, the poor girl's worn out. I guess Archer's got the stamina of a bull."

"Archer?" Weber asked incredulously, trying to stifle a laugh and failing miserably.

"It's not funny, Jimmy!"

"Archer?"

"Look, if Kallie Jo knew I told you this, she'd be mortified. You promised you wouldn't say anything about it."

"Oh come on, Robyn, how can I keep this to myself? Archer's a stud? Nobody's ever going to believe it."

"They're never going to believe it because you're not going to say a word about this to anybody. I swear, Jimmy, if you say one word to Parks or the rest of the guys, Archer will be the only one around here *with* any sex life for a long, long time!"

Weber finally managed to stop laughing, and though Robyn tried to look vexed at him, she couldn't completely hide a small upturn at the corners of her mouth before she looked away in exasperation.

Later, as they were snuggled together in her bed, Robyn said, "So tell me about this lady Fire Marshal. Just how easy on the eyes is she?"

Chapter 12

"If our guy runs true to form, we'll have another fire today," C.C. said at the staff meeting the next morning. "In fact, he's overdue."

"God, I hope not," Steve Harper said.

"Oh, you can count on it. This is the longest between fires since he started escalating."

"You know what makes these guys tick better than I do," Harper said. "But I've already got people asking me when I'm going to put a stop to all this. And that damned newspaper yesterday didn't help things one bit."

"So where do we go from here?" Weber asked. "You say he'll strike again today. Any idea where, or when?"

C.C. shook her head. "I'm good, but I'm not psychic."

"Even with our new volunteers, I don't have enough manpower to blanket the whole town," Weber said. "So what do we do?"

"Do you do any hunting, Sheriff?"

"Not in a long time," Weber said. He had grown up on a small ranch just outside of town and had hunted the mountains for deer, elk, and even bear as a young man. But as time went on he had been too busy and gradually lost interest. Even though hunting was a big part of life in the mountain community, it had been years since he had put in for a deer or elk tag.

"The first thing a hunter has to do is understand his quarry. What are its habits? How does it react to different things like rain, or a cold front, or people suddenly trampling through the forest? It's the same thing here, so let me share some generalities about the mind of a pyromaniac," C.C. said.

She stood up and faced the assembled deputies and volunteers, brushing her hair back as she did so. Weber noted that Robyn was studying the other woman carefully, and made it a point not to allow her to catch his eyes lingering on the redhead for too long.

"Pyromania is an established psychiatric diagnosis. True pyromania is a lack of impulse control, just like kleptomania. The person acts out, even though they know on a practical level that what they are doing is wrong, because they can't resist. But true pyromania is actually pretty rare, it's less than one percent of all diagnosed disorders, though the term is used loosely for anyone that starts fires."

"So what does he get out of it?" Harper asked. "I mean, at least a klepto has something to show for it."

"Oh, they get something out of it," C.C. assured him. "A true pyromaniac experiences arousal, pleasure, and gratification when setting a fire, or from watching it burn, or even helping put it out."

"Putting it out?"

"That's right, Chief. Sometimes a firebug gets his satisfaction from being a hero. They set a fire and then report it. Or…. they respond and help extinguish the blaze."

"Now wait just a damn minute, lady," Harder said, standing up so quickly that his chair overturned.

"Take it easy, Steve," Weber cautioned.

"Bullshit, Jimmy! It's bad enough I've got that asshole at the newspaper going on the attack. Now she's implying that one of my men is involved in this? No way! I'm not going to sit here and listen to this for one minute."

"Calm down," C.C. said, "I didn't accuse any of your men of anything, Chief Harper."

"Then you're accusing me, is that it?"

"I'm not accusing anybody," C.C. told him. "All I'm doing is…."

"All you're doing is pissing me off," Harper said. "I'm out of here. I thought you came to help, not spread rumors that are pure bullshit."

C.C.'s own temper was about to flare and she started to say something, then stopped herself and took a deep breath.

"Steve, listen to me, okay? I don't think you or any of your people are involved in this. I don't. I'm giving an overview so we all know what we're dealing with. And I *am* here to help. Just hear me out, will you? We're all on the same side here."

Harper stared at her for a long moment, his jaw clenched tightly, and the tension in the room was palpable. The assembled deputies glanced at each other uncomfortably, nobody meeting anyone else's eyes. Finally the fire chief relaxed slightly and righted his chair and sat down, but kept his arms crossed in defiance. It felt like the room let out a collective sigh of relief.

"Okay," C.C. said, "Where was I? Oh yes, the true pyromaniac. They're all different, but they all have some of the same characteristics.

Just like the kleptomaniac, or the compulsive gambler, or an alcoholic, setting fires fulfills a need in them. They may start out doing it for the thrill, thinking it's just a one time thing, if they think about it at all. But just like with a junkie, once they have that first shot or snort, they're hooked. They have to have more. And the more they have, the more they want. It's a downward spiral."

A couple of people shuffled in their chairs, and C.C. took a sip from a bottle of water before she continued. "But like I said, actual pyromania is really pretty rare. And I don't think that's what we're dealing with here."

"Then what *are* we dealing with?" Ted Cooper asked. Retired after 20 years as an Army MP, Coop was a good, solid lawman who brought a lifetime of experience and investigatory skills to the Sheriff's Department. At 40 years old, he was in excellent physical shape and still wore his hair short, in the military fashion. Having served as an Army MP himself, Weber had felt an affinity with the man as soon as he signed on, and Coop continued to impress him with the way he handled the job.

"People set fires for a variety of reasons," C.C. said. "Sometimes it's to get back at somebody who they think wronged them in some way. A disgruntled employee quits a job or gets canned and comes back at night and sets the place on fire; or a woman gets mad at her boyfriend for cheating on her and torches his car. Other times it's for financial gain, like insurance fraud or to get out from under a car payment. Then there are those who set a fire to hide some other crime; that happens a lot with murders and burglaries."

"But I don't see that happening in any of these fires," Coop said. "Nobody's turned up dead at any of them, and the last one was the only one that destroyed anything of value, unless you count Max Woodbury's old truck. And even he didn't put any value on it."

"Do you know if Max fired anybody lately, Jimmy?" Dolan Reed asked. "Or if he had a customer who was mad at him?"

"As a matter of fact, I asked him that," Weber said. "He couldn't recall any customers who were mad. And he doesn't have any employees that I know of."

"He doesn't," Harper said. "Once in a while I help him out on a job when he needs a hand, but that's it."

"No, I don't think any of that is what's happening here," C.C. said. "Those things I just described are usually a one time thing. The employee either gets caught or gets another job and moves on with his life. The woman and her boyfriend go their separate ways or kiss and make up. Or the cops catch whoever killed somebody and set the fire to destroy the body."

"Then what *do* we have here?" Weber asked.

"Here we have a pattern," C.C. said. "These fires are repeating, and escalating. First it was a shed, then it was a barn. Then the plumber's truck, and next it was a cabin. I think what we have here is a serial arsonist, but not a pyromaniac."

"What's the difference?"

"Like I said, with a pyromaniac, it's a compulsion they can't resist. You might say that, like a junkie, they start out doing it for kicks and suddenly they're hooked and can't stop. A serial arsonist has an agenda. Maybe it's a thrill, maybe it's to make a political statement, maybe they *are* covering up a crime, or a crime they intend to commit. But once they achieve whatever goal motivates them, they stop. Unless we catch them first, which we intend to do."

Chad Summer cleared his throat and all eyes turned to him. Chad was the department's senior deputy and had seen it all in his years wearing a badge. "I hesitate to say this, and don't you all start laughing at me, considering the source, but the other day at the bakery, George Holman was spouting off about developers being behind the fires so they could then set fires to their own places to collect the insurance money."

"George Holman," Dolan said, shaking his head derisively. "That fruitcake's got a conspiracy theory for everything."

"I agree," Chad said. "Like I said, considering the source…"

"Maybe not," C.C. said. "I don't know this Holman you're talking about, but *could* he be onto something? How's the market up here? Do you know of any developer or small builder who's about to lose his shirt?"

"It seems to me like it's booming," Weber said. "Every time I look there's some new place going up."

"And not necessarily for the better," said Walter Alford, one of the new volunteers. "It's getting to where you have to stand in line everywhere from the bank to the grocery store. I wish they'd all go away."

There were a couple of murmurs of approval, and Weber asked, "So where are we at now? You don't think we have a card-carrying pyro, but we *do* have somebody who's going to keep this up. How do we stop him?"

"I'd suggest several things," C.C. said. "Take a long hard look at who has anything to gain by these fires. Is the boom starting to bust? Could there be some builder out there in over his head who is starting these fires as a cover for torching his own places? I don't think that's the case, but you never know."

"I'll get somebody on that as soon as we're done here," Weber said. "What else?"

"Is there any tie-in between the victims of these fires? For example, did Max Woodbury do any work on a project where the builder is behind the eight ball? Is there a builder looking at the property where that barn sat? Did whoever built that cabin have a connection to anybody else touched by these fires? And finally, and I know you don't want to hear this, Sheriff, it may just be somebody who gets off by setting fire's and may or may not evolve into a full fledged pyromaniac."

"Either way, how do we catch him?"

"Sooner or later, he's going to trip himself up. He may fit the hero profile to some degree," she said, holding her hand up to ward off another outburst by Steve Harper. "That doesn't mean I think he's a firefighter. But how did you get notice of the different fires? Were they all called in? Did a passerby see them? Has a spectator shown up at the fires more than once? Maybe gotten themselves interviewed by the news media?"

"I know the truck fire was spotted by an old lady on her way to church," Weber said. "I'll check on how we got word about the rest. Our news media consists of the *Big Lake Herald* and this new rag. Paul over at the *Herald* is tired and lazy, he doesn't usually chase down the big stories, he prefers to sit and wait for us to bring him the police reports whenever he can."

"What about this new guy?" Dolan Reed asked. "This Tovar jerk? He was out at that cabin. He's looking to make a name for himself. Could he be tied up in all this?"

Weber shrugged his shoulders. "He's working hard to be a pain in the ass and doing a damn good job of it. But does that make him an arsonist?"

"I'd sure like to get my hands on him," Harper said. "I went by his office after I read that crap he wrote yesterday, but it was locked up and nobody was around."

"Probably, just as well," Weber said. "I need you out here helping me wrap this case up Steve, not sitting back there in one of my cells for strangling that kid."

"So what next?" Weber asked C.C. "I'll put some people to work looking at the background stuff you asked about, but what else? Do we just sit here watching for smoke and waiting for the phone to ring?"

"The chances of catching this guy in the act are pretty slim," she said. "But it wouldn't hurt to have as many sets of eyes as you can muster out on the street. Who knows, we might get lucky?"

Chapter 13

"She *is* easy on the eyes," Robyn said after the meeting broke up, as she and Weber watched C.C. and Steve Harper talking, out in the parking lot.

"Really? I hadn't noticed."

She punched Weber lightly on the shoulder. "You need to get your eyes checked, mister, or else go to church and pray for forgiveness for being a lying dog. Because that is one hot woman."

"Hey, when you've got steak at home, you don't stop for burgers at the drive-through window," Weber said.

"Oh come on, do you really think you can put me off with that old line, Jimmy?"

"It was worth a shot."

"Just so that's the only shot you take," Robyn said.

"I never know when you're joking and when you're serious," he told her.

"I know. That's part of the fun, isn't it?"

"Not always."

"Well, if it's any comfort to you, I don't always know myself," Robyn told him, then sat down at her desk and logged onto the computer to start researching builders and developers who might have a reason to want to see their projects go up in smoke.

***

"So where are you and Steve at with things?" Weber asked when Harper climbed in his truck and drove away.

"We're good," C.C. told him.

"Sorry about him blowing up back there in the meeting. He's a good guy, very loyal to his volunteers and dedicated to the job. He's just in over his head."

"Well then," she said, "the quicker we wrap this thing up, the sooner things will get back to normal around here."

"Or whatever passes for normal, anyway," Weber said. "So what do we do now?"

"I think we're going to have another fire any minute now. I told Steve it's not a good idea for him to be too far from the Fire Station because response time can be critical. He's got a couple of volunteers who have arranged their work schedules to be there too, just in case."

"I hope not."

"Sorry, Sheriff," C.C. said. "It's going to happen."

"And what are we supposed to do in the meantime?"

"Let's go for a ride. I'd like to take another look at that old barn and the cabin."

***

They spooked a pair of deer as they walked up to the barn, a doe and her spotted fawn bedded down in the high grass, who leapt to their feet and bounded away toward the forest. They watched them go and Weber said, "Try getting a sight like that in the big city,"

"Yes, but we do have Starbucks," C.C. said. "Everything in life's a tradeoff."

"I'll trade you a five buck cup of coffee for two wild critters any day. Besides, up here I can breathe the air," Weber told her, taking a deep breath.

"Now there you go getting all manly on me again," C.C. teased. "Careful you don't pop the buttons on your flannel shirt with that macho chest of yours."

"About the only way I pop my shirt is across my belly if I order the Cattleman's Cut rib eye at the Roundup," Weber replied, referring to Big Lake's most popular steakhouse.

C.C. laughed and said, "I'll tell you what, once we catch this guy I'll let you buy me one."

"You've got a deal," Weber assured her. "But first we have to catch him."

"Well, we're not going to do it standing out here breathing all this fresh air of yours," C.C. said, leading the way to the barn. "Let's go in and get dirty."

They had donned coveralls when they got out of Weber's Explorer, which was a good thing since they spent the next two hours crawling on, under, and over everything inside the old barn.

Weber was pawing through some blackened metal that looked as if it had once been part of a plow when he heard C.C. call out triumphantly, "Found it!"

He wiped the sweat off his forehead with his arm and walked over to where she was on her knees in the corner where the fire had started.

"What did you find?"

"This," C.C, said holding a small sieve in her hand toward him. All Weber saw was ashes and some bits of charred rubble.

"I'm sorry, I still don't see whatever it is I'm supposed to see," Weber said.

"This," C.C. said again as she held up a black object a little over an inch long.

"What is it?"

"It's the bottom part of a matchbook," C.C. told him. "See, here's where the matches were attached, and here is the striker, the abrasive strip you scratch the match across."

Once she explained it to him, Weber recognized it for what it was.

"So what does this mean?"

"It means our boy struck a match, set the rest of the book on fire, and dropped it here in the corner, just like I said. Probably on a pile of trash, or even some old hay if there was any around."

"How did this survive the fire?" Weber asked. "It's just cardboard."

"It happens more often than you'd think," C.C. told him. "It's small and something falls on top of it and protects it from burning all the way up."

"Okay, now we know how the fire started. I still don't know what it means as far as catching whoever set it."

"Do you remember what I said this morning about a hunter knowing his quarry? You don't learn that overnight, Sheriff. I wish there was a shortcut but there isn't." She extended a hand and said, "Help me up."

Weber took her hand and pulled her to her feet and they were face to face, inches apart. Even covered in soot and with her hair damp with sweat, Weber was aware that C.C. Callahan was a beautiful woman and he felt uncomfortable. If she noted it she didn't comment, and he stepped backward to put some distance between them.

***

After a quick pass through the drive-through lane at McDonald's for sandwiches they drove to the cabin on Beaver Creek road. They pulled into the driveway and ate their lunch.

"So what do we know now?" C.C. asked, then answered her own question, "Our perp has used three different methods to start fires; matches, a flare, and here, the gas and candle. There's no way of telling how he set the first one."

"Is that important, that he uses different methods?"

"Many serial criminals follow a pattern, and that eventually trips them up. The serial killer that preys on prostitutes, or blondes, or whatever."

"I figured that was because they don't have much imagination," Weber said.

"Sometimes, but sometimes it's because that target is a trigger, or fulfills a need. The guy who got laughed at by the blonde cheerleader in high school when he asked her for a date. Whatever the reason, it's that pattern thing we talked about before."

"And our guy here?"

"We're still trying to find that pattern. He doesn't just burn sheds or barns or trucks or cabins. He uses different methods to start the fires. He's very smart and thinks he's going to confuse us."

"Well then he's succeeded," Weber told her. "Because I'm confused as hell."

C.C. drained the last of her iced tea and said, "Let's get at it and see what we can find. Were your people able to figure out how the perp got inside?"

"Mary talked to the owners down in Glendale," Weber said. "They said they left a spare key on top of the back door sill. Wouldn't be hard to find."

"People really do that up here?" C.C. asked. "Amazing."

"It's a small town," Weber said. "Remember? No Starbucks."

Weber really didn't know what he was looking for or what C.C. hoped to find in the burned out cabin, but he dutifully poked around for the next hour. He was in the kitchen when he heard C.C. yelp from the master bedroom, followed by one word, "Shit!"

He walked down the hall and was greeted by a look of pain on C.C.'s face.

"You okay?"

"No. I cut my knee. I wasn't paying attention and knelt on a piece of broken mirror."

Weber saw the wet patch on her right knee. "How bad is it? Can you walk?"

"I think so," C.C. said. "Let's get outside and take a look."

She limped down the hall, through the kitchen and out onto the back deck, which had been spared the worst of the fire's damage.

"I've got a first aid kit in my unit," Weber told her and went to retrieve it as C.C. sat down on a wooden chair.

When he returned, C.C. had peeled off her coveralls and boot. She tried to pull up the legs of her jeans so Weber could get to her knee, but they were too tight. After two failed attempts, C.C. said, "The hell with it, I'll give the wild things a show." She unbuckled her belt and slid the jeans down to her ankles.

The cut was wide, all the way across her kneecap, but didn't appear too deep. Weber wiped it clean and then held a gauze compress tightly to her knee to stanch the bleeding.

"It doesn't look like you're going to need stitches, but we better run you by the medical clinic to get it cleaned up good and get you a tetanus shot."

"I don't need a shot," C.C. said. "In this line of work we get them when we sign on, and boosters on schedule. Can't you just clean it up and tape it? I hate doctors."

"You sure?"

"Yeah, otherwise I have to fill out an incident report and all that crap."

No fan of paperwork himself, Weber understood and set about cleaning the wound. C.C. winced when he applied an antiseptic wipe, but never complained. The bleeding had stopped, so Weber put antibiotic cream on it and then covered it with fresh gauze and taped it tightly.

When he was done he looked up for the first time, then blushed.

"What did you expect, Sheriff? Granny panties?"

"Well, it is a small town."

"In case you're wondering, yes, the carpet matches the drapes. But it's a well trimmed carpet."

"Yeah, well uh…"

C.C. laughed as he stood up awkwardly, tripping over himself and trying to look anywhere but at her. "Relax, I didn't plan to grab you by the ears or anything."

"I didn't… I mean I wasn't…"

C.C. laughed harder at his discomfort. "So much for that whole overconfident cowboy image I had of you. Or are you wondering what somebody would have thought if they had walked around the corner and seen you in that position? I mean, you *have* been in that position before, haven't you?"

Instantly a vision of Robyn being the person walking around the corner flashed through Weber's mind, and even though there were no close neighbors and they were out of sight of anybody passing by on the road, he couldn't help but look around guiltily.

C.C. stood up with a slight grimace and pulled her jeans up. "If you're not going to take advantage of me or at least let me take advantage of you, I might as well close up shop," she said as she buckled her belt.

"Look, C.C., if I ever gave you the idea that…"

She held up her hand and laughed again. "Relax, okay? And stop being so noble. I was just pulling your chain. I know about you and Robyn and I don't pick flowers from another woman's garden."

"How do you know about that? You've only been in town two days."

"I told you, Sheriff, I'm good at what I do. And remember, it *is* a small town."

There didn't seem to be anything else to be learned at the cabin, so they decided to head back to town. Weber had just started the Explorer's engine when his radio came to life.

"All units, we've got a fire at 10161 Pine Knoll Road. Repeat, 10161 Pine Knoll."

Weber stared at the radio for a moment, then grabbed the microphone and said, "Repeat that address."

"You heard it right," Mary replied. "10161 Pine Knoll. It's burning bad, Jimmy."

Weber threw the gearshift into reverse and backed out in the road, then hit the lights and siren as he floored the gas pedal and raced toward town.

"What is it, Jimmy?" C.C. asked, buckling her seatbelt and bracing her arm on the dashboard as they entered the curve along the creek.

"It's the house where I grew up."

Chapter 14

Flames were pouring out of the windows and crawling up the outside walls of the old family home when Weber slid to a stop behind the Suzuki Samurai that belonged to Dave Brock, one of Steve Harper's volunteers.

The firemen were pouring water onto the house, but one look told Weber it was a futile effort. He stood in the driveway watching it burn and a flood of memories rushed through his mind. Sitting on the front porch on summer nights drinking his mother's sweet and tangy lemonade and listening to his father talk about the good old days growing up back before the government got involved with their rules and regulations and pushed so many small ranchers out of business. Playing cops and robbers and cowboys and Indians with Paul Lewis. Snowball fights and building snowmen. Climbing the big old tree in the front yard and falling out and breaking his arm when he was nine. Playing hide and seek with his younger sister Debbie. Debbie… He couldn't go there. He wouldn't go there!

"Do you think anybody was in there?" C.C. asked.

"No, it's been empty for a while now." He didn't add that he had not set foot inside the house since the day he had confronted his sister about her involvement in an armored car hijacking that left two guards dead, and that two more people would die before the investigation was over. He didn't tell her that an irrational fear had made it impossible for him to do anything more than pull his vehicle into the driveway ever since that day when Debbie had pointed Weber's own pistol at him and made her escape.

Chief Harper saw them and walked over, shaking his head. "I'm sorry, Jimmy, we're doing everything we can, but…"

"I know you are," Weber told him. "All you can do is all you can do, Steve."

"Who called it in?" C.C. asked.

"Mail carrier was driving by and spotted it. He had to drive a couple miles toward town before he could get a signal on his cell phone. By the time we got here… well, you can see."

Chad Summers parked his car on the shoulder of the road and joined the trio. "Damn, Jimmy. I'm sorry."

"It's just a house," Weber said. Even as he said the words, he knew that they were false. It wasn't just a house. It was his family home. It was his past, his memories good and bad. It wasn't just the walls and plumbing and wiring. It was the pencil marks on the kitchen wall where his mother had recorded he and his sister's growth. It was the bedroom where he built model cars and stared out the window at night, dreaming of a life far away from the tiny mountain town and the constant work a small ranch demanded. It was the smell of the evergreen trees the family cut on the mountain behind them and dragged back home to stand up in the living room and decorate as Christmas carols played on the stereo every year. It was all that and more, and yet Weber had not been able to force himself to set foot on the porch in almost two years.

His memories were interrupted when Darron Tovar walked past them and started taking photos of the fire. When Harper saw the young man he swore and started toward him, but Weber grabbed his arm.

"Not now, Steve."

"I want to wring that little jerk's neck."

"Wrong time, wrong place," Weber told him. "Do your job here. His time will come."

The fire chief's temper was as hot as the inferno that had been the Weber family home, but to Weber's relief he didn't push the issue with the reporter at that time. Instead he turned to one of his firemen and asked, "How are we doing for water, Stan?"

"Less than a minute, Chief."

"Squeeze the last drop out that you can."

"Will do," the man said as the flow of water out of the fire truck's tank began to slack off and then stopped. The firemen quickly uncoupled the hoses and sped away toward the lake to refill.

"I'm sorry, Jimmy. I hate this shit."

"I know," Weber told him. "Doesn't look like it would do much good anyway."

"Afraid not."

"How soon are you getting your new truck?"

"As soon as I can arrange for somebody to pick it up."

There wasn't anything they could do then but watch the house burn.

***

It was dark by the time the blaze was extinguished and Harper's men mopped-up any stray embers and put their equipment away. As the tired, dirty volunteers left the scene, each paused to shake Weber's hand, to put a hand on his shoulder, to tell him they were sorry they couldn't have done more. Weber knew they all felt like they had somehow failed him and he assured each man that he appreciated their efforts and that they couldn't have done any more, given the situation and the tools at their disposal. Chief Harper seemed to be more disturbed than anyone else, much like a dedicated coach might be if another team had defeated his in a major playoff game.

"I'm sorry, Jimmy. Damn. We tried. We really did."

"It's okay," Weber told him. "I'm thankful for everything you and your guys did. At least the place was empty and nobody got hurt."

All of Weber's deputies had come by the fire scene at some point, and several had stayed by his side until he told them to go home to their families, or back on patrol. "Whoever's doing this is still out there. You can't help here, but maybe we can nail his ass before he starts another fire."

Finally only Weber, C.C., and Robyn were left.

"Are you all right, Jimmy?"

He had been staring at the ruined hulk of the house he had grown up in, looking surreal in the moonlight.

"Jimmy?"

"Huh? Oh, sorry, I wasn't paying attention."

"Are you okay?"

"Yeah, I'm fine."

"What's she looking for?"

C.C. had been prowling around the property with the four-cell Maglite flashlight from Weber's Explorer. "I don't know. But whatever it is, if it's out there she'll find it. She's good."

They watched the light move as C.C. explored the property for another thirty minutes, then made her way back to them.

"Did you find anything?" Weber asked.

"No. It would be nice if our perp did something stupid like dropping his wallet or checkbook as he was making his escape, but no such luck."

"We're not going to accomplish anything out here tonight," Weber said. "Let me drop you off at your motel and we'll hit it again in the morning."

"I don't know about you guys, but I'm starving," Robyn said. "You go home and grab a shower. I'll drive C.C. back to town and then pick up a pizza and come by your place."

Though he had nothing to hide, Weber felt a momentary discomfort at the idea of the two women alone together. In the past Robyn had exhibited signs of jealousy more than once. C.C. agreed and started toward Robyn's patrol car. Before joining her, Robyn paused and asked in a low voice, "Unless you'd rather drive her and "hit it" tonight?"

Weber wasn't sure how to respond, but then he saw the smirk on Robyn's face and she said, "God, you're easy! Go get cleaned up. I'll see you soon."

Chapter 15

Weber's dreams were filled with visions of the past, of growing up at the house on Pine Knoll Road. It had been a good life centered around hard work and family. There was never time or money for vacations or for many luxuries, but John and Patricia Weber were loving parents who gave their children everything they could.

He had never enjoyed working with cattle and wanted more than the hard life of a small rancher, and when Weber graduated from high school he joined the Army. He knew it hurt his father that he didn't want to take over the ranch someday as he himself had done from his own father, but John Weber knew a man had to follow his own destiny.

That destiny had been as a lawman, and the young soldier found himself being trained as a Military Policeman at Fort Leonard Wood, Missouri. He was good at the job and quickly earned the respect of his peers and superiors for his dedication and common sense. After a tour of duty at Fort Eustis, Virginia, and a promotion to corporal, Weber had just arrived at his second assignment, at Fort Campbell, Kentucky when news of his parents' tragic death in an automobile accident reached him.

He took emergency leave to fly home to Arizona to settle his parents' affairs and make arrangements for his twelve year old sister. Running the ranch and a thousand head of cattle and trying to raise his young sister from afar was an overwhelming task, and though he loved his job as a military policeman, Weber reluctantly applied for and received a hardship discharge only six months into his second enlistment.

But just as ranching and livestock had never appealed to him as a teenager, it still did not as a young man, and he soon remembered why he had joined the Army. Before two years had passed Weber had sold off the cattle, leased out the acreage with the exception of the family home and surrounding ten acres, and taken a job with the Big Lake Sheriff's Office. A few years later, when Pete Caitlan retired as Sheriff, Weber was his handpicked successor. His heart had been broken a few years later when Debbie, the sister he had given up his dreams for and come home to raise, had committed her terrible crimes.

Debbie and her husband Mike had lived in the family home after their wedding, and Weber had built the smaller cabin he lived in, careful to locate it a couple of miles away to give the newlyweds plenty of privacy.

Even after seeing a psychologist in the wake of Debbie's crimes and his own on-duty shooting of a young suspect, Weber had still not been able to force himself to enter the family home, and now that it was gone he felt no sense of loss as he stood staring at what was left of it the next morning.

Weber had never really understood the term "closure" before, but he did that morning. He would always have his memories, both good and bad, of this place, but now he felt like whatever demon had kept him away had perished in the fire.

He heard the sound of a vehicle behind him and C.C.'s red Chevrolet Suburban with State Fire Marshal emblems on the doors pulled into the driveway.

"How's the knee?" he asked her as she got out.

"Sore, but I'll live," C.C. said as she handed him a Styrofoam cup of coffee.

"Thanks."

"It's not Starbucks, but your little Stop and Go makes a pretty good imitation," she admitted as she took a sip from her own cup.

"What is this, some kind of mocha latte cappuccino espresso?" Weber asked skeptically.

"No, it's black coffee. Sorry to disappoint."

"That's no disappointment," Weber said, taking a sip. "We might make a mountain woman out of you yet."

"That's probably not a good idea," C.C. told him. "Love triangles never work out and somebody might get themselves shot before it's over."

"What do you mean?" Weber asked warily. Robyn had seemed perfectly normal when she got to his cabin the night before, after dropping C.C. off at her motel.

"Relax, Jimmy, your girlfriend knows I'm not a threat and she isn't planning on going on a shooting spree. I'm talking about Gordon Hahn. Bumped into him while I was getting the coffee. Or I guess you could say he bumped into me. From behind."

"Tell me he didn't catch you unaware and do the old bump and grind."

C.C. laughed. "I guess if he had two more inches on his legs and fifteen inches less on his gut you could call it that. This was more like a belly bump, which was disgusting enough, trust me."

"Somebody really does need to shoot that loser," Weber said.

"Well not today," C.C. told him. "He's had a bad enough morning, what with that hot cup of coffee I *accidently* spilled all over him. At least his Buddha belly protected his little old winkie from getting scalded."

"You didn't?" Weber said, laughing at the visual picture.

"I've got to admit, he dances pretty good for a guy his size," C.C. said with a chuckle.

A moment later Steve Harper arrived and joined them. "Have you seen the latest edition of that new rag?"

"Haven't been to town yet," Weber said. "What's young mister Tovar have to say today?"

"I'm no lawyer, but this looks like slander to me," Harper said, handing Weber the latest edition of the *Big Lake Truth* and pointing to the front page, which had a photos of the fire the day before. Weber read the story under it:

While Fire Chief Steve Harper continues to twiddle his thumbs as our community burns down around him, it would seem that Sheriff Jim Weber prefers to spend his time giving an investigator from the State Fire Marshal's office a back road tour of our area. Who knows what the Sheriff and the very attractive female outsider were up to instead of doing their jobs? But given Weber's womanizing past, which includes an ongoing affair with Big Lake's only female deputy, one can only guess.

Then again, maybe this publication is being too suspicious of the Sheriff's intentions. Or maybe not suspicious enough? Could it be possible that yet another female conquest hasn't been the only thing on Weber's mind? What better alibi could somebody have than a Deputy Fire Marshal when an arson fire destroys a very nice home that has sat vacant for many months? Could a single payoff from an insurance policy be more lucrative than rental income to some people?

"Maybe I should have let you wring his neck yesterday after all," Weber said after reading the article, which went on for another three paragraphs, accusing the Fire Chief of incompetence again and strongly hinting that the sheriff himself might be responsible for the string of arson fires.

"Can you sue him for slander, Jimmy? Maybe that would shut him up."

"Actually, slander is spoken, libel is written," Weber said.

"Slander, libel, whatever. Can you sue him?"

"Not for this. He's hinted that I did something wrong, but he hasn't outright said I did anything. I'm no lawyer either, but I don't think there's a case here. And even if there was, it would probably drag out in court forever."

"Well somebody needs to do something! This guy is making both of us look like fools, and worse!"

"The best thing we can do is catch whoever is setting these fires," C.C. said, pulling on latex gloves. "That might shut him up."

"Then let's get to it," Weber told them.

***

"He's getting sloppy, or else overconfident," C.C. said less than thirty minutes after they started the fire investigation.

"What do you mean?" Weber asked.

"Look here."

They were in the kitchen, or what was left of it. "Do you see that glass there?"

Weber looked at the broken glass just inside the opening that had been the back door. "Yeah?"

"Now go outside and look at where the windows were in this part of the house. What do you see?"

Weber did and returned a moment later. "The glass is all on the outside."

"That's right," C.C. said. "The fire blew the glass out. "Somebody broke the glass in the door and sent it inside. This was your point of entry."

"Couldn't that have happened when Steve's men started pouring water on the fire? Or could they have broken the windows to get water inside?"

"Could have happened if the glass from other windows was inside. But it wasn't, at least not back here. Why would they do that to just one window? Especially a smaller door window?"

"It wasn't my people," Harper said. "I was second on the scene, right behind Kevin, and the place was burning hard when we got here. The windows had already blown out."

"Now come over here," C.C. said, and led them into what had been the dining room. She pointed at a blackened one gallon metal can on the floor near what was left of the table where Weber's family had eaten all of their meals.

After taking photographs and measurements from all angles, C.C. picked up the can and pulled the paper mask down from her face and held the opening to her nose, then extended it to Harper. He sniffed and passed it on to Weber. The faint odor of gasoline was detectable even amid the smell of soot and ashes.

"Like I said, either sloppy or overconfident."

"Do you think you can get any fingerprints off of that?" Harper asked.

"If your guys can't, our lab down in Phoenix may be able to," C.C. told him.

"If nothing else, maybe somebody at one of the convenience stores remembers someone buying a can full of gas," Weber said.

"Steve and I can do our thing here, why don't you get started on that?" C.C. suggested. "This may be the break we've been waiting for."

Chapter 16

"I don't know," Buz Carelton said as he looked at the gas can skeptically. "I think a good lab could do it but I'd be afraid to try. How about you, Dolan?"

The other deputy shook his head. "I'm afraid we'll destroy any evidence there may be. Buz is right, this needs to go to a lab. Sorry, Jimmy."

"That's all right," Weber told him. "C.C. said her people might have a chance." Buz and Dolan were his best crime scene technicians, but it was a small department and they were limited in both training and equipment.

"Are we making any headway on finding a connection between the fire victims and developers and all that?" Weber asked Robyn, who was busy at her computer terminal.

"Not really. The couple that own the cabin built it themselves and seem to be in good financial shape. There are a few small builders who are overextended but it doesn't look like any of them are on the verge of bankruptcy. Tom Cotter and Max Woodbury are both working guys, but in both of their fires there wasn't enough damage to file an insurance claim. All Max had on that old truck was minimum liability coverage so there wouldn't have been a payoff anyway."

"It was worth a shot," Weber said.

Robyn looked up at him and asked, "Are you okay?"

"Yeah, why?"

"With the house and all, I just wondered."

"You know, it's crazy. All this time I couldn't even go in the place, and today I didn't even give it a thought."

"That's a good thing, isn't it?"

"I think so," Weber said. "Who knows? Maybe this was the final thing I needed to happen to move on."

"Be careful with that kind of talk," Robyn warned. "Who knows what that idiot running that new paper would make out of that idea? He's already hinting that you had some involvement in the fire."

"He hinted at a lot of things," Weber said. "Are *we* okay with all that bullshit he wrote in today's paper?"

"I'm not okay with it," Robyn said, "it embarrasses me when my private life, *our* private life, is exposed to the public like that. I don't know why I should be, it's a small town and it's not like our relationship is any secret, but still…"

"I'm sorry, Robyn."

"For what? You didn't write the damn article."

"Not just the part about us. I'm talking about him suggesting that me and C.C.…."

"Jimmy, *we're* okay. I know I'm a jealous head case sometimes, and believe me, I hate myself for it, I really do. There are some women out there I don't trust, but that's my problem and I'm trying very hard not to make it *our* problem. I'd like to find this Darron Tovar and kick his butt, but that's probably not a good idea, right?"

Weber laughed and said, "I guess it depends on how you look at it. A good ass whoopin' might be just what he needs. But from a public relations standpoint, you probably shouldn't. I've got enough paperwork to deal with."

He wanted to touch Robyn, to show his appreciation for her faith in him, but they had a strict policy of keeping their personal relationship out of the office as much as possible. So he just nodded at her and straightened up as Mary Caitlin brought him a thick stack of telephone memos.

"Here's the good news," she told him. "I sorted through these and the first 27 you're going to throw away anyway. I stapled them together to make your life easier. That leaves eleven that you eventually need to deal with, but not right now. I paper-clipped them together. The six that are left do need your attention."

"Now you see, Mary? That's what I've been wanting all along," Weber told her. "Can you do the same thing with all of those forms and reports you're always sticking in my face, too?"

"Don't get used to it," Mary said. "I felt sorry for you because of your parents' house. Once you catch this firebug all bets are off."

***

"Why do you look so glum?" Weber asked Larry Parks as they ate lunch at the ButterCup Café. "Paul here ought to be the sad one, what with this new newspaper putting him out of business."

"Hey, I hope that kid is a success," Paul said as he stirred the fourth packet of sweetener into his iced tea. "I hope he makes a lot of money and builds a big house and finds a good woman and they have a whole passel of yuppie kids just like he is. And I hope that every night when he comes home, his mother runs out from under the porch and bites him."

"Do we still have yuppies?" Parks asked. "Aren't we up to generation XYZ or something? I can never keep track."

"I don't know about yuppies, but we still have hippies," Paul said.

"Don't change the subject. What happened to that smiling young man from Oklahoma we all know and love? Seriously, are you okay, man?"

"Yeah, I'm good. I had to spend the morning with your buddy Gordon Hahn. Some woman on the Rez caught her old man with another woman and cut them both pretty bad. She took off and the Tribal police caught with her in McNary and she sent two of their officers to the hospital before they subdued her. Hahn took great delight in briefing me in complete detail. I swear, if I would have had to listen to him say the words squaw or blanket ass one more time I was going to cut *him*!"

"He is a peach, isn't he?" Weber asked.

"So when you joined the FBI, did you ever think you'd wind up here, holding Jimmy's hand and whatever it is you hold on Hahn?"

"No, Paul, we all think we're going to do glamorous things like busting counterfeiters and fighting domestic terrorism when we're at Quantico," Parks said. "But I've come to love life here in Dogpatch. And I like working the Rez. But I'll tell you what. There are times that I just want to take Hahn out in the forest and bust a cap on him."

"If you did, Chairman Goshay would probably make you an honary Apache," Weber said. "By the way, did you notice a big coffee stain on his shirt today? C.C. told me that he got a little too close and she poured a cup of hot coffee on him at the Stop and Go this morning."

"I knew there was a reason I love that woman," Parks said. "Now that I think of it, Hahn did look more stained than usual. And that's saying a lot."

"Go fishing," Paul said. "Best way in the world to get rid of stress. Well… maybe the second best way."

"I may have to try that one of these days," Parks said. "Lord knows Marsha does all that she can, but on a day like today that stress really builds up. I'm not much of a fisherman, what kind of line do you use, Paul?"

"I'm partial to Stren. Four pound will do the job for the trout we have around here."

"Now you see, that just goes to show you how wrong a man can be. I thought maybe being a newspaper man and all it would be a byline."

"Funny man," Paul replied. "How long did it take you to think that one up? And how long have you been saving it?"

Before Parks could answer, the waitress was back to clear their plates. When she left, Paul said, "I see you got raked over the coals in the *Truth* today. Maybe when Parks here takes Hahn for that one-way ride he can take Tovar with him. Kind of a two for one deal."

"Hey, Uncle Sam pays for my ammo," Parks said. "Let's take a whole carload of jerks and cretins."

Weber started to suggest that he could have Mary draw up a guest list when his handheld radio crackled to life. "All units. Citizen reports a police officer has been shot at the boat launch on Rim Road. Repeat, officer shot on Rim Road."

Chapter 17

Weber's mind flashed back to the same call a few months earlier when Robyn had been shot by a frightened old man when he mistook her for a killer on the loose in Big Lake. The memory of her on the ground, the paramedics working over her, tore at his heart. Steering with one hand, he punched the button on his microphone.

"Who is it, Mary? Do you know who's been shot?"

"Negative," Mary said. "All the caller said was that a deputy was sitting in his car covered in blood."

His car. His. Weber felt a flood of relief that it wasn't Robyn, and just as quickly guilt for what he was thinking, at least Robyn was safe. He cared about all of his deputies. In a department as small as theirs, they were all family. But still, if he had to choose…

He forced those thoughts out of his mind as he pushed the Explorer to its limits, covering the three miles to the boat launch in a blur, hoping no careless citizen would ignore his siren and flashing lights and pull out in front of him, or that a dog or squirrel wouldn't scamper into his path. Beside him, Parks was quiet, thinking his own grim thoughts.

There were two vehicles in the parking lot of the boat launch, a blue conversion van and a marked Big Lake Sheriff's Department car.

"He's over there in the car," a distraught older woman said when Weber and Parks exited the Explorer. "It's horrible. There's blood all over. I stopped to use the porta-potty there and I saw him. Oh, it's terrible! "

"Get inside your vehicle and stay there," Weber ordered as he and Parks drew their weapons and approached the car, scanning the area for any threat that might still be lurking about to ambush them. Weber made mental notes as they went. There were no bullet holes in the car's windshield or anywhere else he could see, and there were no empty cartridge cases on the ground near the car.

The driver's side window of the car was down and Archer sat upright behind the steering wheel. His head hung down and the front of his uniform shirt was soaked in bright red blood.

"Damn!" Weber said. Who would shoot Archer? He was as harmless as the family dog. A big, clumsy dog, but harmless nevertheless.

Weber holstered his .45 and reached through the window and placed his index and middle fingers on Archer's neck to the side of the deputy's windpipe. The skin was still warm and Weber was relieved to feel a pulse. Not just a pulse, but a strong pulse. He was amazed that the man could still be alive after losing so much blood.

The blood. Another police car roared into the parking lot, siren screaming, and Dan Wright jumped out. The sound of more sirens was coming closer. Weber dipped a finger into the blood on Archer's shirt and held it to his nose, then stuck out his tongue and tasted it.

"Son-of-a-bitch!" He pulled his handheld radio from his belt and keyed the microphone button. "All units. Stand down! Stand down. This is NOT an officer down call! Repeat, NO officer is down! Everybody return to regular duties. Call off the paramedics."

He reached in the window again and shook his deputy's shoulder. "Archer. Archer! Wake up!" He shook him again, then slapped the side of his face. "Wake up, damn it!"

Archer's head jerked upright and he looked around in confusion for a moment, then focused on Weber.

"Hi Jimmy. What's going on?"

"You tell me, Archer. A tourist found you sitting here and thought you were dead!"

"Dead? Why…"

Archer looked down at his shirt, and then at the empty plastic 48-ounce Slushy cup on the seat next to him.

"Uh… I think I must have fallen asleep."

"Get out of the car," Weber ordered, jerking the door open. When Archer didn't move fast enough, Weber grabbed him by the arm and yanked him out. The cup and a half-eaten corn dog fell out with him. He marched Archer over to the witness and said, "You scared the hell out of this lady. She thought you had been shot."

"He hasn't been shot?" the woman asked in amazement.

"No ma'am, he's fine," Weber assured her. "He fell asleep and spilled his drink all over himself. Archer, apologize to this woman for what you put her through."

"I'm sorry," Archer mumbled, his head hung low.

"I really thought he was dead," she said. "Now I feel like such a fool for…"

"No, you did the right thing," Weber assured her. "I'm sorry you got such a scare. But he's not dead. At least not yet, anyway!"

***

Weber steered Archer past the rest of the staff and into his private office, his grip firm on the flabby deputy's arm.

"Sit," he ordered, pointing at a chair. "And try not to fall asleep, okay?"

Weber sat down in his own chair and stared hard at the other man. "Christ, Archer. You're a mess! Look at yourself. I should have shot you just for scaring us all to death. Do you know that every deputy in this department was on their way to the boat launch? Do you know how scared we all were? Do you know how many people's lives you put in jeopardy? Any one of us responding could have hit somebody and killed them!"

"I'm sorry, Jimmy."

"Yes you are, Archer. You are absolutely the sorriest excuse for a deputy I've ever seen. As much as I like Steve Harper and as good a job as he's doing as Fire Chief, I just might get behind your dad's push to get you the job. It'd be worth it to have you out of my hair."

Archer didn't reply. He just hung his head as Weber lectured him.

"Damn it, Archer, you've pulled some real stunts in your time, but this takes the cake. What were you thinking?"

Archer shrugged and mumbled something.

"What? I can't hear you, Archer. And look at me when you're talking."

"I've just been really tired lately. Half the time I can't keep my eyes open. I remember pulling into the launch parking lot to have my lunch and the next thing I knew you were there. I don't remember falling asleep."

"Why are you so tired all the time? Do you need to see a doctor?"

Archer shrugged and Weber remembered the information Robyn had shared with him about Archer and Kallie Jo's sex life.

"You have no idea why you have been so tired these days, Archer?"

The younger man blushed, and then shrugged his shoulders. "I don't know," he mumbled.

"You don't, huh?"

Archer shook his head, avoiding the sheriff's eyes.

"Let me ask you something, Archer. How's married life going?"

"Married life? Oh, it's great." He brightened and smiled. "Kallie Jo's wonderful. I can't believe how good she is to me. Sometimes I think it's all just a dream, Jimmy. But if it is, I don't want to wake up."

"So things are good, huh?"

"Yes sir. I never expected it could be this way."

"Let me ask you something," Weber said. "Just between us, how are things in the bedroom?"

Archer's face was as red as the Slushy that covered his shirt. "It's ah… it's good?"

"Good?"

"Really, really good."

"You know, Archer, when a couple first gets together, there's this hot passion. I mean, they can't keep their hands off each other. And like you said, that's good. It's real good. But after a while things start to slack off."

"They do?"

"Yeah. And that's okay too. Otherwise you wear each other out. That's not so good."

"It's not?"

"No, it's not. A woman's body needs time to recharge. A man's does, too. Otherwise bad things can start to happen."

"What kind of bad things, Jimmy?"

"Well, for instance, a wife might begin to resent her husband. She might start to think that that's all he wants her for. Just the sex. That's a bad thing, right?"

Archer nodded his head.

"And a man, he starts making mistakes."

"What kind of mistakes?"

"All kinds of mistakes, Archer. Hell, he gets so worn out that he might even fall asleep at work."

Archer's face flushed again.

"Sometimes maybe a husband thinks his wife expects him to be that way all the time, so he feels like he has to keep that hot passion I talked about going 24 hours a day. Maybe he doesn't notice that he's wearing them both out."

"But won't the wife think he doesn't love her anymore if he… you know?"

Weber shook his head. "Not if he remembers that making love isn't just between the sheets, Archer."

"Oh, we don't just do it between the sheets," Archer assured him. "Yesterday we...."

Weber held up his hands to cut off the rest and to block the mental image that he really didn't want to have.

"That's not what I mean, Archer. See, there's a big difference between making love and having sex. There's nothing wrong with sex. It's great. Really great. But making love? That's something else entirely. Making love includes a lot of little things. Opening car doors for her, holding her hand when you sit together watching TV. Complimenting her on how nice she looks, or how good dinner was. Helping her with the dishes. Listening to her when she says things. Really listening, not just nodding as you stare at the TV. Holding her at night when you sleep. When a man does those things, that's when he shows his wife just how important she is to him. That's what you build a relationship on, Archer."

Archer sat in silence as he pondered what Weber had told him.

"But, Jimmy... about the sex thing? Does that stop when the lovemaking starts?"

Weber laughed, then leaned forward and slapped Archer's knee. "No son, trust me, that's when it really starts!"

Archer looked relieved and Weber said, "Go home and clean up, Archer, and then go to bed. To *sleep*. Come back tomorrow ready to get back to work, okay?"

"Yes sir," Archer said, and scrambled to his feet. He paused at the door and then turned back to Weber. "Thanks, Jimmy. I'm going to work hard at being a better deputy and a better husband."

"You do that," Weber told him.

A few minutes after Archer was gone, Mary Caitlin came into Weber office and said, "I didn't hear any shouting or shooting, and Archer came out with a smile as wide as the Grand Canyon spread across his face. What happened in here?"

"We had us a little talk, and then I sent him to his room," Weber told her.

Chapter 18

"What did you find out?" Weber asked C.C. when she came into the Sheriff's Office late in the day. It was obvious that she had gone back to her motel and cleaned up after another day of rummaging around in ashes. She was wearing jeans and a pastel yellow blouse, her hair pulled back in a ponytail.

"The fire started in the dining room, just like I thought. But this one is different than the others."

"Different? How so?"

"Do you remember when I said that our perp was getting sloppy or overconfident this morning?"

"Yeah?"

"Well, I don't think it was overconfidence. I'd almost think this wasn't the same person, to be honest."

"A copycat?" Weber asked. "Please tell me that we don't have two idiots running around here starting fires!"

"It happens. Especially in a case like this that is getting a lot of publicity. To be honest, I don't know," C.C. told him. "All I can say is that this fire changes the pattern."

"What do you mean?"

C.C. went to the map that held the yellow stickers with the fire sites. "We have to ignore the first fire, the shed at that truck driver's place. Since he cleaned it all up, there really isn't anything we can learn there. So let's look at the others, starting with the barn. Some planning went into it. Our perp started the fire in the corner to get that double burn effect I talked about, and there was enough trash or straw or whatever to get the fire going good. Then we have the truck fire. It was almost too easy but it was effective. Light a flare, throw it in the cab, and run like hell. It was almost a target of opportunity."

C.C. paused to take a drink from her water bottle, then pointed at the fourth dot on the map. "The cabin was the most sophisticated. He thought that one out. That candle was well planned."

"So where are you going with all of this?" Weber asked.

"Patience, Sheriff, I'm getting there. At yesterday's fire it was a step backward."

"The broken window?"

"Not that so much as the gas can. Why leave it there?"

"He was in a hurry?"

"Yes. But why?"

"I don't know," Weber said. "Maybe a car came by and scared him off. There isn't a lot of traffic out there."

"If I were this perp, I'd have poured that gas in the living room like he did. But I would have made a trail out to the door and lit it as I went out. That didn't happen yesterday. The burn pattern is wrong. It started right there in the dining room."

"Why?"

"I don't know. I think maybe you're right, something scared him off."

"I talked to the mail carrier that phoned it in," Chad said. "Jerry Glenwood. He said he had not seen any cars out there. But he was coming back toward town from the Baldwin place, where the road dead ends a mile or so past your old place, Jimmy. So whoever started the fire could have been ahead of him."

"Did he remember seeing a vehicle parked in the driveway on his way up?"

"No, nothing out of the ordinary. But there are dirt roads and tracks all through the woods out there. Whoever did this may not have come up the main road at all."

Weber pulled a topographic map out of his file cabinet and unrolled it. "There's a Forest Service fire road less than a mile behind the place. And do you see this little line here? That's the old dirt track we used to take up to our pasture here, on the other side of the road. I haven't been on it in years but anybody with a 4x4 or ATV could come in from that direction and drive right up to the back door if they wanted to."

"They didn't drive up to the door, but I'll bet that's the way they came in," C.C. said. "I remember seeing that track you're talking about when I was out there."

"We're going to run out of daylight before long," Weber said. "Chad, why don't you meet me at the house tomorrow morning and we'll see what we can find."

Chad was an avid hunter who knew the mountains well, and if anybody could find the perpetrator's trail, it would be him.

"Hold your horses, Jimmy," said Bob Bennett, who had come in while C.C. was talking and looked uncomfortable.

"What do you mean, Bob?"

"Jimmy, you have to distance yourself from this case. You shouldn't have even been out there this morning."

"What? What are you talking about, Bob?"

"Think about it, Jimmy. This last place was your property. You can't be involved in an investigation that you have a personal and financial interest in. It's a conflict of interest."

Weber felt his temper rising, but kept his voice low when he asked, "What are you saying, Bob? And think long and hard before you answer."

"You know exactly what I'm saying," Bennett replied.

"Are you implying I had something to do with these fires? Are you buying into that bullshit that Darron Tovar had in his paper today?"

"Of course not," Bennett said, shaking his head. "Jimmy, we're friends. And I'm telling you both as the Town's attorney *and* as your friend, you have to recuse yourself from this thing. I know you haven't done anything wrong. We all know that. And anybody with half a brain knows that this Tovar kid is a joke. But that doesn't matter. What is the insurance company that covers that place going to say? Remember, Jimmy, your insurance company is not your friend. They're in business to make money. Look at it from their standpoint. The insured is spearheading the investigation into his own loss. How does that look?"

Weber knew that Bennett was right, as much as he hated to admit it. They *were* friends, and he knew Bennett had his best interests at heart.

"Jimmy?"

Weber sighed. "You're right, Bob. I know that, but damn it…"

"Actually," C.C. said, "Sheriff Weber isn't the lead investigator on this case, I am. And he was not out there this morning in his official capacity, he was there as a witness, to tell me how the house was laid out and to answer any questions I might have had about things that may have looked out of the ordinary. That's how my report is going to read. That should handle any objection the insurance company might have about the fire at his property.

"And as for the whole case, like I said, there's a good chance yesterday's fire was set by somebody else. Things don't quite add up. Technically, I'm considering that a separate investigation. As long as Sheriff Weber stays away from that, is there any reason he can't continue with the original case?"

Bennett thought about what she had said for a minute, then nodded. "Okay. I'm not 100% sure this is a good idea, but as long as he stays away from yesterday's fire I think he can squeak by. But seriously, Jimmy, step back from this one, okay?"

Weber nodded, and the meeting broke up.

"Hey, thanks for that, C.C.," he said when they were alone in his office. "I owe you."

"Yes you do, and you can make it up to me by taking me to dinner," she said.

C.C. looked at him for a moment and then laughed. "I've always heard that term about a "deer in the headlights look" but I had never really seen it before. Relax, Sheriff, I'm not trying to get you into trouble with your girlfriend. When Robyn drove me back in last night, she suggested we all get together for dinner tonight. She'll be there, and your buddy Parks and his girlfriend too, so you'll have plenty of protection in case I do decide to try to jump your bones."

Weber shook his head and C.C. laughed again. "God, Weber, do you know *anything* about women at all?"

"Not nearly as much as I need to," he admitted. "Not nearly as much."

Chapter 19

At 9,000 feet elevation, the town of Big Lake, Arizona is a popular summer getaway for desert dwellers and a winter destination for skiers. Main Street is the center of activity in town, housing a myriad of small shops catering to both the tourist trade and full time residents, several restaurants, and most recently, an art gallery or two. The Sheriff's Office is located in the middle of town, with the Big Lake Town Offices located next door across a small parking lot. The *Big Lake Herald* newspaper office is directly across the street. Looking south, Main Street seems to end at the foot of Apache Mountain, an imposing monolith that towers over the town, but in reality the street turns left sharply at the last minute, and connects with the state highway a mile away, completing a loop begun on the north end of town.

The Roundup Steakhouse is Big Lake's most popular dining spot with residents and tourists alike. The restaurant's rough cedar walls are decorated with western memorabilia; old saddles, steer horns, and branding irons. Several old Winchester rifles hang from hooks high up on the walls.

Weber, Robyn, Parks, Marsha, Coop, and C.C. were seated at a round table in the main dining room, working their way through thick slabs of medium-rare beef grilled to perfection over a mesquite fire, accompanied by heaping mounds of wedge cut potatoes, ranch beans, and fresh baked bread.

"So let me get this straight," C.C. said. "This Archer fell asleep and never felt that iced drink soaking into his shirt? Was he in a coma?"

"You have to understand Archer," Parks told her. "That boy was born lazy, and never grew out of it. I think he could sleep right through a tornado."

"Be nice now," Marcia scolded him. "Archer's not that bad. And besides, Kallie Jo is a sweetie."

"Kallie Jo's great," Parks acknowledged. "No question about that.

But I do wonder what she sees in Archer."

"Stop! We don't know what goes on behind closed doors."

Weber was tempted to say that *he* knew what went on behind Archer's closed doors, but Robyn shot him a warning look and he held his tongue. Instead he said, "I'll tell you what, he sure looked dead to me when we got out there to the boat launch this afternoon."

"Me, too," Parks said.

"So why do you keep him?" C.C. asked.

"His daddy's the mayor," Parks said. "And him and Jimmy here, they go way back. Why, the two of them are darned near Siamese twins, aren't you, Jimmy?"

"I'm trying to decide if it would make less of a mess if I shot you, or just stuck this steak knife in you," Weber said.

"Many tried, some died," Parks said with a grin. "But what the hell, give it a shot. You might get lucky."

"Okay, that's enough red meat for you two," Marsha said. "The testosterone is getting knee deep in here."

"*Something's* getting knee deep, that's for sure," C.C. said.

They all laughed, and Coop said, "Ignore these two, C.C., they can't help it. We're hoping they'll eventually get through puberty and turn into halfway decent men."

Their revelry was interrupted when a man approached their table and said, "Jimmy, you've got to do something about this new newspaper. Scandal sheet is a better name for it! Have you seen what that kid running it wrote today?"

"Yeah, I saw it, Edgar. I'm not worried about it."

"Well I am! This kind of publicity could put me out of business. Why, let one of these do-gooders that want to come up here and turn this place into Los Angeles or San Diego get ahold of this and the next thing I know, I'll have the EPA knocking on my door."

Edgar Driscoll was one of the thinnest men Weber had ever known, even though he consumed huge quantities of food at every meal. So much so that the kids in high school had nicknamed him Tapeworm, sure that a massive parasite inhabited his intestinal tract, eating everything that came its way. They all knew that sooner or later it was going to devour Edgar from the inside out, or else make its exit from some orifice in a way that was sure to be horrific. Edgar didn't appreciate the nickname and it had soured his attitude early on to the point that by the time he began his junior year, most of his fellow students were rooting for the creature they knew lived inside of him.

"The EPA? Like the Environmental Protection Agency? Why would they care about the fire out at my parent's place?"

"I'm not talking about that nonsense he wrote about you. Everybody knows that's crap. But look what he said about *me*!"

He laid a copy of the *Big Lake Truth* on the table, not seeming to notice or care that it covered at least two of their dinner plates, and pointed at a story on an inside page. "See there? That's what I'm talking about."

Small Business Or House Of Horrors?

As we said in the inaugural issue of the *Big Lake Truth*, there are businesses in this community whose owners have long curried favor from the press and some members of the Town Council. How long will this be allowed to continue and at what cost to the good people of Big Lake and the tourists who come to this mountain hamlet? Just one example of this willful neglect on the part of those who should be monitoring the welfare of our town is Hi-Land Antiques & Treasures on Main Street. The owner of this establishment, Edgar Driscoll, routinely displays hazardous materials, making no attempt to prevent a health catastrophe or worse. Who has to be seriously injured or even killed before something is done to bring this rogue businessman into compliance with established health and safety codes?

"What the hell is he talking about, Tape… I mean Edgar?"

If Edgar noticed the slip, he let it pass, and said, "He came in and tried to sell me an ad the other day and I told him I wasn't interested. He wandered around for a few minutes, then came back to the counter and asked me what kind of training I had in handling hazardous materials. I asked him what he was talking about and he pointed at some old thermometers hanging on the wall and said they were full of mercury. Well yeah. They're thermometers, for God's sake. Then he saw some old cap guns and rolls of caps, like we all played with when we were kids, and said the caps had gunpowder in them."

"You're kidding me," Weber said. "That's what he's talking about?"

"That's it. This is payback because I wouldn't buy an ad. It's blackmail is what it is! I want him arrested."

"I'm not sure it qualifies as blackmail," Weber said. "Did he tell you he was going to print this if you didn't buy an ad? That might make a case for extortion."

"No, he didn't say a thing. He just mentioned the thermometers and the caps, then he gave me this smug look like he was so smart and I was so dumb, and he left."

"I'll tell you what, talk to Bob Bennett," Weber said. "He'll know if there's a case, either civilly or criminally."

"That's it? Talk to Bob?"

"It's the best I can tell you."

"And you're not going to do anything about this?"

"There's nothing I can do," Weber told him. "Trust me, I'd love to kick his ass all the way back to Flagstaff or wherever he came from, but my hands are tied."

Edgar shook his head in frustration and picked up the newspaper. "Well, that kid's right about one thing, I guess. You *are* worthless!"

He stomped away without a backward glance and it was quiet at the table for a long, uncomfortable minute, then Parks said, "So anyway, has anybody else noticed Jimmy's voice is changing now that's he's in puberty?"

***

Later, as they were getting undressed, Robyn said, "I like C.C.."

"I do, too," Weber said.

"Do you think Coop likes her too?"

"Coop? I guess he… wait a minute. Was that what this was all about?"

"What do you mean?"

"You know what I mean. Dinner. Were you and Marsha trying to fix up Coop and C.C.?"

"Why would you ask that?" Robyn asked innocently, shucking her jeans off.

"Because I'm a trained investigator, maybe?"

"Or maybe you're just naturally suspicious."

"Call it what you will," he said, "Setups are never a good thing."

"It wasn't a setup, okay? But even if it was, would that be such a bad thing? Coop is a nice guy and C.C. is a neat person."

"Okay, so let's say they hooked up and fell in love. Then I'm out a good deputy."

"How do you figure that?"

"Because it's a long ways from Phoenix to Big Lake."

"That's ridiculous, Jimmy. It was just dinner, and you've already got them setting up housekeeping. And even if that did happen, how do you know C.C. wouldn't move up here?"

"Because there's not a Starbucks within 75 miles," Weber told her.

He watched as Robyn crossed the room naked and went into the bathroom. As she stood at the sink brushing her teeth, Weber could see the scar on her hip where the bullet had torn a crease in her skin, and again the memory of that terrifying day came to mind. Not that it was ever far away. He felt a lump in his throat and swallowed.

Robyn spit into the sink, rinsed her mouth, and looked at him.

"What?"

"Huh?"

"What are you looking at?"

"You."

She frowned and walked to where he sat at the foot of the bed, slipping her arms around his neck.

"Sometimes when you look at me that way, it's like you think I'm just going to magically disappear."

"Please don't ever do that," Weber said.

"I'm not going anywhere, Jimmy. I promise you that."

He buried his face in her breasts, and before either of them realized it, he was sobbing.

"Jimmy? What is it?"

He couldn't find the words to tell her. He had lost so much, and yet in her arms he had found everything. All he could do was hold her tighter. Finally the tears stopped and they crawled into bed together, where he held her close all night long.

Chapter 20

"Somebody definitely was on the fire road and came down that trail to the house," Chad told Weber the next day. "There are some overturned rocks on the road that indicate something was driven over them, and the brush was crushed where they parked near the trail. I saw a couple of broken branches on the trail, but the ground's too hard for any footprints or tire tracks. But that's about it. Sorry, Jimmy."

"Thanks, Chad," Weber said. "Write it up and pass it on to C.C., if you will."

Weber understood why he had to step back from the case but it still riled him to do so. Crimes were being committed in his town and it was his job to put a stop to them. At least Bennett had not told him he couldn't continue the investigation into the other cases, thanks to C.C.'s statement that in her opinion they were separate crimes.

Under Mary's watchful eye Weber groused his way through a stack of paperwork that had accumulated in the past few days. With that finished, he escaped from the office, thinking that he would spend some time driving around town, adding another pair of eyes to the deputies and volunteers who were spread thin looking for any suspicious activity that might lead them to the arsonist. He was surprised to see Leslie Stokes' old Toyota pickup in the Town Offices side of the parking lot, since they were closed on weekends.

Weber walked over and tried the door, but it was locked. He put his face close to the door glass and saw Leslie working at her computer. She looked up at his knock, then came to the door and opened it for him.

"Putting in some overtime, Leslie?"

"I'm on salary just like you, Jimmy, such as it is. I don't get overtime. Shoot, with Chet as my boss, I don't even get an attaboy now and then."

"The man's too busy patting himself on the back to notice anybody else's efforts," Weber said.

"Don't I know it," Leslie said. "I'm trying to get this darned old computer system to work better. It just gets slower every day. I swear, I could enter everything in a ledger by hand quicker and it would be more accurate. Every time I turn around I find something that didn't save when I entered it or something else that just got deleted for no reason. I realized yesterday afternoon that when I entered this week's data, it overwrote all of last weeks, so now I have to go in and reenter all of that. And asking Chet to spend anything to replace it, well, you know how that goes. He's having fits over the money the Town Council allocated to the Fire Department. But those guys sure need it. Especially with everything that's going on lately around here."

Her voice softened and she added, "I was so sorry to hear about your parents' house burning Jimmy. That's just terrible. I'm just glad they weren't here to see it. They took so much pride in the place."

"Yes, they did," Weber said. "Mama always said that it didn't matter if you were rich or poor, your home made an impression on the world and said a lot about you. There was no excuse for not keeping it tidy."

"I loved your mom. And Mr. John, you couldn't find a better man than him. Salt of the earth."

"Thank you," Weber said, then noticed that her left hand was wrapped in a thick gauze bandage. "What did you do to yourself?"

"Oh this?" Leslie held her hand up and grinned ruefully. "If I tell you, promise not to laugh?

"I'll do my best."

"I slammed it in a door."

"Ouch! How did you manage that?"

"Oh, you know me, Miss Clumsy. I was trying to get a cobweb off the wall above the door of the spare bedroom and couldn't quite reach it. I was too lazy to get a stepstool, so I used a little wooden coffee table instead. I was standing on my tiptoes reaching up with one hand and holding onto the open door for balance when the darned table collapsed. It pitched me forward and slammed my hand in the door."

Weber couldn't help but chuckle, and said, "I'm sorry, but I can just picture that."

Leslie laughed with him. "What can I say? Like I said, Miss Clumsy."

"It must make typing even slower," Weber said.

"And that combined with this antique Chet calls a computer is why I'm here on a Saturday instead of at the casino in Hon-Dah feeding nickels into a slot machine."

"Well, I'll leave you to it," Weber said. "Do you need anything?"

"A young, handsome computer techy kind of guy who can fix this machine," she told him, then added as he went out the door, "And if you can find one that gives good foot rubs, that's a plus!"

***

"I've got an opinion about these fires," Hazel Fuller told Weber when she flagged him down as he drove past her small home on Chestnut Lane. That didn't surprise the sheriff at all. *Everybody* seemed to have an opinion, and before she said a word, Weber knew what Hazel's would be. But he humored her anyway.

"What's that, Miss Fuller?"

She looked around to be sure nobody was within earshot, then leaned in the window of his Explorer to say "prostitutes" in a stage whisper.

"Prostitutes?"

"That's right, Sheriff. Harlots. Strumpets. I think they're setting up shop in these places to do their filthy business and then burning them down afterwards to destroy the evidence."

Weber never thought much about Heaven or Hell, or what happens after people die, but if reincarnation was possible, he sometimes wondered if Hazel had been a working girl in a past life. The woman suspected prostitutes were setting up shop everywhere from the boat launch to the library bookmobile to the Town Pump, Big Lake's new 24-hour convenience store. He didn't bother to point out that hookers could probably find a better place than a backyard shed or an old barn or the cab of a derelict truck to ply their trade.

"That's something to think about," Weber told her.

"I'm just sure of it," Hazel said. "How could it possibly be anything else?"

"You may be right," Weber agreed. "Let me get back to the office, I want to pass this on to my deputies. Thank you, Miss Fuller. It's good citizens like you that make our job easier."

"Well, I'm just doing my civic duty, Sheriff. That's all." She stepped back, Weber put the Explorer in gear and waved as he drove off in search of firebugs and soiled doves.

***

"Big Lake One?"

Weber was almost out to the ski lodge on the north end of town at Cat Mountain when dispatcher Kate Copley called him on the radio.

"This is One."

"Can you call me on your cell?"

"Sure, hold on," Weber said. He pulled off the road and pulled his cell phone out and pushed the speed dial for the office number. "It's Jimmy," he said when Kate answered.

"I've got somebody here who says she has some information about the fires, but she will only talk to you."

"Who is she?"

"Stand by a sec," Kate said, and he heard her talking to somebody, then she was back. "Her name's Sharleen Collins."

"Tell her I'm on my way," Weber said and made a U-turn to drive back to town.

Sharleen Collins worked in the high school cafeteria, and her husband Rocky was a carpet layer when he wasn't busy drinking, hunting, or fishing with his brother Mitchell. Usually the siblings multitasked, combining drinking with their pursuit of wild game and trout. Every time he heard the term "school lunch lady" Weber thought of Sharleen, who seldom smiled and seemed to be disappointed with every aspect of her life. This day was no exception.

"Can we talk in your office?" she asked him, and Weber led her into his office and closed the door.

"The dispatcher said you had some information on these fires?"

"I think I know who's setting them," Sharleen replied. "I think it's that no good brother-in-law of mine."

"And what makes you think that?"

"He can't hold a job, for one thing. That's a family trait. Rocky managed to get himself fired a couple of weeks ago for drinking on the job. The idiot spilled beer on a brand new carpet he was installing and then tried to say it came that way from the mill." She shook her head in disgust.

"Just because he doesn't have a good work history doesn't make him an arsonist," Weber said.

"It's not just that. Mitchell always has money. If he's not working, where is it coming from?"

Weber looked at her and then folded his hands open on his desk. "I don't know. You tell me."

"I think he's robbing those places and using the fires to cover it up."

"I'm sorry, I'm not following you," Weber said. "Only two of the fires were places where there might have been something worth stealing."

"I don't know about the others," Sharleen admitted. "But I do know that just last night Mitch was showing Rocky a new shotgun he bought. Or said he bought, anyway. I bet if you were to check it out, it either came from the fire at your old house, or else that cabin that burned."

Weber knew there were no firearms in his parents' house. Dolan and Buz had brought him his father's old bolt action .30-06 Springfield and 12 gauge Ithaca shotgun when they had cleaned out the place for him of the things he wanted. All that had been left was some furniture, housewares, and things Weber had no room or use for. Still, he remembered C.C. saying that some arsonists set fires to cover other crimes. He would have to get in contact with the owners of the cabin on Beaver Creek Road and ask them if they had a shotgun there.

"Anything else?"

"Well, I know that Mitchell and Max Woodbury had a big fight a while back."

"A fight? What was that about?"

"I don't know, I just know that Mitchell was bragging about kicking his ass. And one other thing, Sheriff, I heard that somebody used a road flare to set fire to Max's truck? Is that true?"

Weber didn't care to discuss details of an open investigation, although he knew that in a town as small as Big Lake, few secrets survived for very long.

"Why do you ask about flares?"

"Because I know Mitchell has some in the back of his Jeep. I saw them when him and Rocky pulled a deer out of the back of it last week."

"A deer? It's still a couple of months from hunting season."

"Do you think a season is going to stop those two fools from jacklighting a deer, Sheriff? They butchered it in the garage and put it in our freezer. And it's not the first time."

"You do realize that if they poached a deer they could both get fined, maybe even arrested?"

"That would serve them right," Sharleen said, standing up. "And if you do lock them up, I hope you throw away the key. I'm sick of supporting Rocky while he plays. He needs to grow up. Maybe this will do the trick. If not, you can keep him!"

Chapter 21

"I've known Rocky and Mitch since they were kids," Dolan said. "And both are about as useless as tits on a boar. I have no doubt that they would shoot a deer out of season. But burglary and arson? I just don't see it."

"I've got a call in to Mark Santos over in Pinetop," Weber said. "The deer comes under Game and Fish's jurisdiction, so I'll see what he says about that. Meanwhile, I'm going to drive over and have a talk with Max Woodbury about that fight Sharleen told me about. I'm wondering why he never mentioned that to us."

Chad hung up the telephone and said, "According to Mrs. Fetter, who owns the cabin, they didn't have any firearms, and nothing else of real value was in the cabin except the car they left up here to use when they spend time here. Otherwise, just some furniture, a small TV, pots and pans, that sort of thing."

"I remember seeing what was left of the TV," Weber said. "I really don't think there's anything to the story except a wife that's fed up and wants to make life hard for her husband and his brother. But I'm going to go over and talk to Max, see what he has to say about the fight. We don't have anything else to go on at this point, do we?"

"Not really," Chad said. "C.C. went back to Phoenix this afternoon to take care of some stuff at home and said she'd be back Monday. Or sooner if anything else pops up."

"Or burns down," Weber said dryly as he headed for the door.

***

Max Woodbury was cutting lengths of heavy black PVC pipe when Weber pulled into his driveway and got out of the Explorer.

"Afternoon, Jimmy. Did you come by to tell me you caught that firebug, or do you need to borrow a plunger?"

He laughed at his own joke and Weber gave an obligatory chuckle.

"Neither, Max. But I need to talk to you if you've got a minute."

"Sure," Max said, setting his saw down. "What's on your mind?"

"Last week when I was out here after the fire, I asked if you knew anybody who might be mad at you or be holding a grudge."

"Yeah, and I told you. Not anybody that I know of."

"What about Mitchell Collins?"

"Mitch? What about him?"

"Somebody said you two had a big fight a while back. What was that about?"

"A fight? Me and Mitch?" Max looked perplexed, then suddenly laughed and asked, "Who told you that bullshit?"

"Did you guys get into a fight?"

"No! Not really. More of a shoving match than anything else."

"What happened?"

"We was playing pool at the Tap Room and Mitch had that girlfriend of his with him. What's her name? Linda? No Lynette, that's it. She wanted to play too, and she was wearing one of them blouses with a loose top and no bra, and every time she bent over to take a shot I could see everything she had. And I'm here to tell ya' Jimmy, that old gal bent over a lot, if you get my drift."

Max paused to take a drink from a water bottle, then said, "Well, I guess Mitch got kind of jealous and asked me what I was doing looking at his woman that way. I told him I figured if she was putting it on display it'd be rude of me not to enjoy the view." He laughed at the memory.

"And he didn't like that?"

"Naaa. I guess he felt like he needed to defend her honor or something, because he started to get up in my face about it. Hell, Jimmy, we was both drunk. We shoved each other a little bit, but nobody ever threw a punch or anything like that. Finally he gave me a good shove and I fell on my ass right there next to the pool table. He told me to stay there and not get up or else. So I did just what he said. I laid there on the floor and I started laughing, and I guess that made him even madder. Thing was, I wasn't laughing at him at all."

"Then what were you laughing at?" Weber asked.

"Mitch got all pissed off because I was looking at his gal's titties, and when he pushed me down I looked up and there she was standing right there in a skirt with no panties on, and I could see everything she had. So I just stayed right there like Mitch told me and kept right on looking!"

Weber couldn't help but laugh at the picture, too.

"So that was it?"

"Yeah. Wasn't nothing else to it. Just a couple drunks and a woman who can't seem to afford any underwear."

"Let me ask you this, Max, and I'm not accusing anybody, I'm just thinking out loud. Do you think Mitch would have been mad enough to torch your truck?"

"Mitch? Hell no! Shoot, he came by a couple days later and apologized for gettin' all het up like that and we had a beer or two. Fact is, I told him what I was laughing about down there on the floor, and when he heard that, he about busted a gut laughing about it, too. I wouldn't trust Mitch to build a doghouse unless I was standing right there watching him, otherwise he'd get drunk and forget to leave an opening for the dog to get in and out of. But he ain't got a mean bone in his body. He's just a good ol' boy."

"Well, I thank you for your time," Weber said. "I'll let you get back to work."

"All right then," Max said, picking up his saw. Then he added, "Say, Jimmy. I was real sorry to hear about your folks' old place going up in flames like that. I remember going out there to work on things a time or two, back when I was just starting out. Your daddy kept that place going on spit and baling wire, but he was a good, hardworking man. And your mama, Miss Pat? There wasn't nobody in this would that could make anything as delicious as her peach pie. That crust just melted in your mouth. Yes sir, I can close my eyes and taste it even after all these years, just like it was yesterday."

Weber smiled at the memory. "Me too, Max. Makes my mouth water just thinking about it."

***

Mark Santos, the game warden assigned to the Big Lake area, worked out of the district office in Pinetop. He called Weber's cell phone while he was driving back to the office. Weber pulled into the parking lot of what was once the video rental store and was now empty. A big sign in the window announced a new boutique called Mountain Mystique was coming soon. One more place for the summer crowd and ski bunnies to spend their money, the supply of which never seemed to run dry.

"I hear you've got a firebug over there," Santos said when Weber answered.

"Yeah, and I'd sure like to catch the bastard," Weber said.

"Anything I can do to help?"

"Maybe so," Weber said, and then related what Sharleen Collins had told him.

"And she said the venison is in her freezer?"

"That's what she said."

"So how do we want to play this?" Santos asked.

"Well, I'm thinking if we catch Rocky with the illegal meat, maybe we can convince him to roll over on his brother if Mitchell really is involved in these fires of ours."

"Sounds good to me. How does tomorrow morning sound?"

"You tell me when and I'll be ready," Weber assured him.

"Do you think we'll need a search warrant?"

"I'm thinking the wife is just mad enough to let us in without one."

"How about we meet at the ButterCup at 7:30? You can buy me breakfast."

"I'll see you there," Weber told him and put the phone back in his pocket. He didn't expect much to come out of the search that would help with their case, but as he had said earlier, they didn't have anything else to go on.

Chapter 22

"Tell me about these two guys," Coop said as he poured syrup over a stack of buttermilk pancakes the next morning. The restaurant was crowded with fishermen and locals who nodded at them as they came in, but they had found a small table in a back corner.

"A couple of local losers," Weber said. "Neither one can keep a job, both have been nabbed for DUI. In fact, Rocky, the one whose wife snitched them off, got his license suspended for a while. But we've never had any major problems with them."

"I cited Mitchell Collins for fishing without a license last year," Mark Santos said. "He didn't give me any trouble over it, didn't even try to make some lame excuse. Just said "Yes sir" and "No sir" and that was it."

"After talking to Max Woodbury yesterday, I'm pretty sure this is a waste of time as far as these fires are concerned," Weber said as he wiped a drip of egg yolk off his chin. "But if nothing else, we'll get Mark here a bust and make him look good to his boss."

"That and a free breakfast. What more can a guy ask for?" Santos asked.

"Wait a minute. You're really going to make me buy you breakfast *and* hand you a bust on a silver platter, too? Both in the same morning? You should be buying *me* breakfast!"

"That's the way it would be in a perfect world," Santos agreed. "But life isn't fair, Jimmy. You know that."

Before Weber could reply, a man wearing jeans and a black T-shirt that said "Spotted Owl Tastes Like Chicken" in white block letters approached their table, a scowl on his face. "This is what my tax dollars are paying for, so you can sit here and shoot the shit while the whole town is burning down around us?"

"Morning Doug," Weber said.

"Morning? That's all you've got to say? Why aren't you out tracking down the maniac that's starting these fires instead of sitting in here on your ass?"

"A man's got to eat."

"Yeah, right, what do you care if the rest of us are burned out of house and home? You've got a big insurance settlement coming."

"If you've got something to say, out with it," Weber told him.

"I just did. You don't give a rat's ass about the rest of us, you know the insurance company is going to take care of you."

"I think you'd better go now," Coop said.

"It's a free country. I'll go where I want, when I want," the man snapped.

"You're causing a public disturbance. Move on. This is your last warning."

"What, you're not man enough to speak for yourself, Weber? You've got to have your robot here do you're talking for you?"

All conversation at the tables around them had stopped as people turned to watch the confrontation. Coop started to rise, but Weber put a hand on his arm and he sat back down.

"Look, Doug, we're doing everything we can. But unless you can point me in the direction of somebody who you think is responsible for these fires, you're not helping things coming in here making a scene. It may not look like it to you, but we're working on this. As for my folks' old place, I don't even know what it was worth or what kind of payout the insurance will be. I've been a little too busy trying to catch whoever's doing all this to worry about that right now."

The man started to respond, but Weber cut him off. "I know you're worried about these fires. All of us are. But be reasonable, we *do* have to eat, and we have to plan our next step. And every minute I sit here yacking with you is a minute I'm not working on the fires. So how about you go on about your business and let us tend to ours?"

Weber had hoped that he could defuse the situation but it wasn't meant to be. The man leaned over, jabbing his finger at the sheriff as he said, "You can eat my shit for all I care, because that's all you're worth. Shit!"

Weber leaned his head back to avoid being poked in the face, and Coop asked, "Now?"

"Yeah, now," Weber told him.

Coop moved quickly for a man in his forties, rising fluidly out of his chair and pulling the angry man's left arm behind him before he could react.

"Ouch! Let go of me," Doug said.

"Give me your other hand," Coop said, and when Doug tried to resist, Coop applied more pressure to the arm he was holding, getting a howl of pain from the other man. "Your other hand, do it now!"

"I didn't do anything. Let me go," Doug protested, but he did comply and put his other hand behind him, which was quickly handcuffed.

"Take him outside and call Dispatch to have somebody come pick him up," Weber said. As Coop hustled the man out of the restaurant, the sheriff said, "Sorry folks. Go on and finish your breakfasts, show's over."

"Who was that?" Santos asked.

"Doug Weems. We've had a couple of run-ins before. He likes to beat on his wife and mouth off to anybody who gets in his way."

"Well let's hope the Collins brothers are in a better mood than that clown when we get there."

"The thing with Doug is, that *was* his good mood," Weber said. "When he's in a bad mood he can be downright irritating."

***

Rocky Collins was sleeping off a Saturday night of drinking when they pounded on the door of his rundown frame house on Aspen Lane. Sharleen let them in and pointed to the bedroom.

"He's in there if you want him. I damn sure don't."

"This is Mark Santos with the Game and Fish Department," Weber said. "The first thing we'd like to do is see the meat from that deer you told us about, if we could."

She led them through the house to a small utility room off the kitchen and lifted the lid on an old Frigidaire chest style freezer.

"There it is," she said, pointing at bundles wrapped in white paper.

"Do you mind if I open a couple of them?" Santos asked.

"Suit yourself."

The Game Warden opened three packs of frozen meat and said, "Looks like venison to me."

"The hide's hanging in the garage," Sharleen said.

As they returned to the living room, Rocky Collins called from the bedroom. "What's going on? Who you talkin' to, Shar? Do we have company?"

"We don't have company," she yelled back. "*You* do!"

A moment later a shirtless and barefoot Rocky came into the room. He was bleary eyed and badly in need of a comb and a shave, but one look at the three lawmen in his house seemed to wake him right up.

"Oh crap."

***

"No way," Rocky said shaking his head emphatically. "Mitch don't have nothin' to do with those fires, and he ain't no thief."

He was sitting at the kitchen table, a Formica and chrome thing that reminded Weber of his childhood. Two cups of black coffee and the fact that Santos had read him his rights had driven away the last vestiges of his partying the night before.

"What about that deer?" Weber asked. "Poaching is stealing, Rocky."

"Yeah, but it ain't like breaking into somebody's place and ripping them off. And setting those fires? Like I said, no way."

"Let's cut to the chase," Santos said. "We found three deer hides out there in your garage. You're looking at a $750 fine and six months in jail for each violation. If you know something about these fires, you need to man up and tell Sheriff Weber. If you think you're protecting your brother, you're wrong. Because he's getting busted, too."

"Is that what you want?" Sharleen demanded. "Because I'm telling you right now, Rocky, if they take you out of here in handcuffs you're not coming back. You can sit in jail and rot. I'm not bailing you out. I'm done with you."

"I can't tell you anything because there ain't nothing *to* tell," Rocky insisted. "Yeah, me and Mitch might have jacklighted a couple of deer. Do what you gotta do. But I didn't have nothing to do with them fires and neither did Mitch!"

"Why should we believe you?" Weber asked.

"Why shouldn't you? I've got no reason to lie to you," Rocky said. "Did I deny that we killed those deer? No. Did I try to blame it on Mitch and make like I didn't have nothing to do with 'em? No. I may not be everything Sharleen here wants in a husband, but I'm man enough to own up when I've done something wrong. And so is Mitch. Find him and ask him."

"That shouldn't be too hard to do," Coop said. "I think he's here now."

Chapter 23

Weber had to admit that Mitch was a stand up guy, pulling into his brother's driveway with two police vehicles and a Game Warden's truck parked there. Either that, or else he was a total idiot. He parked his battered old primer-gray Jeep Cherokee in the yard, or what would have been a yard if any grass would have survived Rocky's lack of attention and the junk cars and pickup trucks scattered around, and walked into the house without knocking.

"I heard you were asking about me, Sheriff," he said. "Max said you and him had a talk."

"That's true," Weber said, "and this gentleman from the Game and Fish Department has some business to take care of with you, too."

"Hey, Warden," Mitch said, shaking hands with Santos. "I guess you want to talk to me about those deer hides piled up next to your truck."

"I do. But first I need to read you your rights," Santos said.

"You don't need to go through all that. I killed those there deer, my brother here didn't have nothing to do with them. I take full responsibility."

Instead of stating the obvious, that Rocky's possession of the venison and the hides meant that he was involved in the poaching, Santos read Mitch his Miranda rights, and then said, "Okay guys, you talk to Sheriff Weber and then we'll take it from there."

They nodded, and then Weber said, "Mitch, somebody suggested that you might be involved in these fires we've had around town. Is that true?"

"Somebody?" Mitch cast a suspicious eye at his sister-in-law, and Sharleen glared back at him defiantly.

"Did you have anything to do with the fires, Mitch?"

"No! Max told you he knew I didn't set fire to that old truck of his. Sure, we had a couple of drinks and butted heads a little bit, but there weren't much to it. We been doing that since we was in grade school."

"So why did you go around telling people you two had a big fight?"

"I never said that. I was laughing and telling these two about it. If somebody said I called it a fight they were making things up to make me look bad. Now, I wonder who that would be?"

Sharleen's jaw was set, and it was obvious that there was no love lost between the two of them.

"Somebody said you had some road flares in your Jeep. Is that true?"

"You don't miss much, do you Sharleen?" Mitch asked, then turned back to Weber and said, "Yeah, I got three or four in the back end. That ain't illegal, is it?"

"Do you mind if we take one for comparison with the one that started the fire in Max's truck?" Weber didn't know if C.C.'s lab could match the flare with the remnants from the truck fire or not, but figured he had nothing to lose.

"I don't care. Do what you have to. Like I said, I didn't have anything to do with that truck burning, or none of those fires."

Even though Weber knew that no firearms had been stolen in the fires, he asked, "Where did you get the new shotgun you were showing off?"

Mitch shook his head. "Where would a guy get a new shotgun? I got it from Matt Wells over at the gun shop."

"And where did you get the money for that?" Sharleen demanded. "You darned sure didn't work for it!"

"Just because you've had my brother under your thumb for the last fifteen years don't mean I have to start answering to you, too."

Weber wondered if it might have been a better idea to take the brothers to his office to interview them, but Mitch looked at him and shrugged his shoulders.

"My birthday was last week. My girlfriend Lynette bought it for me. You can call and ask her, or check with Matt."

Weber realized that his first impression was right, this wasn't going anywhere. He was convinced that for all their shortcomings, the Collins brothers were not responsible for the fires.

"I'm done here," he said to Santos. "They're all yours."

The Game Warden nodded, then said, "Okay, let's talk about those deer."

"Leave him out of it," Mitch said, nodding toward his brother. "I shot all three of those deer in the last month. All he did was let me butcher them in his garage and I gave him some of the meat in return. I'll plead guilty if you let Rocky go."

"Where's the rest of the meat?"

"At my place. Lynette's place, technically, but I've been staying there since…"

"Since you got kicked out of your trailer," Sharleen sneered. "Can't pay the rent if you don't work, can you Mitchell?"

Weber and Santos walked outside, leaving Coop to prevent any violence between Mitch and his sister-in-law. He didn't think Mitch would become aggressive, but he was pretty sure Sharleen would be happy to have both brothers' heads hanging on the living room wall next to the mule deer buck above the fireplace.

"What do you think?" Weber asked.

"They're guilty as sin on the poaching. As to who pulled the trigger, or if Rocky was even there, who knows? He says he was, and Mitch says he wasn't. I've got to give Mitch credit for being willing to take the fall for his brother."

"I'm not sure which would be worse punishment, taking Rocky in or leaving him here with his wife," Weber said. "What do you want to do with them?"

"I'm not going to arrest either one of them," Santos said. "I think I'll cite Mitch for two counts of poaching and give him a pass on the third one, since he owned up to it. And I'll cite Rocky for illegal possession of a game animal."

"Sounds good to me," Weber said, "Let's get back in there before that woman butchers one of those guys and sticks him in the freezer, too."

"Here's the deal," Santos said once they were back in the kitchen. He explained what he planned to do and both brothers nodded in agreement. "What I'm *not* going to do, which I could, is confiscate your Jeep or Rocky's freezer or the one at your girlfriend's house, since all three were used in the crimes. I could also confiscate your rifles. So you're getting a break because you cooperated with us."

"That's fair enough," Mitch said and Rocky nodded.

"You're not taking them to jail?" Sharleen asked incredulously.

"No ma'am, I'm giving them citations and they'll have to appear in court."

"Then you can take your brother with you when you go, Mitchell," she said. "I don't want to see either one of your faces around here again."

"Awww, come on baby," Rocky said. "I know you're upset but…"

"Whatever," Santos said. "You guys can hash that all out once we're done here. Jimmy, can you have a deputy round up some boxes and dry ice? We'll take the venison from both places to the women's shelter and food bank once I photograph and inventory it."

"Wait a minute, you're taking the meat?" Sharleen asked.

"Of course," Santos told her. "It's contraband."

"I don't get to keep it?"

"No ma'am. That's against the law. You would be profiting by your husband's involvement in a crime."

"You're taking all of it? Don't I get to keep some of it as a finder's fee or something?"

"Sorry," Santos said. "You can file for a reward under the Game and Fish Department's Operation Game Thief program, but to be honest, I'm not sure if you can collect since you're married to one of the offenders."

"That's it? I don't get anything?"

"Well, you *do* get to keep your freezer," Santos reminded her.

While Sharleen released a stream of invective that he was sure could be heard all the way over at the Game and Fish office in Pinetop, Weber left Santos to absorb the abuse and made his escape before *his* head got added to the woman's potential trophy wall.

Chapter 24

Weber was almost back to the Sheriff's Office when a silver blue Mazda M5 minivan pulled out in front of him from a side street. He slammed on the brake pedal to avoid a collision and cursed at the other driver, who seemed unaware of his presence as he continued down the street. Weber turned on his overhead light bar and accelerated to catch up with the Mazda. When the driver did not seem to notice the police vehicle behind him with flashing lights, the sheriff gave the siren a bump to get his attention.

The Mazda pulled over to the curb and Weber stopped behind it while he radioed dispatch and ran the license plate.

"Big Lake One, that plate number comes back to a 2012 Mazda M5 registered to Darron Tovar, with an address in Payson, Arizona."

"10-4," Weber said and got out of his Explorer. Tovar had not rolled down his window, so Weber knocked on the glass. The young man looked up at him, then pointed his digital camera at the sheriff before lowering the window.

"License and registration, and proof of insurance, please."

"Why are you stopping me?"

"You failed to yield back there and I almost rear-ended you."

"I don't think so."

"License and registration," Weber repeated.

"Why are you harassing me, Sheriff Weber?"

"I'm not harassing you. You committed a traffic violation and I'm enforcing the law."

"I disagree. It's obvious that this is your way of paying me back for things you don't like that have been in my newspaper. And for the record, I'm recording this entire encounter."

"That's fine. That's your right," Weber said. "So be sure you get this part. I've asked you twice now for your license, registration and insurance card. Under Arizona law you face a criminal penalty for noncompliance with the obligation to identify yourself. You can show them to me or I can take you into custody. Which is it going to be?"

Tovar smirked and said, "I'm sure you'd love to get me into one of your jail cells where nobody can see what happens. But I don't think I'll give you that pleasure today, Sheriff. I'm reaching for my wallet now to get my license, and my registration and insurance card are in the console. I am not making any hostile moves so you don't have a reason to shoot me."

Shooting the sneering young man had not entered Weber's mind, though he desperately wanted to reach through the window and pull him out into the street and throttle him, camera or no camera. But he was a professional so he pushed his emotions aside and took Tovar's paperwork and returned to his vehicle.

Weber could play the passive-aggressive game, too. He took his time asking the dispatcher to run the young man's drivers license and was not surprised when Judy Troutman radioed back that there were no outstanding wants or warrants. Weber slowly and carefully wrote a traffic citation for failure to yield the right of way and strolled back to the Mazda.

He handed Tovar's license and registration back to him along with his insurance card. "Mr. Tovar, I'm citing you for failure to yield. Please sign here and press hard, there are three copies. Your signature is not an admission of guilt, just a promise to appear in court at the appointed time."

Tovar took the citation pad and pen, but did not sign it.

"What if I refuse to sign this thing?"

"Then you'll get to see that jail cell you talked about."

"Maybe I should talk to an attorney first."

"That's certainly your right," Weber told him. "You can make a phone call after I'm done booking you."

"Or beating me up back in that cell where nobody can see what you're doing? Or are you too cowardly for that, Sheriff Weber? Maybe you'll have a couple of your deputies do your dirty work for you."

"Are you going to sign the citation, sir? Or should I take you into custody?"

"Oh, I'm going to sign it. But I'm kind of a slow learner, so first, explain to me what I did again and what it means when I sign this thing?"

"A slow learner, huh?"

"Yes sir. I think my pediatrician called it attention deficit disorder, maybe with a touch of dyslexia."

"Those are big words for a slow learner," Weber said.

"Yeah, well, I'm what they call a *gifted* slow learner."

"You know what I think?" Weber asked.

"I wasn't aware you were capable of thought," said Tovar. "Most animals seem to just operate on primal instinct. In fact, I'm surprised that you can communicate with more than grunts and primitive gestures."

"You're a funny man," Weber told him. "And I don't think you're a slow learner at all. A full scholarship to NAU, a master's degree... no I don't think you're slow at all. In fact, I think you're pretty darned smart, to tell you the truth. There's just one problem. You're not nearly as smart as you think you are."

"Really?"

"Yes sir. Because you think you're a real hotshot, but the truth is you're just a kid trying to make a name for himself, and you think you can make it at my expense."

"Fascinating, Sheriff. Among your many talents, you're a mind reader too!"

"Let me give you some advice, Mr. Tovar. You can write whatever the hell you want about me. You can make your half-assed implications that I'm incompetent, or that I set fire to my parents place, or whatever makes you feel like a crusading journalist out to change the world. But you need to get a smaller camera."

"Why's that, Sheriff."

"Because the other day you embarrassed Deputy Fuchette in your paper. You don't get to do that. It can be very uncomfortable."

"Uncomfortable for who?"

"For you," Weber said. "Because if you ever do that again, I'm going to take that camera of yours and stick it so far up your ass it's going take a team of surgeons a week to get it back out again. That's why you need a smaller camera."

"You do know that I'm recording all of this, don't you?"

"And you do know I don't give a shit, right? Because if you ever embarrass Deputy Fuchette again, if you ever even use her name in your rag again, I'm going to hurt you. Do we understand each other?"

"I could have your badge for this, Sheriff."

"Fine, I'll put it right up there with your camera. Now sign the damn ticket or go to jail. Your choice."

Chapter 25

C.C.'s red Suburban was parked at the Sheriff's Office when Weber arrived Monday morning, and he found her and Coop huddled together at a desk in the back. For a moment Weber wondered if Robyn's matchmaking attempt had worked but as it turned out, they were just going over the fire reports once again, looking for anything they might have overlooked the first dozen times they had done the same thing.

"You must have got off to an early start," Weber said.

"I couldn't sleep so I left Phoenix about four this morning to beat the traffic," C.C. told him.

"Admit it. You missed all this fresh mountain air, didn't you?"

"That or she was hoping to run into Gordon Hahn again," Coop teased.

"Oh spare me," C.C. said. "The only time I want to run into that pig is when I'm doing sixty miles an hour."

"Did you find anything new there?" Weber asked, nodding at the fire reports.

"Nothing that jumps out at us," C.C. said. "But you never know."

"Always the optimist, right?"

"Right," she said. "By the way, I dropped that gas can we found at your parents house off at our lab. If anybody can find something on it, our techs can."

"And I gave her that flare we got from Mitch Collins yesterday," Coop added.

"I'm pretty sure that's a dead end," Weber said. "I think Sharleen was hoping we'd lock both brothers up and she would be done with them."

"That was one very unhappy lady," Coop told him. "After you left I don't think she stopped cussing long enough to take a breath until after Santos and I boxed up all of that meat and left. And speaking of pissed off people, I had Dan put that guy Weems that was in the restaurant hassling you in a cell so he could cool off, but when I got back here to let him out he wanted to argue about it. So I left him there until after dinner and then called Tommy and had him cut him loose. He said you'd be hearing from his lawyer."

"I can hardly wait," Weber said, then added, "With any luck at all Chet Wingate will get the Town Council to fire me before it ever gets to trial and whoever replaces me can deal with it. In the meantime, can we please figure out who's starting these damn fires and put a stop to them?"

"How about if we brainstorm any possible suspects we might have," Coop suggested. "Just throw names out there and see if anything strikes a nerve. Does anybody who is even a remote possibility come to mind?"

"You mentioned somebody that set fire to his bulldozer or something," C.C. said.

"Dutch Schmidt," Weber said. "I had Robyn check. He's working for a well drilling outfit in Heber, a good 90 miles from here."

"And his boss confirms he was on the job when the barn and cabin burned," Robyn added.

Looking toward the door before he spoke, Tommy Frost said, "I have to ask, before Chief Harper gets here, are we a hundred percent sure it couldn't be somebody connected with the fire department? Didn't you say sometimes people have a hero complex or something?"

"True. There have been many cases where a fireman was responsible for setting fires and then responding to them. As I recall, ten years or so ago a Bureau of Indian Affairs firefighter over in Cibecue was charged with setting a couple of fires. His motivation was the money he earned fighting them. We've had similar cases in other places in the state. Some were for the money, others were motivated by that hero complex thing. So it's not inconceivable."

"I just don't see it," Buz said. "I've known every volunteer on the force for years. I can't think of one who'd do something like that."

"As long as we're just spit balling, and please don't let it leave this room, what about Chief Harper himself?" Robyn asked.

"Steve? No way! Why would *he* do it?"

"Hear me out, Buz. We know that the Fire Department is underfunded and the mayor treats it like a redheaded stepchild, no offense intended, C.C. Could this be a way to raise awareness of the needs of the Fire Department?"

"Hey, my biological parents raised me and I've got the psychological scars to prove it. No offense taken," C.C. said with a smile. "But you raise a valid point. *Could* it be? Stranger things have happened."

"I don't buy it," Buz said, shaking his head.

"Could your response be based upon your friendship with him?" C.C. asked, "And again, no offense meant."

"It probably is," Buz said. "But I think I'm a pretty good judge of character."

"Okay, how about his number two man, Upchurch? Do I see some hero worship going on there? Could he be behind this, trying to make Chief Harper look good?"

"Kevin may look like a moose, and he's probably not the sharpest knife in the drawer," Weber said. "But again, I just don't see it. He's as dedicated to the Fire Department and the welfare of this town as anybody could be."

"I don't disagree, from what I've seen of him," C.C. said. "But could that be the reason for him to do something like this? Kind of like surgery to remove a cancerous tumor? A little bad has to happen for the greater good?"

"Two reasons why I don't think so. First; like I said, he's a good guy, but I don't think he has the smarts to plan something this elaborate. And second; you live in a city in the desert where wildfires are not a constant threat. Up here, we're all very aware of the fact that millions of acres of forest surround us. We all know that something like the Rodeo–Chediski Fire could happen again at any time," Weber said, referring to the massive wildfire that consumed over 280,000 acres in the White Mountains in 2002. "I don't think any firefighter who lives here would risk that happening again."

"What about Darron Tovar?" Coop asked.

"The newspaper guy? What would he get out of it?"

"Think about it," Coop said, "the fires started just about the time he hit town and we know he has an ax to grind with Jimmy and the Fire Department. And we know he'll stoop to just about anything to sell newspapers and make a name for himself. Could a newsman be *making* the news he reports?"

"He's not a newsman, he's Chet Wingate's puppet," Weber said scornfully.

"No question about that," Coop agreed. "But he's a devious little son-of-a-bitch."

Weber thought that what Coop was suggesting was entirely possible, but he wasn't sure if that was because of his own problems with Tovar or if it was based upon professional thinking. He had to admit that, of all the possible suspects they had discussed, the brash young newspaper editor might well be the most likely one at that point in the investigation.

The impromptu meeting ended there with the arrival of Fire Chief Steve Harper.

"Now there's a man wearing a smile I haven't seen in a while," Weber said, as Harper came in the door.

"You're darned right I'm smiling," Harper said. "Even as we speak our new fire truck is on the back of a flatbed trailer heading here just as fast as eighteen wheels can roll."

"You found somebody to haul it up here?"

"Yep. Tom Cotter."

"The fellow whose shed burned?" C.C. asked.

"The one and only," Harper said. "He's a trucker and dropped a load off in El Paso over the weekend. He was going to deadhead home, but agreed to borrow a flatbed from a freight broker he knows there and pick up the truck in Deming. Should be here by late this afternoon."

"It's nice to have some good news for a change," the sheriff said. "I guess it's too much to ask that we don't have to use it for any fires for a long time?"

"We can only hope," C.C. said.

"Well, enjoy that good feeling while you can," Mary Caitlin said grimly, handing him the latest issue of the *Big Lake Truth* and pointing to the bold front page headline:

Don't Shoot Me, Weber!

While the good citizens of Big Lake worry about whose home or business will be the next to go up in flames, Fire Chief Steve Harper stumbles around like a blind man in a corn maze. As terrifying as that is, there is an even more dangerous threat lurking among us waiting to strike. Ever since the day he pinned on his badge, Sheriff Jim Weber has been an arrogant bully preying on the weak and sleeping his way through the available women, including some women that may not have been available.

Like some modern-day gunslinger, Weber seems to think that slapping leather and shooting it out is the way one deals with problems, even in today's world. Consider the fact that he was on the scene when a woman named Tina Miller and her unborn child were killed. Consider that he was the officer in charge when elderly Anthony Wilson was shot to death in a business he owned by one of Weber's deputies. Consider the tragic death of Steve Rafferty, a teenage boy Sheriff Weber killed with not one, not two, but three shots as the poor boy tried to escape the sheriff's violent wrath. Weber was also the officer in charge when an elderly couple were shot to death in their car during a standoff with deputies. And then there is the latest death that Sheriff Weber had a role in, when a prisoner was shot three times while inside his cell at the Sheriff's Office.

Given all of that, one can certainly understand this reporter's fear when he was stopped on Main Street yesterday and threatened with physical violence by this psychotic lawman. Will I be the next person to die at the hands of Sheriff Jim Weber?

"That's bullshit," Dolan Reed said, reading over Weber's shoulder. "The FBI shot Tina Miller. And Anthony Wilson was a crazy old coot trying to kill somebody when Wyatt Trask shot him. And Steve Rafferty? Why didn't this guy mention that that "poor boy" was a stone cold killer who had just shot one of our deputies? And as for…"

"It's okay," Weber said. "It's not worth getting all upset about, Dolan."

"But damn it, Jimmy, this idiot is making it sound like you're Charles Manson or something. I want to find him and kick his ass."

"Get in line," Harper told him. "A lot of us want to kick his ass."

"If this is the worst thing I have to deal with all day, it's worth it," Weber said.

"Don't count on it," Coop said. "We're long overdo for another fire, according to the pattern C.C. told us about."

"Maybe he decided to stop?" Weber suggested.

"I've been thinking about that," the Fire Marshal said. "Remember when I said that sometimes a perp has an agenda and that when they reach whatever goal they set for themselves they stop?"

"Yeah?"

"What if getting back at you was the goal?"

"Me?"

"Think about it; you've no doubt made some enemies in your time as sheriff. What cop doesn't? The last fire was at your parents' house on Thursday and today is Monday. Four days. That's the longest time between fires except between the first and second. Could they all have led up to torching your parent's house?"

"I don't know," Weber said. "Yeah, I've made a few enemies, no question about that. But if they wanted to get to me, why not burn the place where I live? My cabin's not three miles away."

"Who knows? People who do these things aren't rational, after all."

"So what now?"

"This is all only a guess on my part," C.C. said. "All we can do is wait and see if we have another fire."

"I hope not, Weber said. "It'd be worth losing the old family place if it put an end to all this."

The sheriff would not get his wish. As it turned out, there would be more fires, and the next one would be that very day.

Chapter 26

Patrick Watson was mowing his grandmother's lawn that afternoon, a chore he enjoyed because he liked driving the Cub Cadet riding lawnmower. At thirteen, Patrick was almost two years away from getting his learner's permit, but with the ear buds from his iPod blasting away and his Ironman wraparound sunglasses on he could pretend that he was cruising Main Street in a tricked out Mustang GT, or maybe boonie hopping in a Ford F-150 XLT 4x4.

His best friend Beau Ellis hoped to inherit his older brother's Toyota pickup when Rob went off to college next year, and Patrick had to admit that the Tacoma was cool with its lift kit and roll bar, but it wasn't for him. He'd buy American or walk, a message that his Grandpa Jack had drummed into his head from as far back as Patrick could remember. And not just American, but a Ford. Grandpa had been a proud union man, retired from Ford's assembly line in Flat Rock, Michigan, and Patrick would rather push a Ford than drive a Chevy, let alone a rice burner like the Toyota. Grandpa had died last summer, but Patrick knew he'd be proud to know his lessons had taken hold when he was looking down from heaven. No, Patrick planned to get a Mustang or an F-150. Maybe both. He bet Tara Breslin would notice him then.

Patrick had only recently discovered girls. Well, he'd known that girls existed for a long time, of course, but they had all been prissy, giggly creatures that he had pretty much ignored until a few months ago. That all changed the first day of school after Christmas break when Tara had been assigned the seat next to him in History class. Tara was the most beautiful girl Patrick had ever seen, which surprised him because they had been classmates since first grade and he had never really paid any attention to her. Patrick wasn't sure how it had happened, but over the holidays Tara had grown boobs. Or maybe there really was a Santa Claus and he had brought them to her, in which case Patrick felt like Santa had blessed them both with a wonderful gift.

However they had arrived didn't really matter as much as the fact that they *were* there. Patrick knew, because that first day in class Tara had leaned over to get something out of her backpack and he had turned to see what she was doing and had an unexpected view right down her blouse to her bra, which had small blue and yellow polka dots on it. Suddenly Patrick was in love with polka dots, bras, boobs, and most of all, Tara Breslin. She had found whatever it was she was searching for in her backpack and started to sit back up when she had caught Patrick looking at her. He was mortified, but instead of slapping him or shrieking, Tara had just smiled at him and said, "Perv."

Patrick tried to work up the nerve to talk to Tara after class, but she was with Trish Baker and Suzie McConnell and he had chickened out. Besides, what would a girl like Tara see in a guy like him. What was he going to do, give her a ride to McDonald's on the handlebars of his bicycle? But he knew that would all change the day he got his drivers license and a set of wheels.

In the meantime, he pointed the Cadet at the far end of Grandma's wide lawn and made another pass. As he neared the back end of the property, movement across the utility easement caught his eye. What were those guys up to at the Oswald place? As Patrick watched, two older boys were doing something at the back of the house, waving their hands around like they were painting or something. But what was in their hands? Something white, but it couldn't have been paintbrushes because the color of the house didn't change, it was still light pink.

The boys dropped whatever it was and then one of them dug into his pocket and pulled something out. A moment later Patrick saw a small flare and the boy threw it against the house. Nothing happened, so he struck another match and tried again. This time he was successful and a line of flames erupted. The boys slapped a high five and ran around the corner of the house as the flames climbed the wall.

The Cub Cadet might not have been a Mustang GT or a four-wheel drive pickup, but it shot across the easement and into the Oswald yard. Patrick turned off the key and stared at the fire for a second in horror. What should he do? He pounded on the back door, feeling the heat of the flames, and when no one responded he started to run around to the front of the house. That's when he spotted the hose coiled up next to the garage.

Grabbing the green garden hose, Patrick frantically twisted the knob of the water faucet sticking out of the side of the garage and dragged the hose to the house and started spraying the wall. By now the flames were halfway up the wall and growing. Patrick could see the paint blistering as he tried desperately to extinguish the fire.

"Help," he yelled. "Help! Fire! Fire!"

Were his efforts doing any good? Patrick wasn't sure, but he didn't know what else to do. Should he abandon the hose and run back to Grandma's house to call 911? Was anybody home at the Oswald's? Should he try pounding on the door again?

"What in the hell are you doing?"

Suddenly a large man was there. He grabbed the hose from Patrick's hand and started spraying the wall, moving in closer to saturate the wood. Patrick stood there dumbfounded for a minute, then decided to go around to the front and pound on the door again. But as if reading his mind, the man pointed a finger at him and said, "Don't you move, you little bastard, or I'll break your legs. I've already called 911."

And sure enough, Patrick could hear the sound of sirens. He was rooted in his spot out of fear of the angry man, though his bowels felt loose and he wanted to run as far away as he could as fast as he could.

The sirens were loud now, closer, and before he knew it, two sheriff's deputies were there with fire extinguishers helping the man with the hose, and then firemen seemed to appear out of nowhere with a big canvas hose and shot a strong stream of water against the fire. Through it all, Patrick just stood there, his mouth hanging open.

Chapter 27

"You sit right there and wait until your parents get here," Weber told the frightened boy, pointing toward a chair in the interview room.

Patrick sat down obediently and hung his head, staring at the table. "Keep an eye on him," Weber told Robyn. "Mary's called his mom and dad. They'll be here soon."

She nodded and Weber went back down the hall to where Coop and Chad were writing reports on what they saw when they arrived at the Oswald house.

"Do either of you know this kid?" Weber asked.

"I've seen him around town," Coop said. "Never had anything to do with him."

"Same here," Chad told him. "I know most of the local young miscreants, can't remember ever having any problems with him."

"His father is Stanley Watson."

"The music teacher over at the school?"

Mary nodded, "His mom is a nurse at the medical center. His grandmother is Ruth Everett, she lives behind the place that was on fire. She and her husband used to volunteer at the animal shelter until Jack passed on last year."

"Did the boy say anything?"

"Just that he didn't do it," Weber told her. "But I told him not to say a word until his parents got here. I don't want there to be any question about his rights being violated or something."

"Damn, a kid like that, never been in trouble, and then this. You never know," Chad mused.

"Well, he's in a lot of trouble now, that's for sure," Coop said.

***

Stanley and Jennifer Watson wore frantic expressions on their faces when they pushed through the door of the Sheriff's Office.

"We got a call about our son," Stanley said. "Something about him being involved in some kind of criminal activity. What's going on?

Where is he?"

"Is he all right," Jennifer asked, barely holding herself together.

"He's fine," Weber said, introducing himself. "Let's go in my office and talk."

"I want to see my son," Jennifer said. "Please, I need to see him!"

"I understand that ma'am," Weber said. "And you can, in just a minute or two, but please, let's go in here first."

He showed them into his office and got them seated, and then explained what had happened, that a witness had caught their son setting fire to the Oswald house, but had been able to call 911 and then contain the fire until help arrived.

"Fortunately, nobody was at home when the fire started," Weber said. "And except for some blistered paint and minor damage, we got it out in time."

"I can't believe it. Patrick?"

"I'm afraid so, ma'am" Weber said.

"There must be some mistake. There has to be."

"Listen, Sheriff, I know parents always say their kid couldn't possibly do anything bad. They all think their kid is perfect. I deal with it every day at the school. But what Mom and Dad see and what happens when little Johnny or Susie are out of sight can be totally different. I get that," Stanley said. "But this just doesn't sound like Patrick at all. He *is* a good kid. And we're involved parents. We keep track of him. We know where he is every minute of every day."

"Where was he supposed to be today?" Weber asked the man.

"Doing some chores at his grandmother's house. Feeding her pets while she's out of town and cutting the grass."

Weber remembered the riding lawnmower in the back yard of the house.

"How about we go have a talk with him, okay?"

He led them back to the interview room, and when Patrick saw his parents he threw himself into his mother's arms and started sobbing. "I didn't do it, Mom. I swear I didn't!"

Weber allowed his mother to comfort him for a minute, and then said, "Patrick, we need to talk about what happened today. But first I have to read you your rights. And Mr. and Mrs. Watson, you have the right to stop this interview at any time, okay?"

They nodded and Weber added, "Before we do all of that, do you want a few minutes alone with your son?"

"No," Stanley said. "Let's get down to the bottom of this."

Weber, C.C., and Chad sat across the table from the boy and his family, and after going through the formalities and turning on the video camera, Weber asked Patrick to tell him what had happened from the start.

"I was mowing the grass at Grandma's house and I saw these two boys messing around the back of Mr. and Mrs. Oswald's house. At first I thought that they were painting it or something, because they had something in their hands and were waving them around. Then I saw one of them light a match and throw it against the house. I guess it went out because he did it again. That's when the fire started."

"What happened then?" Weber asked.

"I pounded on the back door but nobody heard me. So I got the hose and started trying to put the fire out. Then this man was there, I don't know where he came from, but he took the hose and kept spraying water on the house until the cops and firemen came. Then… then you brought me here."

"These guys you said you saw starting the fire, do you know who they were?"

"No sir. I think I've seen them around town a couple of times but I don't know them."

"About how old were they?"

Patrick shrugged. "I don't know. Older than me."

"How were they dressed?"

"Jeans. I think one had a black shirt on. Or maybe like a dark blue. The other one had a lighter colored one."

Weber looked at C.C., then Chad to see if either had anything to ask.

"How did the lawnmower get in the back yard of the Oswald house?" Chad asked.

"I drove it there when I saw the fire start."

"Why didn't you just run across the yard?"

"I don't know," Patrick said, shaking his head. "I was already on it so I just drove it."

"Have you heard about the other fires around town lately?"

"Yeah, I guess. I mean, yeah. Everybody has, right?"

"I'm very well trained in investigating how fires start, Patrick, and I'm very good at it," C.C. said. "There's nothing I haven't seen before. So I have to ask you, are you telling us the truth? Because if you're not...."

The boy shook his head. "I'm not lying! Honest, I'm not. Why would I do something like that?"

"Son, if you did have something to do with this, you need to tell us right now," Stanley said. "It's only going to get worse if you don't."

"I'm not lying, Dad," the boy said, and began crying. "Why don't you believe me?"

"I'm not saying I don't believe you, Patrick. I'm just saying that if there's something you're not telling us, you need to come clean."

"Patrick, we have a witness that says he saw you spraying these on the back of that house," Weber said, pulling two cans of charcoal lighter in plastic evidence bags. "What do you have to say about that?"

"Those are what those guys had that I told you about," the boy said. "They threw them down and left them when they took off."

"*Those* guys had them, not you? Is that what you're saying?"

"Yes sir."

"Then can you tell me why the witness," Weber referred to his notes. "Why Mr. Clarke said he saw you spraying the cans on the house?"

"I don't know. But it wasn't me. Maybe he saw one of those guys I told you about."

"One of those guys. How come he didn't see both of them if there were two guys, Patrick?"

"I don't know! But I swear, Sheriff, I didn't start that fire. I was only trying to help!"

"How well do you know Mr. and Mrs. Oswald?" Chad asked, trying another tactic.

"I just know them because they live behind Grandma. I see them and wave sometimes. That's all."

"Do they wave back?"

"I guess so. Yeah, I think so."

"Do you remember ever talking to them before?"

"I don't think so."

"Did you maybe have an argument with one of them at some point? Or maybe they yelled at you because they thought you were in their yard when you were playing or something?"

"No, never. I just know them because they live by Grandma."

Weber looked at Chad and C.C., but neither had anything else to ask the boy.

"How about you folks sit tight for a few minutes and we'll be right back," he said, standing up. "Does anybody want some water. Maybe a soda?"

The boy and his parents shook their heads, so Weber led Chad and C.C. out of the room.

"What do you think?"

"I don't know. He seems like a good kid," Chad said. The department's senior deputy had coached youth baseball teams for years, he had even been Weber's coach back in the day, and he had an intuition about the younger crowd that Weber respected.

"Still, we've got an eyewitness that caught him red-handed," C.C. said. "That's kind of hard to beat."

"Yeah, about that witness," said Coop, who had joined them in the hallway. "We need to talk."

Chapter 28

"The guy's story doesn't add up," Coop told them when they had adjourned to Weber's private office.

"How so?"

"He said he was working on his car in his driveway when he saw the boy spraying the charcoal lighter on the back of the house and then starting the fire."

"Okay. What's your point?"

"We found two cans of charcoal lighter. But where were the matches or the lighter the kid used to start the fire? We didn't find them on the ground by those cans and they weren't in the kid's pockets."

"I'm listening," Weber said, his eyebrows furrowing.

"Another thing, Jimmy; from where his car was parked in the driveway the angle's wrong. He could have seen the side of the house, but not the back where the fire started."

"Maybe he heard something and walked closer, and that's when he saw him?"

Coop shook his head. "He went through it three times. He says he was under the hood replacing a heater hose and noticed something suspicious, and when he looked up he saw the kid doing his thing. I was out there, Jimmy, if you're on the street facing the house that was on fire, his place is next door on the left. His car was nose into the driveway, next to the house. And the driveway's on the far side of his place from the neighbor there. There's no way he saw where the fire started or where we found those two cans. Here, let me show you something."

Coop sat his laptop computer on Weber's desk and pointed to the screen. "This is a program called Google Maps. See, this looks like an aerial photo of the neighborhood? Actually, it's taken from a satellite."

"Amazing," Weber said.

"Here's the Oswald house, and here's Mr. Clarke's house. Now look at this." Coop clicked the mouse and brought up the street view.

"Whoa." Weber said.

"Cool, isn't it? They have vehicles driving all around the country up and down every street taking pictures. Now, here's Mr. Clarke's house. Pretend you were here in the driveway about where his car was." Coop clicked the mouse again and the image rotated. "See what I mean, Jimmy? "There's no way this guy was standing where he was, doing what he said he was doing, and saw that boy starting the fire, unless he has a periscope that looks around corners over a hundred feet away."

"So why would he lie?" C.C. asked.

"Who knows? Remember what you said about somebody wanting to be a hero? Maybe this guy isn't our firebug, but he saw an opportunity to make himself look good at the expense of some kid and went for it."

"It wouldn't be the first time, Coop," Weber said. "You're pretty sure about this?"

"I don't know if the kid started the fire or not," Coop told him. "But I know our witness didn't see it the way he says he did."

Weber looked at the computer's screen and said, "Get him in here."

Melvin Clarke had been waiting in a chair next to Coop's desk, and when he was escorted into Weber's office he sat down in the chair next to the sheriff's desk without being told to. He was a big man, about six feet tall, and Weber was sure he tipped the scales at well over 350 pounds. A roll of fat protruded from the bottom of his tightly stretched green T-shirt when he had walked into the room, and his face looked like it had not seen a razor in at least two days.

"Mr. Clarke, we sure appreciate your help out there today," Weber said. "Without you that place might have burned all the way down."

Clarke shrugged and smiled. "Just doing what any good citizen would, Sheriff."

"Well, it's commendable," Weber told him. "I've read the statement you gave to Deputy Cooper here, but can you run it by me just one more time so I can get a clear picture in my mind of what went down?"

"Like I said, I saw the kid spraying that stuff on the back of Will Oswald's place and the next thing I knew he set it on fire. So I called 911 and ran over and put the fire out."

"And what was the boy doing all that time?"

"Little bastard tried to sneak away, but I told him if he took one step I'd break his damn legs. That put the fear of God in him, I'll tell you that!"

"You said you put the fire out? Because Deputies Cooper and Summers said the fire was still burning when they arrived and they said they used the fire extinguishers in their patrol cars, and that it was still burning when the Fire Department got there a couple of minutes behind them."

"Well, I didn't mean I *put* it out. More like I tried to contain it until the cavalry got there."

"Okay, that makes better sense," Weber said. "I stumble over my words all the time like that. No big deal. You said you were working on your car when you saw the boy, Patrick, acting suspicious and then starting the fire?"

"That's right. I'm sure glad I was out there. People need to be more aware of what's going on around them instead of having tunnel vision. That's one of the great things about a small town like this. People here care about their neighbors. Not like living in the city. Tucson? Phoenix? You couldn't get me to live in one of those places."

"How do you think that boy got there to the back of the house?" Weber asked.

"I don't know. Didn't somebody say his grandma lives right behind the Oswald's?"

"Yeah. And did you notice the riding lawnmower? One of my deputies said you can see a clear line of mowed grass where he rode from her place to the Oswald's house. Not exactly the world's best getaway vehicle, is it? All we'd have had to do was follow the trail right back to Grandma's house."

"Who knows with kids?" Clarke asked. "It's anybody's guess why they do the things they do. Half of them are on drugs these days."

"Yeah, I wondered about that," Weber said. "I wonder why he decided to set fire to that place in particular. From everything I've heard, the Oswald's are nice folks."

"They are," Clarke assured him. "Couldn't ask for better neighbors. They darned sure didn't deserve this."

"I know," Weber said. "So why their house? I wonder what that boy had against them?"

"Like I said, it's anybody's guess with kids. I blame a lot of it on that rap music they listen to all the time, and those video games they're always playing. I'll tell you what, no kid of mine would be wasting time with that garbage."

"Uh huh." Weber didn't say anything else. He knew that oftentimes silence was the best tool an interrogator had at his disposal.

"I bet when you put some pressure on him, that kid's gonna crack and spill his guts," Clarke said. "I'm glad to help put a stop to these fires. People around here have been scared to death that their place was going to be next."

There was more silence in the room as Weber regarded the man.

"Yeah, it was good timing on my part for sure. I wasn't going to change that leaky hose until tomorrow. Shoot, if I had even stopped for lunch on the way back from the auto parts store it might have been too late. I was just in the right place at the right time."

Clarke stopped talking and seemed to be searching for something else to say. He started to open his mouth, then stopped and shook his head. "Crazy damn kid."

When there was still no response his voice faltered and he looked at the floor. Time seemed to stretch on, and then Clarke looked up and said, "Well, if you're done with me here, I'll get out of your way. I've still got that car to fix."

He stood up and then didn't appear to know what to do next, so Weber ended the tension by saying, "You're not going anywhere just yet. Sit down, Mr. Clarke."

***

"What a loser," C.C. said twenty minutes later. "The guy starts out doing something commendable and then twists it all around like that. He was willing to throw that kid under the bus and ruin his life for what, fifteen minutes of fame?"

"People are funny animals," Weber said.

"I still think we should have charged him for filing a false police report," Coop said.

"I would, but we may need him to ID those two kids when we catch up with them," Weber told him. "Meanwhile, I know a young man and his family that need some good news."

***

Sitting between his parents, Patrick had stopped crying and seemed to be drained when Weber, C.C., and Chad went back into the interview room.

"Son, we all owe you an apology," Weber said. "And not just that, we owe you a big thank you."

"What do you mean?" Stanley Watson asked.

"The witness was confused," Weber said. "He saw two boys running past his house and then he heard Patrick here yelling for help. When he got to the back of the Oswald's house he saw Patrick trying to put out the fire and he jumped to conclusions."

"But he said he saw Patrick spraying that stuff on the house and setting it on fire. Why would he do that?" the boy's mother asked.

"Let's just say that he made an error in judgment," Weber told her.

"He lied? Is that what you're saying?"

"People aren't always perfect," Weber acknowledged. "Your son here, he's a fine young man, and it's not fair that we had to put him through all of this. And to put you and his dad through it, either. All I can do at this point is apologize. But I want you to know that Patrick is a hero. You should be very proud of him."

Weber caught Chad's eye and there was an almost imperceptible nod, then the deputy left the room.

"I'm not in trouble any more?" Patrick asked.

"No sir, you're not," Weber told him. "Like I said, you're a hero and I'd like to shake your hand if you'd let me." He extended his hand to the boy and they shook, then Weber said, "Look folks, you've been through a lot today, and I know Patrick here must be starving by now. Why don't you take him to Mario's for a big old pizza, and I'm going to call Sal and tell him it's on me. Does that sound good to you, Patrick?"

The boy nodded and Weber said, "Great, let's get you out of here."

Coop and C.C. had already left the room, and when Weber escorted the boy and his family into the main office the six deputies and the civilian staff on hand all stood up and applauded, and then the deputies stepped to either side to make room and saluted as a bewildered Patrick and his proud parents passed by and out the door.

Chapter 29

"Dyno-Lite Charcoal Lighter," Weber said, reading the label on one of the cans. "Not Kingsford or any name brand I've ever heard of. So where did this come from?"

"The can looks familiar," C.C. said. "Where have I seen these before?"

"When you were home last weekend?"

"No, I don't think so. Except for stopping for gas and at our lab, I never left my condo. Where else....?"

"Looks vaguely familiar to me, too. I've probably seen it someplace," Coop said. "But where?"

C.C. snapped her fingers. "It was here!"

"Here?"

"Remember when I brought you a cup of coffee the other day, Jimmy?"

"Yeah?"

"I got it at the Stop and Go. I think there's a display of this stuff right by the door."

"Check it out," Weber said.

When Coop left, Weber asked, "So if we find these two, do you think that's it? Are they our perps?"

"You're going to hate me for saying this, but I don't think so," C.C. told him.

"Why was I afraid you were going to say that?"

"It's that same pattern thing all over again," C.C. said. "Except for the first fire at the shed, which we don't know the origin of, and the truck, which still doesn't add up, every fire has been started from the *inside* of the structure. This doesn't fit the pattern. And it's too crude. We go from the barn fire, which was set in a corner to get that double burn effect, to the cabin where we had a timed explosion, to your family home where the perp broke in and started the fire in the living room, to this? Just squirting some charcoal lighter on an outside wall and touching a match to it?"

"Maybe they got in a hurry?"

"Why be in a hurry? Why pick a target where they *had* to be in a hurry? There are lots of places to choose from."

"You're the expert. I'm just a small town boy. You tell me," Weber said.

"Because it's not the same person. Or persons. Our perp has acted alone, I'm sure of it. These guys are copycats. Kids doing it for the thrill."

"Just what we need. More idiots running around playing with fire."

"Oh, make no mistake about it. Our perp, the one we've been looking for all along, isn't an idiot. He's smart and he's put some thought into all this."

"But you still haven't told me why," Weber said. "What's in it for him?"

"I don't know yet," C.C. said. "You'll have to ask him when we catch him."

***

"C.C. was right," Chad said when he returned from the convenience store. "They have a display of Dyno-Lite right by the door, just like she said. It's their house brand and nobody else in Arizona sells it. So unless it came from a store outside this area, we have the source. And then we got lucky. The manager gave me this." He held up a DVD.

"No way, it can't be that easy," Weber said.

"Sometimes it is," Coop said, sliding the DVD into the slot on the side of his laptop. "They have an automatic system that loads a new DVD every twelve hours and recycles the old ones every three days. This one starts at midnight and ends at noon today. The 911 call on today's fire came in at 1:03. So unless they lifted the stuff and ran across town right to the Oswald house, I think we'll find our two young persons of interest on here."

"I don't know many kids that are up too early in the morning during summer vacation," Weber said. "Can you fast forward to about 8 a.m.?"

"Don't need to fast forward," Coop told him. "I can start it about there."

After Coop found the correct starting point on the DVD, it took over an hour of watching the screen at triple speed before C.C. said, "Stop! Right there. No, back it up a little bit. More."

The image showed two teenage boys dressed in jeans, one wearing a long sleeved dark blue shirt and baseball cap and the other a white T-shirt. They came in the store and loitered around for a couple of minutes, then the one in the T-shirt went to the counter with a bottle of soda and a small bag of potato chips. While the clerk was busy with him the camera showed the other boy standing in front of the Dyno-Lite display with his back to the camera, then both boys left the store.

"Back it up slow again," C.C. said. "Stop there."

The screen showed the front of the store, one boy approaching the counter and the other behind him turning toward the door. "Can you zoom in and show the charcoal lighter?"

Coop zoomed the screen in and moved the mouse to center on the display.

"Now go forward to where the boys are leaving the store. Right there. Do you see it?"

"What am I missing?" Weber asked.

"I see it," Coop said. "Here, Jimmy, let me scroll back. Okay, look at the top of the display, five cans on the top row, right? Now look when I jump forward."

Once it was pointed out to him, Weber saw the obvious. When the boys left the store there were only three cans of Dyno-Lite Charcoal Lighter on the top row of the display. The time stamp on the screen said 11:44 a.m.

***

None of the deputies or office staff recognized the boys in the video so Weber instructed Coop to print out copies of stills from the video that showed their faces and hit the streets. Melvin Clarke, still chagrined at being caught in a lie, said they looked like the boys who had run past his house just before he heard Patrick Watson calling for help, but he couldn't be sure. Stanley Watson, Patrick's father, said he knew all of the students at the junior and senior high school and they did not look familiar to him.

Caroline Bryant, the high school principal, stopped filling the hummingbird feeders on her big front porch to study the photographs and shook her head. "I'm sorry, Sheriff. It's a small school and I know every one of my kids. They're not students."

The best they were able to get was from Staci Harbaugh, the clerk who had been on duty at the Stop and Go that morning, who said the boys had been in several times in the last week but she didn't know them.

They even struck out with Mary Caitlin, that vast resource of local lore, who knew everything about everybody. "They're not from here," Mary said, settling the matter once and for all. "And there's no family resemblance to anybody I know from this area."

"I'm thinking they're out-of-towners," Dolan Reed said. "Bored kids looking for something to do. It wouldn't be the first time we've had problems from summer kids."

"No, and it won't be the last," Buz Carelton said.

With the many newcomers who had come to Big Lake in the last few years for summer fun and winter skiing, there had not only been an influx of cash and skyrocketing land values, but also an increase in crime of all kinds. Where once the Sheriff's Office dealt mostly with fights between drunk cowboys and loggers at the area bars, domestic violence calls at rundown cabins and mobile homes, and the occasional lost hunter or hiker, more and more of Weber's deputies were now also dealing with reports of vandalism, drug related crimes, and a host of other "big city" problems. People who fled places like Tucson and Phoenix, or even as far away as southern California, had brought the same problems with them they had been trying to escape. Weber knew that there was a reason many of the locals resented all the newcomers and longed for the good old days. He had found himself thinking the same things more than once.

"Keep at it, guys," he said. "I really want to get these punks in custody. One firebug at a time is about all we can handle."

***

Weber spent the next two hours on patrol, knowing that the chance of catching their mysterious arsonist in the act was very slim, but he wasn't accomplishing anything in the office and figured that the more sets of eyes there were on the street the better.

He stopped at the Town Pump for a Pepsi, and as the man behind the convenience store counter rang up the sale and handed him his change, he asked if there was any news on the investigation.

"We've got a couple of possible suspects."

"The kids in those pictures Deputy Frost brought in here?"

Weber nodded and pocketed his change.

"I've got to tell you, Sheriff, my wife is terrified that our place is going to be next. I'm thinking about buying a gun."

"None of the arsons have been at an occupied structure," Weber told him.

"Not yet, but there's always a first time for everything."

"You've certainly got a right to protect your home and your family," Weber said. "But just having a gun and not knowing how to use it can be more dangerous than the chance of somebody trying to set fire to your place."

"I was in the Army. I can handle myself," the clerk assured him. The man was in his late 40s and Weber doubted he had touched a firearm since basic training. The memory of Robyn being shot by a panicked homeowner went through his mind again.

"Listen. Joe, is it? Listen, Joe, if you do get a gun, and I'm not saying you should or shouldn't, but if you do get one, take a safety class, okay?"

"Like I said, I was in the Army."

"It's one thing to shoot at a paper target and something else to use a gun in a life or death situation," Weber told him. "All I'm saying is that if you decide to get a gun, understand that it comes with a big responsibility too, okay? Chad Summers is our firearms training officer and you can usually find him out at the cinder pit target shooting a couple of Saturdays a month. He'll be happy to give you a few tips."

The man nodded but Weber knew he wasn't really listening. He was afraid, just like all of Big Lake was, and he was desperate to protect what was his. And as the sheriff left the store, he couldn't honestly say he blamed the man.

Chapter 30

The sound of raindrops on the roof of his cabin awakened Weber in the middle of the night. Maybe the rain would keep the firebug at home. Or at least keep a fire from spreading to the forest. Lightning flashed off in the distance somewhere and a moment later thunder rumbled. The rain increased in intensity, drumming loudly on the cabin's metal roof. Getting out of bed and pulling on a pair of jeans, he walked through the darkened cabin to the front porch.

Weber had always enjoyed thunderstorms. He sat in a rocking chair and watched nature's lightshow. An occasional gust of wind brought a few stray raindrops onto the porch, and as the storm passed overhead the trees in his yard were illuminated in the lightning flashes.

He heard the door open behind him and Robyn came out, wrapped in a blanket.

"Couldn't sleep?"

"The rain woke me up."

She sat on the porch swing and patted the seat beside her. Weber moved to her side and she wrapped the blanket around his shoulders and pulled him in closer.

"What would your mother say if she knew you were sitting here naked on the front porch with a man you're not married to?"

"She would be appalled," Robyn said. "Absolutely scandalized, I'm sure."

Weber chuckled and kissed her forehead. Robyn snuggled against his shoulder and sighed in contentment. "This is nice."

"Very nice," Weber agreed.

A nearby lightning strike lit up the porch in a blue-white flash and a second later the thunderclap shook the cabin. They both jumped, then laughed at themselves and settled back under the blanket. Never in his life had Weber felt such contentment as he did at that very moment.

He should have known it wasn't going to last.

***

They had both dozed off and the storm had passed when the ringing telephone roused Weber just before dawn. He stood up, his back stiff from sitting so long, and tucked the blanket back around Robyn before he went to answer the call.

"Sorry to wake you, Sheriff, but I thought you should know that there's been an accident."

"No problem," Weber told the dispatcher, knowing that she would not have called him at home at that hour unless it was serious. "What's happened?"

"A couple of kids hit an elk out on Tucker Road."

"How bad is it?"

"Carl Harris found them when he was riding past. He said one of them went halfway through the windshield. I dispatched Deputies Wright and Wingate, and EMS is on their way."

Weber was pulling on clothes as she talked and said, "I'm on my way. Where at on Tucker Road?"

"About a mile past the turnoff to the Boy Scout camp."

"Radio Dan and Archer and tell them I'll be there in a few minutes."

Robyn had come inside during the phone call. "What's going on?" she asked sleepily.

"Just a bad accident. Somebody took out an elk on Tucker Road."

"Want me to come with you?"

"No, go back to bed," he told her. "We've got it covered."

He kissed her and buckled on his gun belt.

"Be careful," Robyn said as she shuffled toward the bedroom.

Weber didn't hear her, he was already going out the door.

To avoid disturbing his neighbors, he didn't turn on his lights or siren until he was out on the highway. It was normally a ten minute drive to Tucker Road but Weber made it in seven, and five minutes later he saw flashing red and blue lights ahead. Two Sheriff's Department cars were pulled onto the shoulder of the road, and Big Lake's EMS ambulance was backed up between them. A red Yamaha V-Star 1100cc motorcycle was on its kickstand, and at first Weber couldn't see the accident. But a wide swath of blood mixed with green radiator coolant on the pavement told him what had happened there.

He parked and walked up to the ambulance, where one of the EMS personnel and Dan Wright were loading a stretcher with a bloodied young man on it into the back. Dan shook his head grimly, then led Weber down the embankment to where a black Land Rover lay on its passenger side. Archer stood by watching as the other EMT knelt beside a second patient. The boy was moaning but was sitting upright.

"Let's get you up on your feet and see if you can make it up to the ambulance," the EMT said.

The boy yelped as the EMT helped him to get upright and sagged for a moment, but the EMT held him up. "Give me a hand Deputy," he said, and Archer took the boy's other arm. Between the two of them they helped him make it to the road and into the back of the ambulance. A moment later the doors were closed and the boxy vehicle was headed toward town with its siren wailing.

"Fill me in," Weber said.

"Mr. Harris here called it in," Dan said. "I followed the ambulance out and Archer was already here."

Weber thought that was probably the first time in his career as a deputy that Archer had beaten everybody else to a call.

"Morning Sheriff," Harris said. "Not a very good way to start the day, is it?"

"Afraid not," Weber said, shaking his hand. "What happened here, Carl?"

"I was out for an early morning ride and when I was riding past I saw all the blood on the road and those tire tracks. I figured somebody hit something, so I pulled over to see if the animal was down on the shoulder somewhere. That's when I saw the car down there. I helped the driver out, but the other one was halfway through the windshield and I was afraid to try to move him. He didn't look good."

"Is that the one you guys were loading on the stretcher?"

Dan nodded. "I don't think he's going to make it."

"Glad you picked this road for your ride this morning," Weber told Harris. "Not much traffic out here. Who knows when anybody else would have come by, or if they would have even seen the vehicle down there."

"Glad I was able to...."

Suddenly the man's face lost all of its color and he started to tremble.

"Carl? Are you all right?"

"I... I just...."

He started to crumple and Weber stepped forward quickly and caught him under his arms and eased him to the ground. Harris turned to his side and vomited, then began coughing. Weber patted him on the back and felt the man begin to sob.

"Sorry," he managed to get out.

"It's okay," Weber told him. "Happens to all of us."

Dan went to his car and brought back a bottle of water. He twisted the cap off and offered it to the other man. "Here, have a drink, sir."

Carl filled his mouth and spit to rinse it, then took a sip and coughed. He managed to get control of himself and shook his head. "Sorry, I don't know what hit me."

"It's okay," Weber repeated. "We see this kind of stuff a lot and it still gets to all of us sometimes. For somebody who's not used to it....."

"It doesn't make you less of a man," Dan added. "You probably saved at least one of those kids' lives this morning. Maybe both of them if we get lucky."

They heard sirens approaching and Buz Carelton arrived on the scene just as Weber and Dan helped Carl to his feet.

"I'll tell you what, how about you give Dan here your statement and then he'll drive you back to town," Weber said.

"I can ride my bike."

"I'd prefer you didn't," Weber told him. "You just had a massive adrenalin rush and then the letdown that followed it. You're still pretty shaky and I don't want to have to be scraping you off the pavement."

"What about my bike? I don't want to leave it out here."

"If you trust me to, I can come back and ride it back in," Dan offered. "I've got a Harley."

"I'll let you guys work out the details," Weber said, then shook the man's hand again. "Thanks for helping us out, Carl. Like Dan said, you may have saved a couple of lives today."

Weber and Buz walked down to the Land Rover and the deputy whistled when he saw the crushed front end and top. "Looks like they rolled at least once. It's a wonder anybody survived."

"One looked pretty iffy," Weber said.

"Where's the elk they hit?"

"Over in that direction," Archer said from up on the road, pointing to a thick tangle of brush and small trees. "I heard it moving around for a while but it's been a few minutes."

"Let's go check it out," Weber said.

He and Buz followed the matted grass and blood trail for a hundred yards before they found the animal. She was still alive but unable to do more than raise her head feebly at their approach.

"She's a big one," Buz said. "Damn shame. No use making her

suffer any longer."

Weber nodded and drew his pistol.

Chapter 31

It was a little before 9 a.m. when Weber knocked on the door of the big A-frame, and it took a few minutes before he heard someone moving on the other side.

"Who is it?"

"Big Lake Sheriff's Office."

A dark haired man wearing blue boxer shorts opened the door and squinted in the sunlight.

"Yes?"

"Are you Mr. Glissman? Albert Glissman?"

"Yes, what's this about?"

"Sir, do you have two sons?"

"Three. We have three sons."

"Al? Who is it?" a woman called from inside the house.

The man turned his head back inside and said, "It's the police, Paige."

He turned back to Weber and asked, "What's going on?"

"Your sons, Mr. Glissman. You have three boys?"

"Yes, Forrest, Tyler, and Ricky. Please, what's going on?"

A heavyset woman came up behind Glissman, wrapping a multicolored robe around herself. She saw Weber standing on the deck and asked, "What's happening?"

"Can I come in?" Weber asked. "I'm afraid I have some bad news."

***

Paige Glissman cried quietly from the back seat of Weber's Explorer while her husband sat beside her and stared woodenly out the window. They arrived at the medical center and a nurse quickly ushered them into Tyler's room.

"I hate to see a kid die like that," Chad said, handing Weber a cup of coffee. "So much life ahead of him. Such a waste."

"The parents didn't even know they had snuck out," Weber said.

"Apparently this isn't the first time they did it and went joyriding in their dad's car."

A few minutes later the door opened and the Glissmans came out into the hallway, holding onto each other for support.

"Can we see Ricky now?" Paige asked.

"You really shouldn't," Weber said. "I'm afraid he's…"

"I have to see him," she said. "He's my son."

Weber wanted to tell her that no mother should see her child in the condition the accident had left Ricky in, but one look in the woman's determined eyes told him nothing was going to keep her from doing what she needed to do. He nodded and led them down the hall to another room.

***

"Did you recognize them from the store video?"

"I recognized Tyler," Coop said. "The other one…" he shuddered at the memory.

"According to the parents, both boys have been in trouble before, little stuff like vandalism and shoplifting," Weber said. "About six months ago they took their mom's car and went cruising. Ended up rear-ending a city bus in Mesa. He said they've been coming up here for the last couple of summers to get the kids out of the city, hoping they'd stay out of mischief."

"They seem like nice people," Chad observed. "Doesn't seem fair, does it?"

Weber shook his head. "We both know life isn't fair. The dad said that the oldest son, Forrest, never gave them a problem growing up. He's in the Navy, stationed in Jacksonville, Florida. These two, just the opposite."

"It's a terrible time to talk to them about the fires," Chad said.

"I know. Wish we'd have caught up with those two boys yesterday. We could have saved their parents a world of grief."

"I sure hate to put his folks through this right now. You have to wonder how much more they can take."

"Can't be helped, Jimmy. You know that," Bob Bennett said.

Weber nodded and finished the last of his coffee, wondering for the thousandth time what so much of the strong swill was doing to his stomach. "Sometimes this job sucks. Let's get it over with."

***

"How's he doing?" Weber asked.

"The doctor says he got lucky," Albert Glissman said. "His left arm is broken and they're going to be putting it in a cast in a little while. A few cuts and bruises. But compared to Ricky…" His voice broke and Weber's heart ached for the grieving man. Never having any children himself, Weber couldn't imagine the pain this father was feeling, and he hated himself for the fact that he was about to add to it.

"This is Bob Bennett, Big Lake's Town Attorney. We need to talk to your son about the accident and some other things. Do you suppose you're all up to that right now?"

Albert was an intelligent man, and realistic enough to know the character of his two younger sons. He looked across the room to Tyler, who was propped up in bed talking to his mother. "What other things?"

"I hate to tell you this, sir, but we think that Tyler and Ricky were involved in at least one of these arson fires we've been having."

The man closed his eyes for a moment and shook his head. "Can this morning get any worse?"

Weber didn't tell him that it was about to get much worse.

***

"I said all along the truck fire didn't fit with the other stuff," C.C. said. "That takes at least one wrinkle out of the fabric."

For a moment Weber felt irritation at her comment. It almost seemed like she was more concerned with the fire investigation than the fact that a young man was dead and another was in serious trouble, or the agony all of this was putting their parents through. Then he remembered that for C.C., the fire investigation *was* her primary concern. She had not witnessed the gore at the accident scene or been there when he had to tell the Glissmans that life as they knew it was over, or been witness to the crushing defeat in Tyler's parents eyes as they realized that they had lost more than one son this tragic morning.

"I guess the mom and dad enjoy a nightcap or two and sleep like logs. Tyler said they had been taking their dad's car out almost every night and running around," Weber said. "According to him, they started out planning to siphon gas out of Max Woodbury's truck but then found out it was a diesel. He says that's when his brother Ricky got the idea to come back later and torch the truck with a flare Ricky had shoplifted from Todd Norton's auto parts store. Tyler also said that all he did was stand out on the street as a lookout while Ricky started the fire at the Oswald place."

"His brother Ricky did that? All by himself? A one man crime spree," Coop said with a shake of his head.

"That's right. According to him, Ricky was the instigator and he was just along for the ride. He also claims Ricky was driving the car when they hit that elk," Weber said.

Buz shook his head. "The evidence says otherwise. Ricky was through the windshield on the passenger side, and Carl Harris said he helped Tyler get out from the driver's side. And the seat belt bruises on Tyler's chest show that he was in the driver's seat when they hit that elk."

"And at least one of those cans we found at the Oswald house are going to have his fingerprints on them. Not to mention Patrick Watson's eyewitness testimony that he saw *two* boys spraying the house with that charcoal lighter. So the only thing we know Tyler is telling us the truth about is that it was Ricky who actually stole the lighter fluid while Tyler distracted the clerk at the Stop and Go."

"I'd say that young man is in a heap of trouble," Bennett said. "Right now we've got him on accessory to theft, two counts of arson, and vehicular homicide, since he was driving the car."

"What really irks me is that he won't take a bit of responsibility for any of it. It's all Ricky's fault, and Ricky's dead. Very convenient."

"Sociopaths come in all ages, Jimmy. It's not a learned art."

"I know that, Bob. But you don't know how much I wanted to grab that little bastard by the front of his hospital gown and jerk him out of that bed and knock some reality into his head. Or at least some compassion for his parents. Sitting up there crying crocodile tears and blaming his brother for everything and making himself look like the poor victim who was drawn into it all against his will. And all the while he's trying to cover his own ass, he's smearing more crap on his brother's memory for his parents to live with."

"The dad wasn't buying it," Bennett said. "I could see it in his eyes."

"I know," Weber told him. "And I don't know if that made it better or worse."

Chapter 32

"Sheriff Weber, what can you tell us about the status of these fire investigations, if anything?" Councilman Mel Walker asked at Tuesday evening's Town Council meeting. "I understand that you have made an arrest?"

"Not exactly," Weber said. "We have a suspect in two of the fires, but he's not in custody at this time."

"Why not?" Mayor Wingate demanded. "And what do you mean when you say this person is only a suspect in two of the fires? Are you telling us that there is more than one person running around the town starting fires? How do you know that? How do you know that the person you suspect didn't start all of the fires? And why…"

"Chet, let him answer one question at a time," Councilman Kirby Templeton said.

"We need answers, and we need them now, Kirby."

"And we can't get those answers unless you let the man speak, Chet."

The mayor frowned, but sat back in his chair. Templeton gestured to Weber to continue.

"During the course of our investigation into the fires, Deputy Fire Marshal Callahan told me that she believed that there might actually be two different arsonists. After the fire yesterday at the Oswald house on Maple Lane we developed information that two boys had started that fire. Early this morning there was a fatal accident out on Tucker Road," Weber told the Council. "A young man named Richard Glissman, age 18, was killed. His brother Tyler, age 17, suffered relatively minor injuries. I can't go into all of the details at this time because it's an open investigation, but we had evidence that the Glissman boys started that fire. When confronted with that evidence, Tyler Glissman admitted that he and his brother were responsible for both the fire at the Oswald's and for burning up Mac Woodbury's truck."

"And why isn't this young hoodlum under arrest?" Mayor Wingate demanded.

"He's a juvenile and his family just suffered a terrible tragedy," Weber said. "I talked to his father, and he understands the seriousness of the situation and promised me that he'll make sure his son is available to us when the time comes."

"That's ridiculous," the mayor said. "How do you know that will really happen? I want him in jail right this minute."

"It was a judgment call," Weber said.

"The name isn't familiar. Are they from here or summer visitors?" Councilman Walker asked.

"They rented a place here for the last couple of seasons," Weber replied.

"So there's absolutely nothing to keep them from skipping town with their little pyromaniac," the mayor said. "Do you ever think before you make decisions like this, Sheriff Weber?"

"Chet, they just lost one son. I didn't have it in my heart to take another one away from them the minute he walked out of the hospital."

The mayor hated it when Weber addressed him by his first name, which was a big part of the reason the sheriff did it so frequently. The little man's scowl was even deeper as he started to speak again when Templeton held up his hand to stop him.

"Sheriff, you know I trust your judgment, but I have to tell you, I'm not comfortable with this one. With no charges against him, what's to keep this kid from skipping town?"

Before Weber could reply, Bob Bennett made a suggestion. "Our jail doesn't have the facilities to house a juvenile for very long and this isn't a capital crime. How about if we charge this young man and have Judge Ryman release him to his parents custody?"

"I want him behind bars. We don't need another fire," Wingate said stubbornly.

"Like I said, Deputy Fire Marshal Callahan doesn't believe the same person started all these fires," Weber said. "So whether he's in custody or with his parents isn't going to prevent another fire."

"Assuming she's right," the mayor said. "I'm not willing to risk it."

"Something else to consider, Mr. Mayor. We'll have to send the boy to Navajo County's juvenile detention facility until his trial, and that's going to cost us $175 a day."

When Bob Bennett said that, it got the mayor's attention. Chet Wingate hated to spend money on anything, guarding the town's coffers like a miser over his horde of gold coins. He thought about it for a moment and then said, "Maybe you're right, Mr. Bennett. His parents would have to pay some kind of bail to assure that he'd return for trial, wouldn't they? Hmm… yes, I think that's the best course to take given this poor family's recent misfortune."

"Okay, is there anything else you can share with us about these fires, Sheriff?" Templeton asked.

"There's really nothing else to tell," Weber said. "We're following up on every lead we have, but it's a frustrating case. I'm trusting to Ms. Callahan's experience to help us get to the bottom of it. I wish I had more for you."

"We all wish for that," Templeton said. "Keep at it. We're all behind you, Sheriff."

The look on the faces of the mayor and two of his staunch supporters told Weber that not every councilmember was behind him, but that was nothing new so he sat back down as the meeting moved on to other business, including Fire Chief Harper's report on the arrival of the new fire truck and Town Clerk Leslie Stokes's request for the funds for new office equipment, which Mayor Wingate quickly shot down.

After the meeting ended, Bob Bennett called Judge Ryman at home and explained the situation with Tyler Glissman. Ending the call, he said, "Harold doesn't like coming in after hours but you know he's got a soft spot for kids, so he said he'd do it. Let's go have a chat with Tyler's parents."

***

It was close to midnight when Weber finally got home after formally arresting and booking Tyler Glissman and then taking him before Judge Ryman, who set bail at $50,000 and allowed his parents to secure their son's release with a lien against certificates of deposits they kept in a safe deposit box at their bank in Tempe.

The sheriff was worn out physically and emotionally. He stared at the contents of his refrigerator, trying to work up the energy to fix something for dinner, then gave up and closed the door. He got a jar of Jif crunchy peanut butter out of a cabinet and ate four big spoons full, then undressed and climbed into the shower. He turned the knob to hot and stood under the hard spray until the water turned cold, then got out and toweled himself dry. Minutes after his head touched the pillow, he was asleep.

But it would not be a restful night. His dreams were filled with visions of Ricky Glissman spread out across the hood of his father's car, and of Steve Rafferty, another young boy who died violently, with three of Weber's bullets in his body. Twice he woke himself up screaming, sitting upright in the dark bedroom until his breathing steadied and he was able to fight off the demons that plagued him before he lay back down again.

Chapter 33

Judge Ryman's courtroom occupied a large block building on the other side of the Town Offices from the Sheriff's Office. The building also held two small meeting rooms used for various purposes, and in the rear was a depository for records dating back to the earliest days of the community.

The sun was still an hour away from rising over the mountains when David Poole pulled his Dodge pickup into the empty parking lot. The left tire on his boat trailer had a slow leak and every few days he had to pump it back up.

He knew he should have done it the night before but he had forgotten. He *should* get the darned thing fixed and be done with it, but who had the time? He worked long hours as the head of maintenance at the ski lodge, and even in the summer the place kept him busy, making sure the lifts were running for the sightseers to ride to the top of Cat Mountain and that everything in the lodge was in working order.

His boss, Ashley Knott, was a real ball buster, a driven thirtyish woman on the fast track to success. She made no secret of the fact that she hated Big Lake. She considered the lodge just a rung on the ladder to success that she had to climb to get a plum assignment at one of Fairchild Resorts premier properties, preferably in Hawaii, though she would have settled for Miami. Anyplace away from the cold, from small towns, and from the small-minded people who inhabited them.

David's wife Kimberly was a bit of a ball buster herself and did not appreciate him spending the one day a week he had off fishing, so when he got ready to leave this morning and noticed that the tire was low he had cursed himself. Not wanting to wake up Kim by opening the garage and turning on his big air compressor, he had waited until he was in town. There'd be hell to pay when he got home anyway, he didn't need to add any more fuel to the fire.

He retrieved the little 12-volt air pump from the metal toolbox in the bed behind the truck's cab, plugged it into the cigarette lighter socket on the dash board, and ran the cord back to the trailer. Even with the anemic little pump, it only took a few minutes to air the tire up. That chore done, Poole screwed the valve cap back onto the tire stem, unplugged the pump, and was stowing it back in his toolbox when he saw the flames.

***

"Who called it in, Steve?" Weber asked.

"David Poole. He works out at the ski lodge. He stopped to air up a tire and saw the fire. He ran over to your office and told the dispatcher. By the time we got here it was going strong."

C.C. joined them in the parking lot, and in the early morning light Weber noticed that she looked good even without makeup.

"Well, we knew it was going to happen," she said.

"You said he was getting cocky," the fire chief said. "I guess you were right. This is about as cocky as it gets."

They were interrupted when Chet Wingate marched up to them on the sidewalk and got as close as a man of his short stature could get to Weber's face, "What do you have to say for yourself now, Sheriff?"

"Jesus, Chet, you could have taken the time to brush your teeth," Weber said, stepping back and waving his hand with irritation.

"So much for your *judgment call* about that young thug that you insisted on keeping out on the street! I'm holding you personally responsible for this!"

"It's too early for this. Go back to bed, Chet. Trust me, you really need your beauty sleep."

"I want that… that hooligan in handcuffs within the next ten minutes. That's an order, Sheriff."

"And I want a harem of busty college cheerleaders to serve me breakfast in bed. Nether one's going to happen. I don't take orders from you, Chet."

The mayor grabbed Weber's shirt and shouted, "I've had it with your insolence, Sheriff. I demand respect!"

As much as he longed to stomp the little tyrant into no more than an obscene blotch on the sidewalk, Weber made it a point to keep his voice level when he said, "Chet, you just committed assault on a police officer in front of a crowd of people. I'm going to tell you this just once. Take your hands off of me and step back. If you don't I'm going to put you face down, right here on this sidewalk, and then I'm going to handcuff you and haul your chubby ass to jail. And I'm *not* going to be very gentle about any if it. Do you understand me?"

The mayor started to open his mouth, but when he saw the malevolent look on Weber's face he thought better of it. He released his hold on the sheriff's shirt and stumbled backward.

Weber shook his head in frustration, then turned his attention back to the fire. The newly acquired pumper truck, even with its leaky water hoses and weather checked tires, was already proving its worth. The back of the building where the fire was concentrated only had three windows up high on each side, but with one truck in a parking lot on either side of the building pouring water through those windows, the volunteer firemen were able to extinguish the blaze before it spread to the courtroom in front.

"Hell of a way to break in your new truck, Chief," Kirby Templeton said as he joined them on the sidewalk, where several town officials stood among the crowd of onlookers.

"I'm just glad we filled the tank yesterday to check it," Harper said.

"You guys did good. Proud of you. How soon before we can get inside and see what's left?"

"We're going to need a while yet," Harper said. "We'll open it up and set up a couple of big fans to blow the smoke out."

"Sir, I know you all need to get inside and see how much damage has been done," C.C. said. "But before we have a bunch of people tracking through there, I need to investigate the scene."

"Do you think this is the work of our firebug, Ms. Callahan?"

"I do. We were past due for another fire."

"You don't think there's any chance it was a coincidence?"

"Are you willing to take the chance it wasn't?" C.C. asked him.

"No. No, ma'am, I'm not. You do what you need to do. We'll wait." Then Templeton turned to Weber and asked, "Got a minute, Jimmy?"

They walked a few yards away where they could talk in privacy.

"I saw that stunt Chet pulled. I commend you on not knocking his block off. Don't know if I could have shown as much restraint."

"It wasn't the time or the place," Weber said. "He's always irritating but I can usually blow Chet's bullshit off. But when he put his hands on me he stepped over the line. I won't be so calm next time."

"Let's hope he got the message," Templeton said. "Meantime, I have to ask you to do something you're not going to like."

"That kid didn't do this, Kirby. He's a worthless little maggot, but his dad gave me his word that he'd keep an eye on him and I believe him."

"Still, we need to know."

Weber nodded, knowing the man was right.

***

The night had not been kind to Albert Glissman, or his wife. Grief and fatigue had left dark circles under their eyes and etched lines into their faces. Tyler, on the other hand, looked like he had slept very well.

"It wasn't me," the boy told Weber. "I was right here all night long. You can ask my mom and dad, they took turns sitting in a chair in my room like some kind of prison guards."

Weber was tempted to tell him that he was probably going to get to know some real prison guards before things were finished, but instead he just looked to the boy's father for confirmation.

"You're damn right we did, Tyler. And we plan to do it every night until we know we can trust you again."

"Why don't you just get a pair of handcuffs from him and you can lock me to my bed and save yourself the trouble?"

Weber was having a hard time not taking the sneering punk out back and explaining some hard facts of life to him, but just as with Chet, he held himself back.

"I'm sorry to intrude on you in your time of trouble," Weber said, standing up and shaking Albert's hand.

"Sieg Heil," said Tyler from the couch, extending his good arm in a Nazi salute.

Until then Albert had seemed to be in control of his emotions, but the boy had finally gone too far. He turned to his son and said, "Tyler, shut your mouth or I'll break your other arm."

The boy rolled his eyes and gave an exaggerated sigh, but he dropped his arm back beside him.

Oh yeah, that young man's going to get a real education in jail, Weber thought to himself as he walked back to his Explorer.

Chapter 34

"What a mess," C.C. said, stepping over heaps of sodden paperwork and puddles of water on the concrete floor.

"How are we supposed to find anything in here?" Weber asked, looking at the shambles the fire itself and the hoses used to put it out had caused. Decades of planning and zoning records, Town Council meeting minutes, tax records, personnel files, court records, transcripts, businesses license information, invoices, receipts, and all of the other paperwork that town government had generated were reduced to soggy piles and charred trash.

"Surround and drown," C.C. said. "It's the best way to put out a fire in a hurry. If you see red, put water on it."

"The good news is that most of the damage was confined back here," Chief Harper said. "One of the general purpose meeting rooms is going to need new drywall, but the other one and the judge's office and courtroom are fine. Stinky, but no damage to them."

Spying the fuse box on one wall of the cavernous room, C.C. made her way to it and opened the metal door.

"Is the power off to the building?" she asked. "I'd prefer not to get fried standing here in a pool of water."

"I watched the guy from the electrical co-op disconnect it myself," Harper said. "We used to pull the meter off the back of the building, but I saw a training video where somebody doing that accidently grounded the legs of the meter to the metal box or something and the damn meter exploded. It was like a glass hand grenade going off. No thanks."

C.C. studied the electrical box and the wiring leading out from it and said, "Damn! It's a wonder this place didn't burn up years ago. This thing looks like it was put in during the Roosevelt administration. Teddy's, not Franklin. Don't you have building codes in this town?"

"We do now," Harper replied. "But this place was built long before I was born, and it's needed upgrading for years. But our good mayor has a real problem spending money for anything."

"Our town clerk has been begging the mayor for money to replace her computer system for over a year now," Weber said. "If he had his way she'd be using an abacus and a chalkboard to keep track of things. Who knows how much is lost here that she can never re-create?"

"What are you looking for?" Harper asked. "Do you think it was just an electrical fire?"

"A fuse box is a great place to start a fire," C.C. told him. "Remember the old trick of putting a penny behind one of these screw in fuses? If you do that and then plug in an electric heater or something with a big draw, it will overload the circuit. But the penny bypasses the fuse and acts as a conductor, so instead of the fuse blowing, you get a fire. You can do the same thing with modern resettable breakers. Wedge a toothpick in to keep it from tripping, the breaker overheats and starts a fire."

"Is that what happened here?"

"No, Sheriff. See, there's no burn pattern climbing up the wall. The fire started over there where those metal shelves held boxes of paperwork. Notice that along this center aisle you have the most burned debris?"

So much had been washed away and scattered by the pressure of the fire hoses that Weber really couldn't see what she was talking about at first, but when C.C. pointed out that the metal shelves themselves were more blackened than those along either wall and that many of the cardboard boxes full of records on those wall shelves were not burned as much, it was easier to see.

"Any idea how the fire started?"

"It would be a no brainer to throw some kind of accelerant around and touch a match to it," C.C. said. She pulled a Leatherman multi-tool from its nylon sheath on her belt and opened the knife blade. Cutting a piece of cardboard from what was left of one of the boxes, she sniffed it, then repeated the process at several places. "I can't smell anything like gas or lighter fluid, but that doesn't mean something like that wasn't used. He could have used rubbing alcohol. It makes a quick hot flash and burns away, so it's harder to detect than gasoline or kerosene."

"Any idea how he got in here?" Harper asked.

"The door there on the north side was kicked in," Weber said.

"My guys did that with a battering ram to get in," the fire chief said.

"All the windows are broken," Weber observed. "Did your people do that, too?"

"Probably, but I'll ask to be sure."

"Then again, there's not even a deadbolt on the exterior door," Weber said. "And this lock looks like any kid could pick it with a paperclip."

"I'm surprised Chet Wingate wouldn't have at least sprung for a decent lock," Harper said. "After all, he sells them at his hardware store. He could have made a few bucks off the deal."

"Do you think he'll learn a lesson from this and not be so cheap in the future?" C.C. asked.

Considering his encounter with the mayor that morning, and the many times they had butted heads in the past, Weber doubted it.

"We've gone from fires on the edge of town to one at Jimmy's old house, and now just two doors down from the Sheriff's Office. What's next?" Harper asked. "How far is this guy going to go, C.C.?"

"I wish I could tell you," she said. "But if he keeps this up, he's going to hurt or kill somebody."

***

It was mid-afternoon by the time C.C. had completed her investigation. She had photographed the fire scene inside and out, sketched a rough map of the interior of the building, paying particular attention to the storage room, and cut away over a dozen pieces of cardboard from the boxes paperwork had been stored in to send to the laboratory for chemical analysis.

When she relinquished the scene to the Town Council so they could evaluate the damage, Councilwoman Jordan echoed C.C.'s first comment when they entered, "What a mess!"

"I guess," Kirby Templeton said, appalled at the mayhem left in the fire's wake. "Where do we even start?"

"I don't know," Leslie Stokes said, obviously overwhelmed at the sight. She shuffled along the aisle, picking up a piece of paper or a waterlogged ledger book here and there, then, not knowing what to do with them, she would set them down and go on to the next. In the past Weber had occasionally teased the Town Clerk about being mildly OCD, but he knew she was very good at her job and believed in organization. Now years of careful filing and records management had been reduced to the wreckage before them. She had tears in her eyes when she said, "It's so… it's just all… it's just... I can't.…"

"It's okay, Leslie," Templeton assured her, putting a comforting arm around her shoulders. "We'll get a crew of people to come in here and help you get this all sorted out. You're going to need some help for sure, even without that bum hand of yours."

She didn't respond, just looked forlornly at the mishmash that had once been Big Lake's town records and history.

Chapter 35

The mayor called an emergency meeting of the town council to discuss the latest fire, and immediately went on the attack.

"I've been telling you people for as long as I can remember that we need to replace Sheriff Weber and Fire Chief Harper with some real professionals" But would you listen to me? No, and this is what it's come to!"

"Professionals like your son?" Councilman Frank Gauger asked. The retired postal worker was a senior member of the Town Council and had been witness to the mayor's schemes and tantrums for years.

"Yes, I believe Archer could do a much better job than what we have now, as a matter of fact."

"So which job do you think he's qualified for, Fire Chief or Sheriff? Or maybe we should combine the two? I wonder if we can make him Postmaster, too?"

Somebody chuckled, but the mayor ignored it. Weber wondered if he was actually going to suggest that his inept son would be able to handle the combined roles, but before he could say anything, Kirby Tempelton said, "Chet, give it a rest. We have real issues to discuss here."

"Issues? Issues like the Sheriff threatening me today?"

"He didn't threaten you, he told you what he was going to do if you didn't let go of his shirt. I saw the whole thing," Templeton said. "*You* broke the law by touching the man, Chet. And I'll tell you right now, if I would have been in Sheriff Weber's place, I wouldn't have warned you, I'd have knocked you on your hind end!"

There was a gasp from Councilwoman Smith-Abbot and Templeton looked at her. "Did you have something to say, Gretchen?"

"I would expect better behavior from a councilmember," she admonished him.

"And I'd expect better behavior from a mayor," Templeton told her. "Now, can we get to the business at hand, or do you have anything else you want to say?"

"As a matter of fact, I do. Last night I saw a video that was shot by Mr. Darron Tovar in which Sheriff Weber threatened him, too! Right on Main Street in broad daylight."

"Threatened how, Gretchen?"

He said he was going to… well, I won't repeat it," she said primly. "It was disgusting!"

"Do you have any evidence of this alleged incident?" asked Tempelton.

"It wasn't *alleged*, I saw the video."

"Mayor Wingate, if you're prepared to make a motion to dismiss the Sheriff, I'll second it," said Councilman Adam Hirsch. Hirsch, a nerdy-looking little man, had hated Weber ever since high school because he believed the future sheriff had stolen his girlfriend. The fact that Weber had hardly noticed the young lady in question and that she had barely acknowledged Hirsch's existence didn't matter. His resentment was too deep to make inconsequential things like that a consideration.

"Stop it!" Gauger said, shaking his head in frustration. "I can't believe you three. It never ends. Week after week we come in here and waste time listening to the same nonsense over and over. Gretchen, if Mr. Tovar wants to file a complaint with this Council, please encourage him to do so and we'll deal with it then. But since he hasn't come forward himself, this is hearsay as far as I'm concerned. In the meantime, can we put this pettiness aside and get back to doing the job the citizens of this town elected us to do?"

"Agreed," said Tempelton. "Sheriff, do we have any idea how this fire started? Is it related to the other fires we've had?"

"We don't have any proof of it yet, but I think it's too much of a coincidence. So yes, I'm pretty sure this fire was arson, just like the others. We don't know anything for sure yet, but Ms. Callahan believes that some type of accelerant was used to start it. She is sending samples of some of the boxes from the records room to her lab in Phoenix for analysis."

"What about the boy who was involved in that accident and the other fires? Did you confirm that he was home with his parents?"

"I talked to his father. He assured me that Tyler was home all night long."

"We know this boy and his brother snuck out before by his own admission, so how do we know he didn't do it again?"

"I'm taking his father's word on it."

Hirsch snorted, "Like that means anything?"

"The father and mother actually took turns sitting up in his room all night to make sure he didn't try to sneak out," Weber said.

"You don't think it's a coincidence that less than twelve hours after this kid was in Judge Ryman's courtroom, the building is set on fire?" Hirsch asked.

"I don't think he had anything to do with this latest fire," Weber said. "Their place is two miles from here. The chance of him slipping out while his parents were on watch, making his way here, breaking into the building, setting the fire, and getting back home are about impossible. And remember, he's banged up from the car accident and has a broken arm."

"Sheriff, please tell us you at least have *some* suspect in all of this," Hisrch said. "We'd like to believe that you're at least *trying* to earn your salary."

Weber wanted to tell the councilman that he could accomplish a lot more in the investigation out on the street rather than sitting there undergoing an inquisition, but instead he said, "I wish I could, but I'd be lying to you. We're looking at this thing from every angle. We've submitted evidence to the State Fire Lab. C.C. Callahan is one of the best fire investigators in the state, if not the entire Southwest. My deputies and volunteers are all working tons of hours, most of them off the clock."

"And still you have nothing?"

"Not yet."

"And do you think that there is any possibility that you might eventually get off your duff and get around to…"

"Enough Adam!" Templeton roared. "My God, I feel like I'm on the merry-go-round in an insane asylum. Will you please grow up? And you too, Chet. I wish I had that camera that kid from the new newspaper carries around because I'd love to record some of these sessions and post them on that funny video program my wife watches on TV. Except that there's nothing funny about adults, public servants, acting like petulant children. Adam, do you have anything constructive to add to this meeting or do you plan to just sit here baiting Sheriff Weber all afternoon?"

Hirsch's face reddened but he didn't say anything more.

After a moment Templeton said, "All right then, let's move along.

Leslie, I know everything's a big mess next door, and it's hard to know anything at this point, but do you have any idea how much we lost?"

"I don't know," said an obviously discouraged Leslie. "I'll need to get in there and spend some time looking through everything. But it's all so overwhelming right now that I don't even know where to start."

"You can't do it alone," Templeton said. "Like I told you earlier, we'll get you some help."

"And how are we going to pay for it?" Mayor Wingate demanded. "We have a responsibility to protect the taxpayer's money."

"If you didn't obsess so much about every penny, we'd have installed a decent sprinkling system in that warehouse a long time ago and we might not have all of this to deal with," Gauger said. "And just last night at our regular meeting, Leslie was in here again asking for money to upgrade the computer system. And you turned her down, *again*. I've had complaints from citizens about payments for utility fees and traffic tickets that never got recorded properly because when she enters them into that antique you call a bookkeeping program, they just disappear. If she didn't go to the time and effort to manually enter everything on paper too, how would we ever know who actually did pay? And now with this fire.... it's a mess, Chet. An absolute mess. And as far as I'm concerned, we have you to thank for that."

"I object," Councilwoman Smith-Abbot said. "Mayor Wingate is a prudent and watchful steward of this community's revenues. We can't just grant every request that comes before this Council. Just last week we spent a huge some of money on the fire department and look what that got us! Those firemen made an absolute trash heap out of our records facility."

Chief Harper started to say something, but Weber put his hand on his arm and stilled his retort.

"What it got us was a trash heap we can hopefully clean up and salvage something from," Gauger told her. "What did you expect them to do, Gretchen? Run inside and stomp the fire out with their feet? Having that second truck pouring water in from both sides saved the rest of the building." He turned to Harper and said, "Chief, I'm going to make a move for a formal commendation for you at next week's Council meeting."

"My guys are the ones who deserve a commendation, not me," Harper replied. "They're the ones who get out of bed in the middle of the night to respond, or leave their paying jobs to come when an alarm goes out."

"True," Templeton said, "You all deserve to be recognized for your contributions to this community. We'll be addressing that very soon, I promise you."

Weber was proud of his friend's selflessness and dedication to his volunteers, and squeezed Harper's arm to convey that message.

"Back to the cleanup. We've got a whole community full of people who are always willing to pitch in whenever somebody needs anything," Councilwoman Jordan said. "I think if we put out a call for volunteers we'd have people standing in line to help."

"There's a problem with that," objected Councilwoman Smith-Abbot. "Those records contain all kinds of personal information that cannot be shared with the general public. People's tax records, traffic fines, court records, Town personnel files. We have a responsibility to protect our employees and our citizen's privacy."

"Actually, a lot of that is all a matter of public record," Gauger said. "Under normal circumstances, people could come in and request access to the majority of it under the state's open records laws."

"But not all of it," Smith-Abbot argued.

Templeton turned to the Town Clerk and asked, "Leslie, knowing how well organized you always are, is there a section of the storage room where the more sensitive documents are stored? Stuff that wouldn't be available as public records?"

"The personnel records are all along the back wall," Leslie said. "That needs to be kept confidential."

"So if you had some volunteers and they were told to stay away from that area, would it be okay?"

She thought for a minute and said, "There are also court records that are not accessible to the public. Juvenile proceedings, sexual assault victims, things like that."

"Is there a way to segregate that area, too? Or are we pretty much negating any help that we can get you?"

Leslie shook her head. "No, I think if we rope those areas off there is still a lot of material to go through. Any help is better than none at all."

"All right then, let's get out of here and start looking for some able bodies to help. If we get them started first thing in the morning, maybe we can make a dent by the weekend. Let's have Ernie and his guys from the Maintenance Department get busy fixing those broken windows and securing the door before we run out of daylight."

Chapter 36

"You're a sight to see," Weber said to Kallie Jo Wingate when he saw her soot and sweat stained face as she pushed a big pile of trash across the storage room floor with a broom nearly as tall as she was. Archer's wife may have been a tiny woman, a couple inches under five feet tall and barely ninety pounds after a big meal, but she had more energy than any four people he knew. Usually that energy was expended in nonstop dialogue. Kallie Jo also talked more than any four people Weber knew, combined.

"Well, it's like my daddy, Buster, always says, Sheriff. You got to get dirty to get any work done. My daddy, he weren't afraid of hard work from the day he was born. That man just never stops. All the folks from the Phillips side of the family's like that. You take my Uncle Wayne, he's the one who broke his back in that there car accident I told you about? Well now, even when he was layin' there in that hospital bed after they put them there steel rods in his back, not known' ifn he'd ever be able to walk again, Uncle Wayne was lookin' at one of them there correspondence courses for computer programmin'. He said if his legs wouldn't work he'd sit on his tukus and work with his hands. 'Course, he didn't have to do that because that ol' boy, why it weren't but six months later he up and walked out of that rehabilitation facility they put him in over toward Waycross and he's mostly good as new!"

Weber had learned that the best way to handle Kallie Jo's monologues was just to nod occasionally and wait until she paused to catch her breath before he made his escape. The problem was, there were times when she never seemed to stop long enough to inhale. Larry Parks was convinced that as pretty and charming as Kallie Jo was, she was actually some type of mutant that had gills like a fish that provided her with oxygen.

This day he thought he was saved when the woman said, "Well anyway, I better get back to work instead of standin' here yackin' all day long."

"Yeah. Probably so," Weber said. "Where's Leslie?"

"Now I've gotta' tell you something, Sheriff. That is a woman who never stops working. Do you know that even with that hand of hers all bandaged up, she was up on a stepladder goin' through stuff in some of those boxes up there on the top shelves? I told her to get down afore she fell and banged herself up even more but she's just as stubborn as a mule. Did I ever tell you about the time me and my cousin Robert Lee took Grandpappy Phillips' old mule Pete to town for popsicles? Lord, what a mess! Here's a tip for you, Sheriff. Never try to eat a popsicle on the back of a mule on a Georgia summer day!"

Weber spied Leslie and made a quick excuse as he moved past Kallie Jo to where the town clerk was directing a couple of volunteers where to put armfuls of wet paperwork on the long cafeteria tables that had been borrowed from the school district. "Those are dog licenses, Charles. They go there on the end of that table. And what do you have, Allison? Receipts for petty cash expenditures and reimbursement? Over there on the third table."

"You're running things like an army commander with a major task force, only in a nicer way," Weber observed. "How's it going?"

"It's going," Leslie said, "We've been at it for four hours now, and I think we've at least got a system that might help us make a dent in it. But there's just so much, Jimmy."

"I know it must be intimidating as hell, but don't let it get you down. It's like eating an elephant. One bite at a time. That's the only way you can do it."

"But there are going to be things that are just gone. Burned up or shredded by the fire hoses or…"

"All you can do is all you can do," Weber told her. He looked at his watch. "It's almost noon, how about you knock off and I'll buy you lunch?"

"I can't leave these guys in here with the personnel records and other confidential stuff. I know nobody would snoop, but if Gretchen or Chet found out, there'd be hell to pay."

"They both got bitch slapped pretty good at that meeting last night," Weber said. "Maybe they'll calm down for a while."

"Don't count on it. More than likely they're looking for somebody to take it out on, and I don't want it to be me."

"How about you all take a lunch break, then?"

"Jimmy, look at me. Look at Allison Reynolds over there, or Judy Pope, or Kallie Jo. Do you think any of us women are going to go traipsing off to a restaurant looking like this? We'd look like a swarm of girl hobos."

"Was it Shakespeare that said 'Vanity, thy name is woman' or something like that?" Weber asked with a laugh. "How about I give Sal at Mario's a call and have him send over some pizzas?"

"That would be nice," Leslie said. "We probably all need a break."

"I'll make the call," Weber told her. "In the meantime, you need to get that bandage changed on your hand. It's filthy."

***

Weber wasn't surprised when Salvatore Gattuccio refused to take his credit card over the phone.

"No sir, Sheriff Jimmy! Sal can't be there to help with the shoveling and the cleaning up of all that mess, but I can make sure those volunteers don't go hungry! I'll send over some pies, and some cannoli, too. It's on me. For my town."

A huge man with a jovial attitude, Sal had never met a stranger and was loved by everybody. He had grown up in the family business, learning to toss dough before he could ride a two wheeled bicycle, and when his parents retired and started spending more and more of their time traveling in their motorhome, he had taken over the operation of the restaurant.

"Thank you, Sal. You're a good man."

"No, Sheriff Jimmy. *You're* the good man! Me? I just make pizzas."

"And damn fine pizzas," Weber added.

"You know what they say, Sheriff Jimmy, never trust a skinny cook! If they don't like their food, you're not going to like it either."

Weber laughed and hung up just as C.C. knocked on his office door.

"Got a minute, Sheriff?"

He waved her inside and asked, "Are you ever going to call me by my name?"

"Sorry. Old habits die hard. I learned early on in this business that a woman has to maintain a professional distance or there are men who will think she's weak or easy."

"We're not all like Gordon Hahn," Weber told her.

"I know that. I really do. And after I dropped my drawers for you in broad daylight and you didn't try to take advantage, I know you're one of the good guys."

Weber colored slightly at the memory, but took the teasing well.

"Hey lady, I was just tending to your wound. I'm a professional too, you know."

C.C. laughed, then added, "Besides I'd have kicked your ass, and when Robyn found out why you had a black eye and a busted nose, she'd have kicked your ass all over again."

"So maybe I'm not as chivalrous as you think I am," he said. "Maybe I just don't like to get beat up by women."

"Oh, there are places I could go with that line," C.C. chortled, "But I'm a lady."

"A kick ass lady," Weber said.

"Anyway, *Jimmy*, I got a call from our lab on that gas can we found at your parents' place. They were actually able to get a couple of partial fingerprints from it and they're e-mailing them to me. They also found some other biological matter."

"Biological matter? What does that mean?"

"Some kind of bodily fluid. They're sending it to the state crime lab for analysis. They have access to technology that's even better than ours."

"As soon as you get those prints bring them to me," Weber said.

"I should have them any minute, Sher.... Jimmy."

He smiled and said, "That's more like it."

***

"Sorry," Robyn said an hour later, rolling her chair back from her desk. "I didn't get a hit on the prints."

"It was worth a try," Weber said. "I wonder if Parks can do any better with the FBI's fingerprint system."

"Admit it. You just want to hang out in his office so you can fart and tell dirty jokes," Robyn said.

Judy Troutman knocked on his office door. "I'm sorry Sheriff. I got busy fielding calls from people wanting to help out with the cleanup and others calling to ask about the latest fire and I forgot all about this. A fellow dropped this off this morning," she said, handing him an envelope. "He said it was for your eyes only."

"Who was he?" Weber asked, looking at the white business sized envelope. His name was written on the front, but there was nothing to indicate who it had come from.

"I'm not sure," Judy said. "He looked vaguely familiar, but I can't place him. Really skinny, looked like death warmed over, to be honest. Yellow looking skin and he was breathing hard, but not like he had been running or anything. Like somebody who had been really sick for a long time."

Weber used a letter opener with a stag horn handle to slit the envelope open and pulled out a single sheet of lined yellow notebook paper with a note written in blue ink:

Sheriff Weber,

I've fought as long as I was able to but I've come to the end of my rope. Afraid I'm leaving a mess for you to clean up and I apologize for that. Don't bring that lady deputy with you. She shouldn't have to see it. I'm sorry you're going to have to.

Jake Gibbons

Chapter 37

They saw the smoke a mile away when they topped out and started to drop down into the valley where the Gibbons ranch had stood for over a hundred years.

"He did it," Weber said grimly.

Beside him, Chad cursed, then reached for the microphone on the dashboard and called the dispatcher.

"This is Big Lake Three. We need extra units and the fire department at the Gibbons Ranch. Tell them to send everything they have. We're going to need an ambulance, too."

When Judy acknowledged his call, he hung the microphone back up.

"When was the last time you saw Jake?"

"It's been over a month," Weber said. "I bumped into him coming out of the Town Office. He was looking pretty bad then. He was using one of those portable oxygen tanks and looked like he was on his last legs. I kept meaning to get out and pay him a call but you know how it is. I'd get busy with other stuff and forget, damn it."

"Don't beat yourself up over this, Jimmy. I think we all knew it was going to come to this eventually."

Weber knew Chad was right, but it didn't ease his guilt or make what they had to do any easier. They turned off the county road and bumped over the cattle guard and soon turned in under the metal pole sign that stood at the entrance to the ranch. The house was three hundred yards down the dirt road, flames pouring through the roof when Weber stopped the Explorer. The big barn, a shop, and several other buildings were all burning as well. There was a white, dual wheel crew cab pickup in the yard, and a couple of derelict vehicles sitting off to the side, slowly rusting into the ground.

Climbing out of the vehicle, Weber looked toward Chad, who shook his head. "Jake?" Weber shouted, knowing that nobody would answer him. "Let's take a look around."

They found the old rancher sprawled out under an oak tree in the back yard, a Smith and Wesson .44 magnum revolver next to his right hand.

***

"Who was he?" C.C. asked as the ambulance drove silently out of the ranch road with Jake's body in the back.

"Jake Gibbons," Weber said,

"What's his story? Any idea why he did this?"

"Jake and his twin brother Sam were good, hardworking men. Third generation ranchers, hanging on by the skin of their teeth since the day they were born, just like every small rancher I've ever known. Fighting the weather and the bank every season just to keep afloat, selling a few cattle every year to keep the tax people at bay, guiding hunters, whatever it takes just to hang on. And still getting a little further behind every year."

"Where's the brother?"

"In prison."

"I thought you said they were good men."

"They are, or were," Weber told her. "But a lifetime of working your fingers to the bone and beating your head against the wall year after year and not getting anywhere can twist a man all up in his head."

"You sound like you know that life well."

"I did. My father was one of them. And his father before him. I watched them both work and worry themselves to death and I swore I'd never be like them. I loved them and I respected them to the moon and back, but I couldn't live that life."

Chad walked up with a cardboard file box in his hands. "We found this in Jake's pickup," he said. There was another piece of yellow notebook paper taped to the lid that said Family Papers in the same handwriting as the letter Jake had delivered to the Sheriff's Office.

"Just put it in my vehicle," Weber said, then asked, "You okay, Chad?"

The older deputy shook his head. "I grew up with Jake and Sam. They deserved more than this, Jimmy. A hell of a lot more."

"I know," Weber said. "They damned sure did."

"What do you think led him to this today?" C.C. asked. "What was the final straw?"

"The bank was about to foreclose on the family ranch, and Jake had cancer and couldn't afford health insurance. It was getting worse, and I think it was just like his note said. He finally came to the end of his rope."

"He was a veteran," Chad said. "I tried to talk him into going to the VA hospital over in Prescott, even offered to drive him there myself, but he wouldn't go. Said no Gibbons ever took charity and he wasn't going to be the first."

"If he was a veteran he earned it," C.C. said. "It wouldn't have been charity."

"No, it wouldn't," Weber agreed. "But for a guy like Jake, wasting away in some hospital bed wasn't the way he would want to go out. He grew up on this land and he wanted to die on it. I can't say as I blame him."

"I hate to say this, but you know some people are going to say that these weren't the first fires Jake set," Chad said.

"I know it," Weber told him. "Could he have been behind all of these, C.C.?"

"You guys knew him better than I did," she replied. "What do you think?"

"I don't want to believe it," Weber said. "But I learned a while back that you never really know what goes on in somebody's head, no matter how well you think you know them."

Chapter 38

Chad's prediction that many people in Big Lake would blame Jake Gibbons for the arson fires that had made them live in fear for nearly three weeks was quick to come true. The fires ended with the rancher's suicide, and the whole community seemed to heave a collective sigh of relief as they began to relax and once again sleep soundly at night.

Of course, there were a few who could not accept the obvious and looked for a conspiracy under every rock.

"I'm telling you, it was those kids," Dale Burglehaus insisted to the regular group as they drank coffee at the bakery. "Their rich daddy bribed somebody to blame it on poor Jake to get that kid of theirs off."

"I swear, Dale, you're getting dumber every day," Ray McDermont said. "I don't know if you're getting senile or you're growing those magic mushrooms in your basement, but whatever it is, that don't make no sense at all. That kid got arrested, didn't he?"

"Yeah. And now he's out on bail. And you know how Harold Ryman is with kids. He'll get a slap on the wrist and that's it. He should get fifty years as far as I'm concerned. And that dad of his? He should do some jail time, too. Who doesn't know when his kids are slipping out and getting into mischief in the middle of the night?"

"Well hell, Dale, ain't that why you and Shelly had to get married in such a hurry back when we was in high school?" Kevin Sharp asked, drawing a laugh from the crowd.

Burglehaus shook his head. "How the hell should I remember? It's been over forty years. But I'll tell you what. If that's the truth, my old man should have done some jail time, too, 'cause I'm servin' a life sentence!"

There was more laughter, and Ray McDermont slapped the table so hard he spilled his coffee.

***

The outcome of the fire investigation was also talked about at the Sheriff's Office.

"Jake Gibbons. I never would have believed it," Dolan Reed said. "I guess we'll never know what goes on in somebody's mind when their back's to the wall and they can't see any way out."

"I was going through that box he left in his truck," Weber said. "He'd already sold off the last of his livestock and all it bought him was an extra couple of months. But he was already so far behind that the end was inevitable. The bank had foreclosed and there was a letter telling him he had 30 days to vacate the ranch. And the IRS had liens against the property, too. I guess torching the house and outbuildings was his last act of defiance."

"But why set all those other fires?" Robyn asked. "What did those people do to him? And you guys were on good terms, Jimmy. Why would he burn your parents place? Or the courthouse?"

"Who knows? Maybe as the cancer spread it was invading his brain or something," Weber said. "I've heard of things like that changing somebody's personality completely."

"Maybe so," Dolan said. "But it's a terrible legacy for a good man like that to leave, if you ask me."

***

The Glissman family had closed up their summer rental early and gone home to bury their son in Tucson, and six weeks later Albert and Paige Glissman dutifully delivered another son to Judge Ryman's courtroom. Tyler was defiant, still claiming that everything had been his brother's fault, that he was no more than an innocent pawn in Ricky's evil schemes. From the look on his parents' faces, they were as disgusted with the boy's refusal to take any responsibility for his actions as the judge was.

After two days of testimony, during which the attorney defending him could do no more than to plead leniency based upon his client's youth, the judge sentenced Tyler to a blended sentence, which meant that the boy would start his confinement in a juvenile detention facility for the next seven months, until he reached the age of 18, at which time he would be transferred to the adult division of the Department of Corrections until he reached the age of 21.

"Under other circumstances I would be inclined to send you to Juvie until you turn eighteen and then intensive probation for the next three years, but your total refusal to accept any responsibility for your crimes and your brother's unfortunate death dismay me. They tell me that you need a wake up call, young man," the judge said as he passed sentence.

Finally Tyler showed remorse, but it was not for his actions or the loss of Ricky. Rather it was only for the situation he suddenly found himself in when the realization hit home that he was not going to walk away from what he had done without looking back.

"Mom, Dad, do something! They can't do this to me. It's not fair!"

"We love you, Tyler," his mother said, dissolving in tears.

"If you love me you'd make them stop. I want to go home."

Paige reached out her arms to comfort her son, but Tyler pushed her roughly away and made a run for the door. He hadn't gone a dozen feet before Dan Wright, showing why he had been a star on his small college's football team, quickly took him to the floor.

Coop ushered his crying parents out a side door as Tyler cursed and struggled in vain in the deputy's strong grasp.

***

Weber couldn't seem to let go of the contrast between the way the hardworking rancher he had known had lived and the crimes Jake Gibbons had committed at the end of his life. The man's suicide itself had not surprised him. Months earlier he had come upon Jake sitting in his truck one evening, a Winchester carbine beside him. The two of them had talked about life, about how the community they had known was changing so rapidly, about the crimes their respective siblings had committed, and Jake's illness. Weber had asked Jake then if he was thinking about ending his life, and he had told the sheriff that it might come to that at some point.

Like many people who had grown up in their time and place, Weber believed that a person should have the right to die with dignity, and wished that society would have made it possible for someone like Jake to end his life with a combination of prescribed medication instead of a bullet.

But no matter how many times he looked at the case from every angle, Robyn's words stuck in his mind. He could understand Jake burning his home and barns to deny some faceless banking corporation or government bureaucrat from ever entering them, but why Tom

Cotter's shed, or the old barn on the Mayer place, or the cabin on Beaver Creek Road, or the Weber family home?

"I can tell you why he may have set that there fire to the records building," Kallie Jo said as she served her promised dinner of southern fried chicken with "all the fixins.'"

"Why?" Weber asked, wondering how Kallie Jo could have any information about Jake Gibbons' crimes.

"Well, when we was all in there cleanin' up after that fire there was a bunch of past due electric bills that he had, and one of them there notices that they was cuttin' his power off. I think he was mad at the town for doin' that to him and it was his way of gittin' back at 'em."

"Do you suppose that was what finally pushed him over the edge?" Robyn asked.

"I don't know. I probably shouldn't even have said that since we had to swear that whatever we saw in there weren't to be talked about, it bein' confidential and all. 'Course, we didn't have to put our hand on no Bible like you do in court or anything like that. I guess it was more like one of them there pinkie swears like my sister Sarah Beth and my cousin Audrey and me used to make to keep a secret like that time we stole some of Uncle Wayne's Pall Mall cigarettes. Uncle Wayne is Audrey's daddy, the one I told you about that broke his back? Well anyway, we snuck off to this old shed there on Uncle Wayne's place and we smoked them there cigarettes, but first we all made a pinkie swear that we wouldn't tell a soul about it." Kallie Jo laughed and said, "Ya'll should have seen us. We was three sick little girls, I'll tell you what! And when Aunt Thelma, that's Audrey's mama, when she saw how sick we was she didn't even have to ask what we'd been up to 'cause she knew. I was sure we'd get a wuppin' for that, but no sir. All she did was tell us we should be grateful we hadn't tried any of grandpappy's chewin' tobacco."

Kallie Jo passed Weber a bowl and said, "Them's black eyed peas, but don't worry, they ain't really got no eyes. Can you imagine if vegetables did have eyes? No sir, I wouldn't like that at all. Archer took me to dinner at the Roundup one time and the fella at the table next to us had a trout on his plate and that thing still had its head on it!" She shuddered but before anybody could say anything she continued, "Now potatoes do have eyes. 'Course they ain't eyes like you and me have, or that there fish on that man's plate, they's really sprouts. I asked Mama one time why they called them eyes if they's really sprouts and she said the same reason they call it catsup but it ain't really made from cats. My mama, she's a hoot. If you ask her a question you can pretty well 'spect to get an answer like that. I remember one time I asked her how peanuts got their name and you don't even want to know what she told me about that!"

By then Weber had forgotten where the conversation had started, but biting into one of her golden crispy chicken breasts, Weber had to admit that for all of her nonstop talking, Kallie Jo Wingate was a damn fine cook.

***

They were holding hands as Weber drove back to his cabin, comfortably full from their meal and too relaxed for much conversation. When Weber got to the turnoff to his cabin, Robyn said, "Keep driving."

"Where to?"

"Just keep driving."

A few moments later she squeezed his hand and said, "Pull in here."

"Here?"

"Yes, here. And shut off the engine."

They sat for a moment in silence, then Robyn got out of the Explorer. Weber followed and stood beside her. A full moon provided plenty of light, and Robyn leaned back against him as he wrapped his arms around her waist.

"How does it feel to you now, Jimmy?"

"What do you mean?"

"You know, your fear of this place or whatever it was that made it impossible for you to be here after Debbie and everything."

"It's okay. I can't explain it but the fire seemed to be some sort of spiritual cleansing for me. Does that make any sense?"

"Maybe *you* should have burned it down a long time ago."

"Maybe so," he said.

"What does it feel like here?"

"I said it's okay."

"No, Jimmy, what does it *feel* like?"

"I'm not following you, Robyn. What *should* it feel like?"

"Does it feel like home?"

"It hasn't been home to me in a long time, Robyn."

"But *could* it be, Jimmy?" Robyn asked, turning to him. "Could it be home again?"

"I've got a house."

"You've got a house, Jimmy. I'm talking about a home. A home for both of us."

"What are you saying, Robyn?"

"A while back you asked me to marry you and I said it wasn't the right time."

"Is it the right time now?"

"It's getting closer to the right time."

"I'm ready whenever you are, baby."

"Where would we live, Jimmy? My place is pretty small and I can't see myself being a second roomie with Parks at your cabin. But what if we built *our* place? What if we built it right here, Jimmy? Could you live here again?"

"Robyn, I could live in a cardboard box under a bridge as long as I was with you."

"I think I want something more substantial than a cardboard box."

"You tell me what you want and I'll build it," he said.

She took his hand and led him away from the road. Stopping at the small gazebo he had helped his father build years ago, she put her arms around him and kissed him passionately, then started unbuttoning her shirt.

"Robyn, what are you doing?"

"Take your clothes off, Jimmy."

"Here? Now?"

"Yes. I want to break in our new home."

Chapter 39

"Oh yeah, Jake was way behind on his electric bill," Leslie said. "I'll be honest with you Jimmy, I kind of broke the rules by not sending the co-op a shutoff notice before he got so far behind. But I knew he was having a hard time and I gave him some extra leeway. More than I should have."

"Nobody's going to fault you for that," Weber said.

"Well Chet might if he ever finds out. He'd probably make me dock my own paycheck to pay it back."

"I think Chet's skating on thin ice with all that's happened. I hear the Town Council approved the purchase of a complete new state of the art computer system for you. And they're finally going to install a sprinkling system in the records warehouse and rewire the whole place to code, like they should have done years ago."

"They did and they are. And when Frank Gauger recommended that I get a $1,000 bonus for all of the extra hours I've been putting in trying to salvage what records I could and get them organized, Chet didn't even object. But the look on his face sure was priceless. I think he about bit his tongue in half trying not to say anything."

"So what are you going to do with your windfall? Go sit on a beach somewhere and sip piña coladas delivered by a hunky waiter named Raúl? Maybe you'll get lucky."

Leslie snorted and said, "Yeah, right. No, I think I'll stay closer to home and take it to the casino. I'd rather try to get lucky there and save the airplane fare."

"When did you finally have to have the co-op cut off juice to Jake's place?" Weber asked her.

"The Monday of the fire here. Which mean's they'd have cut it off on Tuesday. I guess that's why he finally cracked. I have to tell you, Jimmy, I feel really bad about that. Maybe if I would have figured out some way to...."

"Hey, don't blame yourself," Weber told her. "It sucks all the way around but you had to do your job."

She wiped a tear from her eye and said, "I know, but I feel so responsible."

"Don't" Weber said, shaking his head. "Jake was a good man caught in a bad situation. He didn't cause it, and you didn't either. Sometimes life just deals us a bad hand to start with and it doesn't get any better as time goes by."

"I know, but I felt so bad for him."

"Jake was living on borrowed time," Weber said. "If this hadn't been what pushed him over the edge something else would have."

"I guess he just snapped there at the end," Leslie said. "He'd always been such a nice man, but when his electric got cut off he called and was cussing me out and saying how the whole system was rigged against him from the start. I tried to talk to him, to calm him down, but he just kept screaming at me. I finally had to hang up on him. I just couldn't take it any more. Maybe if I hadn't, he might not have burned the courthouse and shot himself. I just feel like I let him down, Jimmy."

She started crying again, and Weber walked around the counter and held her, offering what words of comfort he could. He had his own feelings of remorse to deal with. He remembered their last meeting and how frail the man had been. Weber had promised he'd stop by the ranch for a visit but never made it. But even in his guilt, he knew that neither his failure to follow through on that promise nor Leslie's actions were the reasons Jake Gibbons had done the things he did. In the end, all of society had let him down.

***

As summer began to draw to a close things returned to normal in Big Lake. Talk of the fires had stopped as the incidents became no more than an unpleasant memory and people had other things to occupy their minds, including the upcoming Pioneer Day celebration and the anticipation of a slower pace as the summer visitors closed up their cabins for the season. Of course, it would be a short lived break; as soon as the snow started to fall there would be a new influx of flatlanders as the ski bums and bunnies started showing up, filling the slopes at the ski lodge and Big Lakes restaurants and shops.

Weber couldn't shake his feeling of malaise, and it wasn't improved any when a package containing a plastic box was delivered to him at the Sheriff's Office. He sat it on top of the gun safe in his private office and didn't say a word.

"What's in it?" Parks had asked. "Contraband Cuban cigars? Kinky porn CDs about farmer's daughters? You're holding out on me, Bubba, and that's not right."

Weber's visits to Molly Bateson, the psychiatrist he had been seeing in Springerville in the wake of the shooting of Steve Rafferty, had decreased as he had learned to deal with the emotional repercussions of the event, but he had called her one morning and said, "I need to see you."

***

There were only three women in the world that Weber knew he could trust with anything; Robyn, Mary Caitlin, and Molly. Each filled a need in him that nobody else could. He was in love with Robyn, and though their relationship had its complications, he was totally devoted to her and he knew that she was to him. Mary and her husband Pete had been almost surrogate parents to Weber and his sister Debbie after their own parents had died. He treasured her common sense approach to life and knew that she'd walk through fire for him. But Molly was the one who knew how to ask the hard questions at the right times and make him search for the answers inside himself, even when those answers were truths he didn't want to admit.

"So what's eating you, Jimmy?" Molly asked as she sat in her rocking chair and knitted. Weber wasn't sure if the knitting was something she did on a constant basis or a tool she used to put her patients at ease and make their visits seem more like a friendly chat, but it worked.

"If I knew that, I wouldn't be here, Molly."

"You mean you don't just show up because you're attracted by my animal magnetism and witty banter?"

Weber smiled and shook his head, but didn't reply.

"Are things okay with Robyn?"

"They're good. No complaints there."

"Still having nightmares about her getting shot?"

"Not about that."

"Steve?"

"Sometimes. We had another young kid that got killed in a wreck. I dreamed about him, too."

"You've seen a lot of people that died in wrecks and don't have nightmares about them, Jimmy. Why this kid?"

"I don't know."

"Sure you do."

"I don't, Molly."

She didn't reply, just looked at him from under arched eyebrows as she continued to knit.

"You know, I know that trick," Weber told her. "I use it in interrogations too."

"Is this an interrogation, Jimmy?"

"Sometimes it feels like it."

"And yet you come back."

Molly continued to knit, the only sounds the clicking of her needles, the occasional squeak of her chair as she rocked, and the ticking of a clock somewhere.

Finally Weber said, "I don't know why I dreamed about the kid. Maybe because he was the same age as Steve Rafferty and a troublemaker, too? Maybe he just reminded me of Steve?"

"Maybe. Is that what's bothering you? That another young man is gone? Another troublemaker?"

Weber thought about it for a minute, then said, "No. That's not it. I'm sorry they're both dead, but they both made the choices that led to it."

"So what is it, Jimmy?"

"I don't..."

"Bullshit. You know."

"Is this what I drive all the way over here and pay you for, Molly?"

"Well, I'm fresh out of brownies and I don't have the hips to give you a lap dance, so that must be it."

Neither of them said anything for a while, and then Weber shook his head. "My head's just still screwed up about Jake Gibbons."

"The man that shot himself?"

"Yeah."

"It's not uncommon to be angry at somebody we care about who dies, Jimmy, whether it was due to illness, accident, or in Jake's case, suicide. It's okay to be mad or feel betrayed. The dead don't mind."

"It wasn't like we were good friends. I mean, I knew the man and I respected him. I even liked him as far as that goes. But it wasn't like we were fishing buddies or anything like that."

"And yet his death angers you. Why is that, Jimmy?"

"I don't know. I think maybe he was the last of the real ranchers I knew. He wasn't as old as my dad, but they were cut from the same cloth. Good men that worked and worked and never saw daylight at the end of the tunnel. And they both died too soon and deserved better than they ever got."

"Jimmy, your dad died in a car accident. You know better than most people that accidents happen."

"Yeah, but…. okay, you're right, with my folks it was an accident. Accidents happen, I understand that. But Jake… damn it, Molly, there should have been a way to help him. He was a good man! Why didn't somebody step in and do something?"

"Like you, Jimmy?"

"Like anybody. We all just went on with our lives while his was becoming a train wreck and none of us lifted a finger to help him."

"What could you have done, Jimmy? Could you afford to pay his taxes? Pick up the tab for his medical bills? Handcuff him and haul him off to a hospital against his will?"

"No, but…."

"But what, Jimmy?"

"But he deserves to be remembered as more than a bitter old man running around setting fires. Maybe if I would have caught him sooner things might have turned out differently."

"Differently how? He'd have still had cancer, and he'd have still been drowning in debt."

"I don't know, Molly. I just hate to think of him doing all of that. The man I knew wasn't like that. He wasn't hateful, he wasn't destructive."

"Sometimes illness and desperation can change a person," she said.

"But what was the point, Molly? Why did he do all of it? C.C., the Fire Marshal who was up here working the case with us, said that when people set fires they have a reason. To get back at somebody, to cover up something, to make a statement, maybe just for a thrill."

"And?"

"And none of that fits with Jake."

"You don't think he was getting back at the town by setting fire to the courtroom?"

"Okay, maybe so in that case, though it still doesn't sound like the man I knew. But why burn that shed? Or the barn, or the cabin? I've even thought maybe he burned my parents place because I had dropped the ball by not visiting like I said I would, but that still didn't fit the man he was. If anybody had respect for a man's home it was Jake, the way he hung on so hard to his family place right to the end. And that still doesn't explain those other fires. I have to know why he did it, Molly. I can't rest until I do."

"Okay, so why are you sitting here? Go find out."

"How do I do that? The man's dead, I can't ask him."

"What, you think just because somebody dies they can't still tell you anything?"

"I'm a cop, Molly, not a psychic."

"That's right, Jimmy, you're a cop and crimes have been committed. Knowing *who* committed them doesn't matter unless you know why. Maybe you'll feel better when you solve them."

Chapter 40

"Who's your buddy?" Mary Caitlin asked the next morning as she set Weber's coffee cup and a stack of telephone messages on his desk the next morning.

"Really? We're going to do this again?"

There was mischief in Mary's eyes but she shook her head. "Uh uh, wrong answer."

"If you think a cup of coffee and some sweet talk's going to get me to return all of these calls, you're wrong," Weber said, flipping through the pink message slips and throwing most of them in the wastebasket next to his desk.

Instead of chastising him like she normally did, Marry just stood there grinning at him.

"You're not going away, are you?"

Mary folded her hands and remained silent.

"Okay, you're my buddy, Mary."

"And who's the smartest, sexiest woman you know?"

"If I say Robyn I might get laid and if I say C.C. Callahan I might get shot. What have *you* got for me?"

Mary turned and headed for the door, saying, "Never mind, I'll just keep it to myself."

"Okay. You win, Mary. You're the smartest, sexiest woman I know."

She stopped but didn't turn around. "How do I know you really mean that?"

"Because when I watch *Jeopardy* on TV I want to call you when the hard questions come up, and sometimes late at night I call your name."

Mary turned around with a big smile and said, "That's better." She sashayed back to his desk, parked a hip on the edge and said, "Darron Tovar is history."

"Really? Did Steve Harper run him over with his new fire truck?"

"Nope, his aunt cut him off and he skipped town. Didn't even pay the last month's rent on his office or the place that was printing his rag over in Gallup."

"What happened?"

"Gretchen was footing the bill for his paper until he got it off the ground and he kept telling her about all of this advertising money he had that would be coming in, but he was blowing it as fast as he got it. He traded his minivan for a fancy Dodge Charger, and then he moved his girlfriend over from Prescott to live with him. I think Gretchen could have tolerated the money thing, but living in sin with some bimbo with a tramp stamp tattoo who smoked? Apparently Gretchen went over to his apartment to talk about the money and walked in on them while they were doing the nasty and was understandably scandalized. Once she got over her hysterics, she told him the young lady had to go or else, and young mister Tovar let the wrong head answer for him. The last anybody saw of him, that pretty red Charger was loaded down with everything he and the girlfriend could cram into it and was headed out of town."

Weber laughed and said, "I'd have given a hundred dollars to have been a fly on the wall to see that go down!"

"You're just sorry that you missed seeing that girl naked," Mary said.

"Well, if Gretchen needs somebody to help her work through her trauma, I can give her the name of a good shrink over in Springerville," Weber told her.

***

"I wish I could turn back the clock," Joyce Taylor said wistfully. "I actually dated Jake years ago. I was a sophomore and he was a senior and I thought he was the handsomest boy in school. But my dad said he was too old for me, and that I deserved more out of life than to be a poor rancher's wife. Sometimes I flatter myself by thinking that that's why he never got married. And I have to admit, Jimmy, Eva Gibbons was a good friend of mine back in school. I saw what a lifetime of too much work and too little money did to her. I know she loved Sam and that he loved her. But my dad was right. It wasn't the life for me."

The Timber Savings Bank manager was a short, plump woman in her late 40s with dyed brown, shoulder length hair and sensible makeup. She was a good businesswoman and a good judge of character. And while the life of a rancher's wife may not have been right for her, she drew the line at ever leaving her small White Mountain hometown. More than once the large corporation that owned the bank had offered her the opportunity for a transfer to Phoenix and advancement, but she was happy where she was in life. She had a nice house and a good family and wasn't willing to trade them for the rat race a promotion would throw her into.

"When was the last time you saw Jake?" Weber asked her.

"He was in here on the Monday of the week when he… when he died." She wiped away a tear and said, "He had gotten the final notice of foreclosure on the ranch and he came in to tell me that he'd be gone by the end of the month. He wanted me to know that he wasn't mad at me and thanked me for all of the extensions I had given him. Oh damn it, Jimmy, I tried, I really tried. But the board down in Phoenix, they don't know these people like I do. To them they're not even people, they're just *accounts*! They don't see the blood, sweat and tears that generations have put into their land."

Her voice broke and she looked away. Weber gave her time to compose herself, then asked, "How was Jake that day, Joyce?"

"If I had to sum it up in a single word? Defeated. He'd given up, Jimmy. I think I knew deep down inside what he was going to do. Not the fire at the courtroom, but that he was going to end his life. I wish I would have said something, done something."

"What could you have done, Joyce? Somebody asked me that same thing the other day. I realized that there wasn't anything I could have done to change the way things ended, and neither could you."

"Ted and I were talking about that on Sunday. He said Jake had always been such a good guy when we were in school and had always treated the younger guys well, not picking on them like some of the upperclassmen did. That was Jake. He never had a bad word to say about anybody. Ted said if nothing else, we could have brought Jake to town, and moved him into our spare bedroom. At least then he wouldn't have had to die out there, all alone."

Ted Taylor, a bald round man known affectionately as T.T., owned a radiator repair shop and was one of the nicest people Weber had ever known. At hearing the kindness he would have extended to his wife's former boyfriend, Weber's already high admiration for the man increased even more.

"You said Jake was defeated. Was he upset, angry, what?"

"Like I said, defeated. Just resigned to his fate. But no, he wasn't upset or angry or anything like that. I don't think Jake ever had an angry day in his life. And if he did, he never showed it. Even back in high school when my dad made me break up with him, he just hugged me and said he understood and that he wanted the best for me. He was always a gentleman. As weak as he was that last time he was in here, barely able to stand up and towing that oxygen bottle on its little wheels, he tipped his hat and wouldn't sit down until I did. He was a gentleman to the very end."

***

"Here's the way I see it," Parks said as he and Weber stood looking at what was left of the old barn. "This Gibbons fellow wasn't himself for whatever reason. Maybe because of the cancer, maybe because he saw his brother go to prison, maybe because he was just fed up, whatever. So he lashed out. It didn't matter who he was mad at, he just wanted to strike back at *somebody*. But at the same time, he had this basic goodness built into him. That's what you admired about him, Jimmy. He didn't want to actually hurt anybody, not physically at least. That's why he picked empty places."

"But if you knew you only had weeks or maybe months to live, is that how you'd want to spend the rest of your time, running around starting fires?" Weber asked.

"Not me," Parks replied. "I'd steal all of your credit cards and run off to Mexico and get myself half a dozen hookers, a couple of gallons of Wesson oil, and go out with a bang."

"You don't have to worry about it ever getting that far," Weber assured him. "If you sneeze twice in the same day I'm planning on shooting you to put you out of your misery."

They were quiet for a minute, then Parks said, "Hey Jimmy, you keep asking why Gibbons did what he did. Maybe it wasn't about the fires. Maybe they were just a means to an end."

"What do you mean?"

"What if he set the fires hoping to get caught?"

"If Jake didn't want to die in a hospital bed, he damn sure didn't want to do it in a prison hospital bed."

"No, but maybe he wanted somebody else to save him the trouble of pulling that trigger like he finally did."

"Suicide by cop?"

"It happens."

"But why not just get stopped for a traffic violation and jump out with a gun? Or walk in front of a logging truck?"

"Don't ask me," Parks said. "I'm still holding out for those hookers and that Wesson oil."

Chapter 41

"Tonight we want to honor some special people," Councilman Kirby Templeton said at the weekly Town Council meeting. "People who have gone the extra mile and then some to make our community a better place to live. Two of them are Town employees and the rest are volunteers, citizens who see a need and respond to it without hesitation because that's the kind of people we have here in Big Lake. It's the reason I love calling this place home."

After applause from the audience that packed the room, he called Leslie Stokes to the front and told the crowd how the dedicated Town Clerk had put in nearly as many extra hours as she worked on her regular schedule to salvage as many as the Town records as she could in the wake of the fire, and was now tackling the brand new computer system that had replaced the antiquated equipment she had been struggling with for so long.

"Leslie, we could never afford to pay you for everything you have done, and continue to do for us, but the Town Council and your fellow citizens hope this Certificate of Appreciation and $1,000 bonus check will be some small compensation."

Not comfortable in front of an audience, Leslie thanked Templeton, waved to the crowd and sat back down quickly to a long round of applause.

"The next people we want to recognize are Chief Steve Harper and the volunteers of the Big Lake Fire Department," Templeton said and was met with even louder and longer applause, along with foot stomping and some cheers from the audience as Harper and his men walked to the front of the room.

"I can't say enough good about these gentlemen," Templeton said. "All of them except the Chief are volunteers, but they drop whatever they're doing and come running when an alarm goes out. They leave their jobs, their family dinner tables, their kids' softball games. I've even known them to get up out of their sickbeds because somebody's in trouble and needs help. And it's not just the emergencies they respond to. They put in hundreds of hours training every year. Let's give them all, and their hardworking Chief, a big hand."

When the thunderous applause finally died down, Templeton said, "Chief, the bad news is that you don't get a bonus, too. But you did get a new fire truck!" Laughter and more applause followed, and then Templeton added, "But we do have Certificates of Appreciation for every one of you, and I hope that the respect and admiration of your fellow citizens will let you all know just how important you are to us."

After the firemen sat down to yet another round of applause, Templeton called forward the 25 volunteers who had assisted Leslie in the cleanup and reorganization of what was left of the Town records after the fire and presented them each with their own Certificates of Appreciation.

It was one of the most pleasant Town Council meetings Weber had ever attended and he hoped the evening would end on a high note, but afterward, as Paul Lewis was lining up Leslie, the firemen, and the cleanup volunteers for photographs for the newspaper, he was accosted on his way out the door.

"Sheriff Weber, what are you doing still wasting time on those fire investigations?" Mayor Wingate demanded.

"Who says I am?" Weber asked.

"It's all over town," the mayor said. "People are asking why you're still stirring up all that dirt?"

"I guess technically I'm stirring up ashes," Weber said.

"This town doesn't pay you to be a comedian," Councilwoman Gretchen Smith-Abbot said.

"Do they earn more than newspaper publishers?" Weber asked. "Because I hear there's an opening for one. I could submit a new resume."

The councilwoman's face colored but her only response was to purse her lips with disapproval.

"Look," Weber said, "I just need to know why Jake Gibbons did what he did. It was so out of character for him. I can't wrap my head around it."

"He did what he did because he was a crazy, spiteful man. A failure who wanted to blame everything and everybody else for his problems. What's so hard to understand about that?"

Weber felt the need to defend Jake's memory but he knew that the mayor was only saying what everybody else in Big Lake was thinking.

Be that as it may, the sheriff still felt compelled to keep picking at the case like a scab that he wouldn't leave alone and allow to heal.

"All of it," Weber said. "It's all hard to understand. In spite of what everybody says, Jake wasn't crazy, he wasn't mean. He was…."

"It doesn't matter what he was. He's dead now. What do you think you're going to accomplish with any of this?" the mayor asked.

"I don't know, Chet. I'll tell you when I find out."

***

Weber had spent much of the morning at a Chamber of Commerce meeting where director Juliette Murdoch was explaining the benefits of a proposed Winter Carnival that would draw even more visitors than the ski crowd and the families who brought their children up from the desert on weekends to see snow and experience the wonders of sledding down a hill or building a snowman.

Juliette was describing the snowmobile parade, the kids' snowman contest, and other events the Carnival would include when his cell phone vibrated. He checked it, and seeing that the caller was C.C. Callahan, he excused himself and went outside to answer.

"Did you get a copy of the report from the crime lab on that gas can from your parents' house?"

"I don't know," he told her. "I've been in a meeting all morning."

"Check and call me back."

***

The report had arrived in a plain 9x12 inch manila envelope and almost got lost in the shuffle of everyday office mail, but Mary had spotted it and left it on Weber's desk. He opened the envelope and read through the report twice, not sure what he was seeing, then he called C.C. back.

"So what does all this mean? It's too technical for me to understand."

"It means be ready to buy me dinner tomorrow night. I'll be there in the morning."

Chapter 42

"I thought I wasn't supposed to be involved with the investigation of the fire here," Weber said the next morning when they pulled into the driveway of the old family home.

"And you always follow the rules, right Jimmy? Besides, it's a closed case, right? Everybody knows that rancher that killed himself was our perp."

"Yeah, about that. I don't buy it, C.C."

She was zipping her coveralls over what Weber could have only described as an amazing chest when she asked, "Why not?"

"That's the $64,000 question. I wish I could tell you," he said.

"Are you allowing your personal feelings for the man to cloud your judgment, Jimmy? Don't take this the wrong way, but when you were describing Jake Gibbons and your father and men like them, I felt like I detected a little bit of hero worship."

"I don't know, to be honest," he admitted. "I'd like to think I'm more of a professional than that but I really can't say. All of this, it just wasn't the man I knew."

"When I was growing up I loved dogs," C.C. told him. "We always had a couple of mutts, and I remember this one, Trixie. She was some kind of mixed breed my dad found on a street corner somewhere and dragged home. A real Heinz 57. Us kids would crawl all over her and dress her up and she'd never growl or show any impatience with us, no matter what we put her through. She was just a lovable old yellow dog. My dad was a softie for kids and dogs and when she was getting up there in years she got some kind of tumor. He really should have taken her to the vet to be put down sooner. It would have been the humane thing to do, but he loved that old dog and just kept hoping she'd somehow miraculously get better. I was about thirteen that winter, and when Daddy finally said it was time, I didn't want him to take her in. I was a selfish little girl and too young to understand that it really was the best thing for her. So I tried to stop him. I wrapped my arms around Trixie and wouldn't let go. We were both crying and Daddy was trying to get me to let go of her when the poor old dog couldn't take any more and bit me right here."

Weber had noticed the scar where C.C. pointed at her arm before, but had been too polite to ask her about it.

"I ended up getting stitches and that just added to my dad's guilt. Later, after he brought her home, I wouldn't go outside when he buried her in the back yard. I was hurt and I was so mad that she had bitten me when all I was trying to do was save her from taking that trip to the vet's. After he was done, Daddy came back inside and sat on my bed with me and he explained that Trixie had not meant to hurt me. That she was already in so much pain and that him and me wrestling over her was too much and she just lashed out. He told me that it didn't make her a bad dog and that I shouldn't let that last act of hers be the way I remembered her. Instead he said to remember all the good times and fun we had together."

"Your dad sounds like a hell of a man," Weber told her. "I think I'd be proud to know him."

"I think that's why I'm still single," she said. "I've never met a man that measured up to my dad, and I won't settle for less. He's a hard act to follow."

Weber thought about Jake Gibbons and the story C.C. had told him about her dog and found some comfort in her words. Maybe, just like Trixie, Jake was a sick man lashing out and his final acts should not negate the life he had lived and the memories of him in better times.

He hefted a big plastic case C.C. had brought with her and followed her into the wreckage that had once been his home.

***

"What are we doing here?" Weber asked as they stood in what had once been the dining room.

"You didn't read the report?"

"I read it, but I'm just a dumb old country boy. That thing had words in it that are longer than an afternoon stuck in an elevator with Chet Wingate. What does it mean?"

"I'm not buying that country bumpkin shit-kicker bullshit of yours for a minute," C.C. said. "But basically, what it means is that one side of the can, the side that was laying against the floor, had traces of human blood on it."

"Blood?"

She nodded and said, "And if I'm right, there's more here."

C.C. carefully walked from the dining room into the kitchen, stepping carefully to avoid the worst of the burned floor and studying every inch along the way. Near the back door, she stopped and said, "Bring me that case."

When Weber sat it down next to her, C.C. opened it and pulled out a cordless drill and reciprocating saw. Using the drill, she bored a hole in the floor and then inserted the saw blade and cut out a section where two boards joined side by side. She repeated the process several times in different places and then they went back outside.

"Look here," C.C. said, pulling the boards apart and turning them over. While the top of each was charred, the sides and bottoms were not.

"See that?" she pointed to dark stains on the edges of four of them. "That's blood. When our perp broke the window he cut himself and was bleeding pretty badly."

"Now what?"

"Now we send these to the state crime lab to see if they can get DNA from these bloodstains and if it matches any DNA they could get from the gas can. Did you say that Jake and his brother were identical twins?"

"Twins, but not identical. Sam was an inch or so taller and had a somewhat rounder face shape and his nose was bigger. You could tell they were brothers, but not identical."

"That would have made it easier, C.C. said, "Since identical twins share the same DNA. But it doesn't matter. All males have one Y-chromosome in each cell and that same chromosome is passed down from father to son in each generation. We could get a sample from his brother in prison and see if there is a familial match. It won't be a positive match to Jake, but it will show a link that will be pretty hard to refute unless there's a third brother running around here."

"They had a kid brother, but he was killed in a farm accident when they were all teenagers," Weber said.

"Damn, that guy couldn't buy a break, could he?"

"It sure doesn't seem like it."

"Do you think the brother would consent to DNA testing? Or will we need a court order for that, too?"

"Actually, I think that some convicted felons in Arizona are automatically subject to DNA testing," Weber told her. "But it may not come to that. Are we done here?"

"I guess," C.C, said. "I've got enough samples for the lab to test.

"Good, we need to get back to town and get cleaned up."

Chapter 43

Leslie looked up from her computer terminal and smiled when Weber walked in the next morning.

"Hi Jimmy, what's up?"

"How do you like your new computer system? A big change from that old clunker you fought with for so many years?"

"It's like night and day. If Chet Wingate wasn't such an ugly toad I'd kiss him for finally giving in and letting the Town Council spend the money. Right before I kicked his butt for making me put up with the junk I did for so long. This thing is so fast it's amazing."

"And now that you have both hands working again you can take advantage of that speed."

Leslie laughed and said, "Yep, good as new. At least as long as I don't do something stupid again."

"You got lucky. I remember when my dad got his hand slammed against a fence post trying to muscle a stubborn horse into the corral," Weber said. "His fingers never did work right again. On cold mornings he couldn't even button his shirt. My mom had to do it for him."

"Well, I'll stay away from horses, too," Leslie said with a chuckle as she wiggled her fingers. "I need these babies."

"Yes, you do. But I guess if worse came to worse you could get one of those dictation programs and talk to your computer."

"Nope, with my luck this is a male computer and you men never listen to a thing a woman says anyhow," Leslie said. "Besides, until they make a slot machine that responds to voice commands I'm still not out of the woods,"

"Do you think you'll ever get all of the old data transferred over?"

"I don't know," Leslie said, shaking her head ruefully. "It's going to take years to figure out what never did get saved to the old system and was lost in the fire that we'll never be able to recover."

"You don't have that much time left," Weber said.

"I don't think they're going to put me out to pasture yet, Jimmy. I'll get it done."

"No, but I don't think they'll let you take your computer to jail with you," Weber said. "Leslie Stokes, you're under arrest for arson, burglary, and embezzlement."

***

"Leslie Stokes? I'd have never believed it for a minute," Frank Gauger said over lunch at Sandy's Subs, Big Lake's newest restaurant. "She was always such a dedicated employee. I can't tell you how many times I'd drive by and see her in the office long after the business day was over. I kept saying we needed to upgrade that damn computer system and hire her some help but Chet wouldn't spend the money and Leslie was almost territorial about those files. I suggested getting a college intern one summer and she wouldn't have it. Said she had a system and didn't want anybody screwing it up."

"That's actually pretty classic behavior for an employee thief," Kirby Templeton said. "A couple years ago a fellow I know from the Arizona Pharmacy Association had a woman working for him at his place in Flagstaff. Kind of the same thing, she was always the first in the door in the morning and the last to leave at night. And whenever anyone started to check the inventory she'd say to go on home, she'd do it. Turned out she was stealing oxycodone and other pills both for herself and to sell on the street."

"I can't excuse it, but I guess when somebody has an addiction maybe they can't help it," Gauger said.

"Oh, Leslie has an addiction," Weber said. "But it isn't drugs. It's gambling. The security folks at the casino over at Hon-Dah said she was in there every payday and never left until she was broke. And she made regular trips to the casinos over in Laughlin, Nevada. She'd get lucky and win once in a while, but anyone can tell you that gamblers always lose more than they win in the long run. Before it was over she had taken out a second mortgage on her house, maxed out all of her credit cards, and had pawned her TV, stereo, and anything else of value she could get her hands on, just to feed it all into a slot machine."

"And when she ran out of her own money, she started stealing." Gauger shook his head in disbelief.

"We made it easy for her," Weber said. "That old computer system *was* on its last legs and Leslie complained often enough to make us all aware of it. So it was simple enough to not enter a payment for a traffic ticket or a utility bill when somebody paid in cash and put that money in her pocket. If somebody got a past due notice and came in to complain she'd go find the hard copy of the receipt that she had given them, blame it on the computer and enter the payment, then make it up out of the next money she skimmed. She just kept getting in deeper and deeper, hoping she'd have that one big win and make it all better. When it got too bad, she realized that sooner or later somebody was going to figure it all out so she started setting those fires, all of them leading up to the big one in the records room. She figured that between the problems with the computer and burning up a big chunk of the records, enough would be lost that she could cover it up."

"But those two brothers did set fire to Max Woodbury's truck and to that house where the boy saw them?"

"Yeah. They were copycats. They heard about the fires at Tom Cotter's shed and that old barn and thought it would be fun to set some of their own. All it did was muddy the water for a while."

"And we were all blaming poor Jake Gibbons. That's a damn shame."

"Yes it was, Kirby. It was so out of character for Jake. That's why I couldn't buy it. But for Leslie it made it even better when he torched his place to keep the bank from having it before he shot himself."

"That breaks my heart," Templeton said. "He lost everything. His brother, his land, and in the end he even lost his good reputation."

"That's one of the things that I found so hard to believe," Weber said. "Leslie said that after his electric got shut off Jake called her, screaming and cussing her out. But that wasn't like him at all. Joyce Taylor at the bank said that he came in a few days before he killed himself to thank her for all she had tried to do for him. She said he was a gentleman, wouldn't even sit down until she did, even though he was on his last legs and using that oxygen tank to breathe. Not to mention that he wouldn't have had the energy to be able to scream and cuss someone out, let alone run around starting all those fires. And his telephone had been disconnected for over two months. That's why he came to town to talk to Joyce and again to drop off that note to me, as sick as he was."

"Is Leslie saying anything?" Gauger asked.

"She's cooperating. She said she researched ways to set fires on the internet from her laptop at home, and Coop thinks we can get somebody with some tech skills to check her browsing history to confirm that. She said she expected to find a key by my parents' back door like so many places, including the cabin on Beaver Creek Road. When she couldn't, she broke the window on the back door and cut her hand. It was bleeding so bad she was afraid she was going to pass out and burn herself up in the fire. Apparently Leslie can't stand the sight of blood, so she splashed the gas around and lit a match, but then she dropped the can. So she threw the match and got the hell out of there. Doc Williams at the Medical Center said he put nine stitches in it and she told him the same story about slamming her hand in a door. When he told her that injury didn't look like it came from a door, she changed her story and said she had a few drinks and locked herself out of her house when she took the trash out and had to break a window to get back in and was too embarrassed to admit it up front."

Templeton swallowed the last bite of his Italian beef sandwich and wiped his mouth, then said, "I feel like we need to do something for Jake. I know this clears his name as far as the fires go, but still, he deserved more."

"What he deserved was a break in life that he never got," Weber said. "There's no excuse for what happened with Jake and we can all blame ourselves for a part of that, but it doesn't change a thing."

"So what can we do?"

"I don't know, Kirby. I'm a cop, not a social worker. Be more aware of the people around us and the load they have to haul? Recognize the pain they try to hide behind their smiles and try to help ease it? Pay a call on a sick friend or somebody who's having problems or just all alone in the world and give them some company? I do know there's one thing I can do for Jake. Maybe the only thing that would really matter to him."

***

That evening Weber drove out to the Gibbons ranch. He stopped at the chain stretched across the entrance road and got out with his long handled bolt cutters and cut the shiny new padlock off, then ignored the No Trespassing signs erected by the bank and drove down the dirt road to the remains of the old ranch house. He sat there for a few minutes looking at what once had been home to a loving family of good, hardworking people and would probably end up being turned into condos or summer cabins someday, then got out of his Explorer.

Tucking the small plastic box that had sat on top of his gun safe for the last few weeks under his arm, he walked to the top of a little hill behind the house and took off his Stetson hat. As an owl hooted off in the distance and a coyote answered with its mournful wail, he faced the setting sun, removed the lid from the box, and scattered Jake's ashes on the land he loved and struggled so hard for so long to keep.

"You're home, Jake," the sheriff said, then he stood there a few moments longer before he walked back to his vehicle and drove away, leaving the land to the night animals and the ghosts of the past.

Here's A Sneak Preview Of Nick Russell's Newest Book, Big Lake Honeymoon, Coming Soon!

Boobs.

Cleve liked boobs. He liked them a lot. He had been fascinated with them ever since his first glance at one when his older sister had a sleepover and he had walked in on her and her friends as Kathy Brewster was changing into her pajamas.

"Get out of here, you little pervert!" Joyce had yelled at him, throwing a hairbrush, as big sisters do to thirteen year old brothers. Especially short, fat, socially awkward little brothers. But the rest of the girls had just laughed, except for Kathy, who had been too busy trying to cover herself to respond. She was quick, but not quick enough, and the sight of her breasts was burned into his memory forever.

From that day forward Cleve had been aware of those delightful things women hid under their shirts, and longed for another look. But the short, fat, socially awkward boy had grown into a short, fat, socially awkward young man with few opportunities to do more than just fantasize about boobs, or study them on the internet. He was an enthusiastic student.

Not that he was fixated on boobs alone. Cleve had many interests, from stamp collecting (he preferred American commemoratives) to ham radio, to tropical fish (he limited himself to freshwater species and was partial to African cichlids and the various types of tetras). Yes, all nerd hobbies to be sure, but perfect for a loner like himself.

Except for his work, Cleve had limited social interaction and that was for the best. He didn't handle himself well when he did. Though he was intelligent (he had been in the top five percent of his graduating class at Big Lake High School) he had always tended to fade back into the woodwork when in a crowd. And to Cleve, a crowd consisted of no more than himself and one other human being. It wasn't that he didn't *like* people, he just could never find the right thing to say at the right time so he just nodded or mumbled some unintelligible response in the hope that whoever it was would go away. They usually did, quickly, realizing that even a rudimentary conversation with the young man was frustrating at best.

That's why Cleve liked working the night shift at the Stop and Go, 11 p.m. to 7 a.m. Business was light most nights, with a little flurry of activity when Big Lake's few bars closed and the drunks stopped for cigarettes on their way home, and then things were usually slow until about 5 a.m. when the fishermen started pulling in on their way to the lake. But Sandee, the convenience store's manager, was always on the job by six to help with the rush. Winters were even better because the skiers stayed at the lodge on the other end of town, partied late, and seldom opened their eyes before his shift ended.

And then there were the boobs.

Cleve had become very adept at checking out the cleavage of the women who came in late at night, many of whom had had a few drinks and didn't seem to notice or care if he sneaked a peek. It wasn't like he was *staring*, after all. And several young women who may or may not have been quite of legal age to purchase beer and wine may have discovered that an extra button or two left open to show a little skin made the store clerk forget all about checking their IDs.

One in particular, an especially well endowed young lady named Sheila Wells, had discovered that if she forgot her bra and wore a tube top into the store and chatted with Cleve, he seemed so intent on studying what protruded from the thin fabric that he never noticed her friends Kari Pogue and Shannon Sharpe walking out with a couple of bottles of Boone's Farm Strawberry Hill and a twelve-pack of Bud. Sheila was pretty sure that if she had ever pulled the tube top down and flashed him, Cleve would have been oblivious to them making off with the store's entire inventory.

Early on this Wednesday morning in mid-September things were slow. It was well after two and the last of the bar crowd had come and gone. Cleve had not had a customer in over an hour and was deep into an online article about the benefits of natural plants in the home aquarium. The glass double doors were propped open to allow the air to get inside since the August heat wave had lasted longer than usual in the mountains. There had not been a vehicle driving past on the road in over an hour, and except for the occasional moth or other flying insect, Cleve was alone. The only sounds were a fluorescent light fixture in the ceiling that buzzed irritably, and the occasional thump when a large bug flung itself into one of the store's glass display windows.

When he finished the aquarium article, still undecided between Lilaeopsis, a grass like plant that grew up to two inches tall, or the versatile African Water Fern, Cleve wandered back to the ice cream freezer and got a Fudgsicle. He rang up the sale and paid for the treat, even though he knew that some of the store's employees cheated from time to time. But not Cleve. He liked his job and respected Sandee too much to steal. Besides, living at home with his mom and dad, he didn't really have any bills, so money wasn't a problem for him.

Cleve picked up his Galaxy Tab computer and logged onto the internet, trying to decide which adult site to peruse. Maybe the one about those horny college coeds, or the one where the young mother of two had webcams set up in every room of her home and did her housework in the nude. Cleve had about decided on the college girls after all when he heard a strangled sound and looked up to see a naked woman running through the store's open doors.

It was his greatest fantasy come to life and Cleve was sure he was dreaming. The first thing he noticed, of course, was her boobs. Cleve thought they were probably 36Bs. No sag to them and well formed indeed. There was a noticeable blue vein on the left one. Since this was only the second pair of female breasts he had ever seen in real life, who could blame him if he stared with his mouth agape for a few seconds longer than was probably polite? But when he did manage to drag his eyes away, Cleave realized that the woman wasn't completely naked after all. She wore a small pair of pastel pink panties, a white bootie sock on one foot, and her hands were bound together with some sort of white plastic strip.

"Please help me," she sobbed.

Made in United States
North Haven, CT
23 August 2024

56380617R00134